TIED IN DEATH

A DCI DANNY FLINT BOOK

TREVOR NEGUS

INKUBATOR
BOOKS

Published by Inkubator Books
www.inkubatorbooks.com

Copyright © 2023 by Trevor Negus

Trevor Negus has asserted his right to be identified as the author of this work.

ISBN (eBook): 978-1-83756-172-8
ISBN (Paperback): 978-1-83756-173-5

TIED IN DEATH is a work of fiction. People, places, events, and situations are the product of the author's imagination. Any resemblance to actual persons, living or dead is entirely coincidental.

No part of this book may be reproduced, stored in any retrieval system, or transmitted by any means without the prior written permission of the publisher.

PROLOGUE

10.00pm, 2 November 1974
Pleasley Vale, Mansfield, Nottinghamshire

The woman on the back seat of the Ford Cortina twisted frantically to try and see where she was.

When the two men had grabbed her outside the Art College in Mansfield, she had been too shocked to fight back.

As she walked alone along the dark street, her head had been filled with thoughts about her night class. The artwork she had done that evening had been highly praised by her tutor and inside she was buzzing. He had told her in front of the entire class that she was a naturally gifted artist, and that her paintings were good enough to be commercially viable. At thirty-eight years of age, it had been exactly what she wanted to hear. Her head had been filled with dreams of living on the South Bank in Paris, earning enough money to survive and enjoying the Parisian lifestyle.

So, when the car had stopped sharply beside her on Wood Street, there had been no time for her to react as the two men wearing black ski masks leapt out and grabbed her. They were only slightly taller than her but much stronger. They had knocked her to the ground. One man had bound her wrists, while the other wrapped a length of cloth around her head, effectively gagging her.

Once she was incapacitated and silenced, the two men bundled her face down onto the back seat of the car. She heard them get back in the car, as the two front doors were slammed shut. The car had then driven off at breakneck speed, gears crunching. Neither man had said a word throughout the whole terrifying ordeal.

The vehicle had been moving at speed for five minutes before progress slowed and the terrain became much more uneven.

Now, as she twisted on the back seat to try and see where the car was being driven, she was alarmed to make out silhouettes of tall trees against the night sky.

She glanced towards her captors. Both men still wore the black ski masks. The passenger growled to his companion, 'Switch the lights off. We've got to pass the farm buildings in a second.'

The terrifying journey lasted another three minutes before the car came to a complete stop, the engine was turned off and the men got out.

The back door was yanked open, and she was dragged out by her feet. The elaborately embroidered suede kaftan coat she was wearing rode up as she was dragged across the back seat, exposing her bell-bottom denim jeans and tie-dyed cheesecloth blouse. Unable to break her fall, as her hands were secured behind her back, she landed heavily and saw stars as her head hit the floor and all the air was knocked from her body. One of the men dragging her away from the car began to chuckle at her misfortune.

She was hauled roughly to her feet, and the two men stood by her side gripping her arms. The chuckling man flicked on a torch before they marched her into the woods.

Terrified, she began shouting and screaming but her cries were muffled by the gag. The men ignored her pleadings and held her even tighter. As her panic and sense of desperation grew, she felt her legs buckle and she half-collapsed. The two men managed to hold her upright as her knees gave way.

The one without the torch growled, 'Don't make us carry you, bitch.'

She regained her footing and walked unsteadily beside the two men, her terrified eyes wide open, her head swivelling from side to side trying to recognise where she was. She was desperate to see something—anything—she recognised.

Illuminated by the beam of the torch, a derelict cottage that had long been abandoned in the middle of these overgrown woods loomed out of the darkness. There were no panes of glass in the windows, and the rotten door was hanging by a last rusting hinge. The rafters of the roof were exposed where the slate tiles had been stripped, and the grey stone walls were stained with damp and covered in graffiti.

One man ripped the door off its remaining hinge, throwing it to the floor, before they both shoved the terrified woman inside.

The interior of the cottage was as dilapidated as the exterior. The rotting wooden floorboards were loose, and rubble from the roof was strewn everywhere. The plaster was peeling from the walls exposing the stonework beneath. It reeked of damp and decay.

The man with the torch forced her to her knees before resting the torch on a window opening. The torch had been deliberately placed so the beam shone directly into her eyes, blinding her.

She screamed, 'What do you want? Why are you doing this? Please don't hurt me.'

Her cries were muffled and unintelligible. The men weren't listening anyway. She could sense their malevolent presence directly behind her. Her head was swimming and she felt as though she was about to pass out. The sound of a match strike focussed her brain, and she could now smell cigarette smoke.

The man smoking the cigarette stepped into the torchlight. She felt the second man grab her shoulders, gripping her tightly from behind with powerful hands. The man with the cigarette took a drag and she saw the end glow red. She watched in horror as he took the cigarette slowly from his mouth and placed the red hot tip on her forehead, just above her right eye. She screamed in pain beneath the gag. Had it not been for the strong hands holding her upright, she would have collapsed. The man took another drag, and she screwed her eyes tightly shut as he stepped forward again. This time the cigarette was placed just above her left eye. The process was repeated several times. Each time the man would suck hard on the cigarette filter before placing the hot tip onto her face.

By the time he flicked the spent cigarette butt away she was in agony, sobbing from the excruciating pain.

The man standing in front of her untied the gag and

whipped it away from her face. He grabbed a handful of her long blonde hair and said, 'How do you like it, bitch?'

She whimpered, 'Please don't kill me.'

'Be quiet, you pathetic twat. If you open your mouth again, I'll have another smoke and use your face as my bloody ashtray.'

Through all the panic and the pain she was feeling, there was something about the voice she vaguely recognised.

Suddenly, through the intense pain, her befuddled brain screamed the answer. She knew exactly who was doing this to her, and she felt even more terrified.

She spluttered, 'I know you. Why are you doing this?'

The man bent forward until his face was only inches away from hers. He ripped off his ski mask and bellowed, 'Yes, you bloody well know me!'

Staring into her terrified eyes, in a quiet voice filled with malice and loathing, he said, 'I'm doing this because I can, because I want to, and because karma's a bitch. You're going to be sorry you ever laid eyes on this face.'

She saw the man straighten up. His eyes were wild now, searching the derelict room for something. She saw him bend down and pick up a length of two by four from the floor. Her eyes widened with fear, and she screamed, 'Nooo!' as he raised the wood high above his head, before bringing it crashing down onto the top of her head.

The six-inch nail that had been hammered through the centre of the floorboard many years ago pierced her skull, penetrating deep inside her brain.

By the time she toppled face first onto the floor, she was already dead.

1

9.30am, 16 February 1989
Cresswell Crags, Crags Road, Worksop, Nottinghamshire

Donna Lucas was already feeling stressed. Taking twenty-one ten-year-old children on a field trip was always a nightmare. To make matters worse, two of the parent helpers had dropped out at the last minute. That meant there were now only three adults supervising, and a ratio of one to seven was never good.

The water was Donna's main concern. The small lake at the side of the path, where the caves were, would be a natural magnet for her curious children. She had briefly considered cancelling the trip but didn't want to disappoint her eager pupils. The term time after the Christmas break had been fun. The topic of prehistoric man and the animals that populated the earth at that time had been lapped up by young, curious minds. The trip to Cresswell Crags, an area that had been the home of prehistoric man, was to be the culmination of the term's work. She wanted her children to experience first-hand the atmosphere of the archaeological site situated between Mansfield and Worksop.

On a bright, cold morning such as today, when the mist was rising slowly from the lake, she hoped it would be easy for the children to imagine cavemen going about their daily lives, emerging from the caves in the limestone rock, wearing only animal pelts, and getting ready to spend the day hunting or gathering food.

Donna had organised the children into three groups of seven, each supervised by an adult. The idea was for there to be a small gap between the groups as they all walked along the pathway that now separated the caves from the lake.

She had ensured that the 'problem' children, the more boisterous, bombastic members of the class were all in her group, where she could keep a close eye on their behaviour. Hers was the last group to start the walk, which meant she could also keep an eye on the other children ahead of her. Although feeling stressed, she was determined not to let that show. She wanted her pupils to get the maximum benefit from the trip.

When they came to the first cave, she supervised her group as they walked up the gently sloping steps to look inside. She talked to the children as she walked, inviting them to imagine they were prehistoric children, and to see the cave and surrounding areas as they would have done. They all stood in the entrance to the cave, and she asked, 'Why do you think early man chose to live here?'

Five of the seven children raised a hand to answer. Donna pointed at one of the girls. 'Gemma?'

'Water and shelter, Miss Lucas.'

'Very good. Exactly that. Anything else?'

The same five hands were raised, and she turned to the only boy of the five. 'Geoffrey?'

'Security and plenty of food.'

'Excellent.'

She peered into the dark recess of the limestone cave and said, 'Those four things were all that was needed by prehistoric man to sustain life.'

As she turned back to face the group, she instantly saw that the two boys who had not raised their hands to answer a question were nowhere to be seen.

Ushering the other children out of the mouth of the cave, she shouted, 'Mark, Andy. Come here now!'

The two boys had disappeared.

She knew they had not passed her and gone deeper into the cave. From her elevated position she could see they weren't on the path at the foot of the steps, or near the water's edge. Her anxiety levels rising, she looked towards the deep vegetation in between the cave sites.

About ten yards to her left she saw movement. The boys were hiding in the bushes.

Feeling a huge sense of relief, she shouted, 'You two boys come out of there now! Don't think I can't see you! Why do you two always have to spoil it for everyone else?'

Knowing they had been spotted, the two boys began creeping back through the bushes towards the path.

Suddenly, one of the boys cried out in panic. Then both bolted towards their teacher, their faces ashen white.

As the first boy reached her, she could see their genuine panic. The anger at their behaviour instantly disappeared and she asked, 'Whatever's the matter?'

One of the boys spluttered, 'There's a man in the bushes. He looks funny.'

Moving the children away from the mouth of the cave back to the footpath she said, 'Geoffrey, I want you to run along the path and ask Mrs Trent to come back here with her group, please. Stay away from the water!'

The young boy scooted off after the group of children twenty yards ahead.

Minutes later, Mrs Trent had returned with her group.

Donna said, 'Marie, look after the children, please. I need to check on something the boys have seen in the bushes.'

She retraced the route taken by the two errant school children into the bushes. With each step into the undergrowth, her anxiety levels rose a little higher. She had no idea what she was about to find. From the demeanour of the two youngsters, she knew it was going to be something unpleasant.

As she stooped to negotiate a strand of bramble, she saw the man just to her right.

He was lying on his side, but his face was turned up. His eyes were wide open and glassy, staring sightlessly up at the green canopy above. She could see what looked like dried blood matting his thinning fair hair. The dark blood had emanated from a gaping wound on the top of his head.

The man was wearing a business suit and tie. His wire-framed glasses were lying on his face, still looped around one ear. She could see his hands had been tied behind his back.

There were small, black marks dotted all over his chalk-white face. His lips were drawn back in a rictus grin, exposing yellowing teeth.

Donna Lucas was only twenty-three years old and had never been exposed to death before. She had never seen a dead body. Yet every instinct inside her body screamed out that this man was not only dead, but that he had been murdered.

Trying to stay calm and suppress the revulsion she was feeling, she walked back to the group being supervised by Mrs Trent and said calmly, 'Marie, keep the children here until I get back. I need to go back to the visitor centre and make a phone call. I'll only be a few minutes.'

'Of course. Is everything okay?'

Donna moved in close and whispered, 'Not really. I need to call the police. There's a dead man in the bushes. His hands have been tied up. I'll be as quick as I can. Watch the kids, especially Mark and Andy. Don't let them wander off again.'

2

9.30am, 16 February 1989
MCIU Offices, Mansfield, Nottinghamshire

Detective Chief Inspector Danny Flint had called a meeting of his supervisors to establish how inquiries were progressing in both the Margaret White and Florence King unsolved murders, and to check on the crown court file preparations for the trials of Sam and Thomas Morgan.

Detective Inspector Rob Buxton was responsible for the Sam Morgan file. He started the meeting by saying, 'We're crown-court ready for Sam Morgan. The defence lawyers have indicated there may be a guilty plea on all charges. I think they'll be going down the diminished responsibility route, as far as any possible defence or mitigation goes.'

'What about Thomas Morgan?'

Detective Sergeant Andy Wills answered this one. 'I've

been supervising the preparation of the file for Thomas Morgan. He'll be going to trial, and we're ready. I've had a couple of meetings with the prosecution barrister, and she's happy that we have everything in place evidentially to convict him on both the rape and incest charges.'

'Did she have any comment on how the DNA evidence was obtained?'

'None whatsoever. She has no problem with the way the samples were obtained from Thomas Morgan. She's convinced it's that evidence that will convict the man.'

'Good work, both of you. Let me know if you encounter any problems further down the line. Have we been notified of any trial dates yet?'

Rob shook his head. 'Nothing yet. I'll let you know when dates are set.'

Danny turned to Detective Inspector Tina Cartwright and Detective Sergeant Rachel Moore. 'How are we progressing with the enquiries into the oil companies?'

Tina said, 'We've now exhausted all the major oil companies and have found no staff being employed on forty-eight-month contracts, either in the UK or abroad.'

'So where does that leave us?'

'We're still working our way through the smaller oil companies and companies that provide specialist agency staff for the oil industry.'

'Are there many?'

Rachel said, 'We have a dozen or so smaller oil companies, then a similar amount of recruitment agencies that specialise in providing workers for the oil industry.'

Danny looked at Tina and asked, 'Do you have enough staff?'

'Including Rachel, I've got four detectives working

permanently on this enquiry, supervised by myself. We'll soon work through the remaining companies.'

'I don't need to remind you of the urgency of your enquiry. Two elderly women raped and murdered in their own homes is horrendous. I know there were a few years between the two crimes but I don't think we can bank on having that again. I firmly believe this maniac will strike soon, so if you need more staff, tell me.'

The telephone on Danny's desk began to ring and he snatched it up. 'DCI Flint, Major Crime.'

There was a pause then Danny said, 'Where? Any other details?'

He scribbled down a few notes on his pad and said, 'We're on our way. We'll be there in thirty minutes. Ask the uniform staff to preserve the scene, if they haven't already done so. Thanks.'

Danny put the phone down, looked at the gathered detectives and said, 'Meeting's over. The body of a man has been discovered at the Cresswell Crags archaeological site, and it's not prehistoric. He's wearing a business suit and his hands are bound behind his back. Rachel, I want you to leave the oil inquiries for now and travel to Cresswell Crags. Apparently, the body was found by a bunch of schoolkids on a trip. I may need your expertise talking to potential child witnesses.'

Rachel began to gather the documentation that was being used in the supervisors' meeting.

Danny looked at Tina. 'I want you to stay here with your three detectives and continue working on the oil companies. I'm still getting pressure from Detective Chief Superintendent Potter on those two cases, so I need you to find something positive from those oil companies, and soon.'

The discovery of crude oil at both murder scenes had been the only forensic breakthrough on the White and King murders. Danny knew if they couldn't progress that lead, there was a good chance the cases would remain unsolved.

The fact that one of the elderly women killed was the mother of a county councillor added to the pressure Danny was already feeling trying to progress the inquiry. To have one woman murdered in such a brutal manner was bad enough, but to have two identical crimes and the prospect of a maniac ready to strike again was daunting.

He felt certain that unless they could locate the killer, he would strike again, and soon.

To add to that intense pressure, it now looked like the MCIU would have another murder inquiry to contend with. He could feel the pressure starting to bear down harder as he would now have to juggle his limited resources to potentially catch two killers.

With a weary expression, he faced his remaining supervisors. 'I want the rest of you travelling to Cresswell Crags. I take it you all know where that is?'

With a mixture of grunts and nods, the supervisors answered Danny's question before leaving the office to gather their teams.

3

10.30am, 16 February 1989
Cresswell Crags, Crags Road, Worksop, Nottinghamshire

Danny and Rob were looking at the body that had been found in the undergrowth. They were patiently waiting for the home office pathologist to attend before examining the body. It was always best practice to disturb the scene around the body as little as possible, and on this occasion, time was no problem.

Tim Donnelly was busy supervising the scenes of crime operatives taking photographs of the deceased in situ.

He said, 'Make sure you get close-ups of the knot that's been used to bind his wrists.'

Danny added, 'That looks unusual. Any idea what type of knot it is?'

Tim studied it for a second longer. 'I'm no expert, but it could be a bowline. It's a knot used frequently by climbers, and that would tie in with the rope that's been used. It looks like heavy-duty nylon climbing rope. Once it's cut off, we'll be able to say for sure.'

Danny stamped his feet on the frosty path, looked at Rob and grumbled, 'How long before the pathologist gets here? My feet are freezing.'

'Not much longer. The control room said Seamus Carter was travelling from Retford, so he should be here anytime now.'

'Has Rachel organised everything with the pupils and staff from the school trip?'

'Yes. She's taken DC Pope and DC Bailey with her back to the Holly Primary School at Forest Town. They'll spend the rest of today interviewing the staff and the children involved. It will be a long process as they'll have to get the parents in, to sit with their kids.'

'How old are the children?'

'Ten.'

'Are they okay?'

'The two lads who actually saw the body are understandably shaken by it all, so patience will be needed for their interviews.'

'Rachel knows what she's doing. Have we any idea who the deceased is?'

'Uniform officers found no identification on him when they first attended. They checked his jacket pockets for a wallet. Nothing. There were no cars left in the car park overnight, so he hasn't driven himself here.'

'Unless whoever killed him stole his wallet and his car.'

Rob shrugged. 'That's one possibility, I suppose.'

Danny glanced down the steps and saw the blue-suited

figures of the giant Seamus Carter and his diminutive assistant, Brigitte O'Hara, approaching along the footpath.

Rob shouted, 'We're up here!'

By the time he got to the top of the steps, the man-mountain pathologist was panting. He took a deep lungful of the frigid air and as he spoke his breath came out in white clouds. 'Your man at the car park didn't tell me it was this bloody far.'

Danny smiled. 'You need to get yourself fitter, my friend. Maybe a few less pints of Guinness?'

The pathologist roared with laughter. 'Like that's ever going to happen, Danny. What have we got?'

Danny pointed to the deceased in the bushes. 'White male, late forties, early fifties. His hands have been bound behind his back. There's extensive, heavy bruising to the face, and what appear to be cigarette burns, also on the face. There's a large wound on the top of his head that has caused a major bleed. We haven't had a close look. We've been waiting for you to arrive rather than trample over everything.'

Seamus spoke directly to Tim Donnelly. 'Do you have all your photographs?'

'We do. If you approach the body on the tape line it will minimise the disruption to the vegetation around the body.'

'Okay, thanks.'

He looked at Danny and continued, 'You might as well stay back here while Brigitte and I examine the body. You'll still be able to see and hear everything from here.'

After examining the man's face for a full five minutes, Seamus said, 'He's taken quite a beating. He obviously didn't want to be here. These other marks are indeed cigarette burns. Whoever killed him either wanted to inflict maximum pain or they were done as a form of torture to try and extract something from him.'

He turned his attention to the wound on the top of the man's head. 'This looks very strange. I'll know better when I'm carrying out the post mortem examination, but this appears to be a single penetrating wound that has gone through the skull and deep into the brain. If that is the case, death would have been quick and there would have been a lot of blood.'

Danny said, 'What sort of weapon could cause that injury?'

'Any sort of metal spike. It must have been delivered with a lot of force, though, to penetrate the top of the skull. Am I okay to remove the bindings around his wrists?'

'Yes. They've been photographed.'

Seamus took the craft knife offered by Brigitte and sliced through the nylon rope, leaving the unusual knot intact.

With the arms released, the pathologist tested the body for rigor mortis. 'It looks like rigor has come and gone. A rough estimate, this man was killed between twelve midnight and six o'clock this morning. There is pooling of jelly-like blood around and beneath the head. This type of blood would indicate a massive cranial haemorrhage. Again, I'll know for sure at the post mortem, but cause of death looks like this large head wound. He also has some recent bruising around his knuckles. That could mean one of two things. He either fought back, or it could be as a result of a fall. Hard to say. Brigitte will take fingernail scrapings and hair samples here, then we're good to move him.'

Rob said, 'The undertakers have been contacted. They'll be here at eleven thirty.'

Carter replied, 'I want the body transported to Kings Mill

Hospital mortuary. It was a toss-up between there or Bassetlaw Hospital. It makes sense to do the examination closer to your offices.'

Danny asked, 'What time are you thinking?'

'Let's say two o'clock this afternoon.'

'I'll see you there. Rob and Tim will remain here to work the scene. Anything else you can tell me?'

Seamus glanced down at the body again and said, 'Did you notice his left shoe is half on and half off?'

Danny looked down at the black brogue. Although the lace was still tied, it had come off at the heel. 'Has he been dragged here?'

'Could be. It's possible the heel of his shoe caught one of those steps on the way up here, I suppose.'

Rob stepped back down and examined the soil between the steps. 'There are some drag marks here.'

Danny said, 'Do you think he was killed elsewhere and this is a deposition site?'

Seamus shook his head. 'No, the blood around the body suggests to me that the head wound was delivered here. He could have been beaten and burned elsewhere, but he was almost certainly killed here. It's possible he was either unconscious or semi-conscious when he was brought here.'

'Okay. I'll see you at the post mortem. Thanks, Seamus.'

Danny walked back down the steps with Rob. 'As soon as the body has been moved, I want this whole area searched thoroughly.'

'It's already organised, boss. Andy has been onto the Special Operations Unit. They're sending a full section to carry out a fingerprint search of the scene and the car park. They'll be here at eleven o'clock.'

'Have we interviewed the staff who work here?'

'I've got detectives interviewing and obtaining statements from the two members of staff who were here this morning. I've also contacted all the local radio stations and asked them to announce the closure of Cresswell Crags for the next twenty-four hours due to a police incident. That should save us some grief with punters turning up to visit.'

'Good work. It does mean you'll have the local press sniffing around, though. I'm sure you'll be able to deal with them. I'm going back to the office to start getting things organised there. I'll see you at the post mortem later. I want everyone to attend a full debriefing at five o'clock this evening. Make sure everyone here knows the time.'

'Will do.'

As Danny walked slowly back to his car, his thoughts were focussed on the sudden, brutal death of this unknown man. *Who was he? Why has he been killed here? What was his story? And most importantly, who was responsible for his violent death?*

4

2.00pm, 16 February 1989
Kings Mill Hospital Mortuary, Mansfield, Nottinghamshire

Danny was the last to arrive at the mortuary. When he walked in, he saw Rob Buxton assisting DC Nigel Singleton with bagging the last of the deceased's clothing.

The dead man was now naked on the stainless steel examination table. A scenes of crime operative was taking photographs from every angle, while another was setting up a video camera to record the post mortem. He was being assisted by Tim Donnelly, the scenes of crime supervisor. On the far side of the examination table stood Seamus Carter and Brigitte O'Hara, already dressed in gowns and gloves.

Danny walked across the room and stood beside Rob. 'Any update from the searches?'

'Nothing's been recovered from any of the searches at the scene. Nigel's just found something that could be interesting, though. In the breast pocket of the dead man's shirt was a folded receipt. It's from a bed and breakfast in Mansfield. The Brambles Guest House, located on Woodhouse Road. There was also a Yale key attached to a small piece of wood in his trouser pocket.'

'We need to explore that lead as soon as we've finished the debriefing this evening.'

Seamus Carter interrupted the two detectives, 'I think we're ready now, so can we make a start.'

The pathologist began by making a full external examination of the body. As he walked around the deceased, he spoke into a Dictaphone, recording his findings, 'The body is that of a well-nourished white male. I would estimate the age to be anywhere between forty-five and fifty-five years. The face and ribs are both heavily bruised. The injuries are indicative of a sustained, savage beating.'

He paused before continuing, 'There are numerous cigarette burns on the man's face. Brigitte will count them, so you have a complete record. Although serious, I don't think any of these injuries to the face and ribs would be sufficient to cause the man's death. That is far more likely to have been caused by the single wound to the top of the skull. I will start the internal examination at that point.'

He handed the Dictaphone to his assistant and picked up the scalpel.

After thirty minutes, the pathologist paused and indicated for Danny and Rob to step in closer. 'I want you to see this. Can you see the hole in the top of the skull? Now I've peeled away the flesh from the scalp and the bone is visible, you can clearly see that the instrument used to inflict this injury has a serrated edge on one side. There are clear striation marks in the skull on one side of the hole.'

As he pointed out the strange injury to the detectives, the scenes of crime man's camera whirred into life, recording the marks in full colour, close-up.

Danny said, 'Any idea what could have been used to kill him?'

Seamus was thoughtful for a moment. 'I once examined a man who had been killed by a jealous husband with an ice axe. There were similar marks in his skull, so that's one possibility.'

Rob said, 'That could also fit with the rope used to bind his wrists. Tim said he thought it looked like the type of rope used by climbers. He also said the knot could be one used by climbers. What was it? A bowline or something like that?'

Danny and Rob stepped back from the examination table as Seamus continued his grisly task. He removed the top of the skull and examined the injury to the brain, measuring the depth of the wound and the angle of penetration before removing the organ altogether.

'This headwound was what killed him. There's massive damage to the brain. Several major blood vessels have been severed, or damaged. He would have bled out quickly. I'll say it purely for the record. This death was not natural causes, and you're investigating a murder.'

Danny nodded and continued to observe as the pathologist completed the rest of his macabre but essential examination.

As Danny saw the pathologist coming to the end of his examination, he asked, 'Have you found anything that could assist us to establish his identity?'

'Everything will be in my written report in greater detail,

but the man has had an appendectomy at some stage in his life. He also has a three-inch titanium plate in his right tibia, that has been used to repair what would have been a seriously bad fracture. Brigitte will obtain a full set of fingerprints and get dental X-rays once the room has been cleared. He's had extensive dental work done, so that could prove useful.'

'Thanks, Seamus. When will I have your report?'

'I'll get it to you by this time tomorrow?'

'Thanks. One last thing. Where was the previous murder you mentioned? The jealous husband and the ice axe?'

'I did some of my training in Scotland. The murder I spoke about happened in a small village just outside Edinburgh. The betrayed husband was a keen climber, and he dispatched his love rival using one of the tools of his trade. I believe the case made the national newspapers back then, as the murderer was a celebrity climber who had scaled most of the world's highest peaks.'

'Not a local case then?'

The pathologist allowed a world-weary grin to form on his lips. 'I'm sorry. It was never going to be that easy, Danny. I think you're going to have your work cut out solving this mystery.'

5

**5.00pm, 16 February 1989
MCIU Offices, Mansfield, Nottinghamshire**

Danny raised his hand and brought the room to a hush. The gathered detectives, who had been discussing the new case, fell silent.

He turned to Rob. 'Let's start with the scene at Cresswell Crags.'

Rob took a deep breath. 'After the body was removed, the Special Operations Unit have carried out a fingerprint search of the area but have drawn a blank. A search was also made of the car park, and the pathways from the car park to the murder scene. Nothing has been recovered. The weather has been unusually dry for this time of year and the ground is dry and hard. The cold, clear nights have meant hard frosts, so there were no useful tyre marks or footprints.'

'Did you have any problems with punters, or the press?'

'Not really. A couple of disgruntled customers who hadn't heard the update on the radio informing people that the attraction was closed for twenty-four hours, that's all.'

'Media?'

'A couple of local newspaper reporters came down. They asked a few basic questions and left. Bit too cold for them to hang around long.'

Danny sought out Tim Donnelly, the scenes of crime supervisor. 'What can you tell us about your examination of the scene?'

Tim read from the notes he had made. 'We've obtained soil and vegetation samples from the scene and the car park. Fibre lifts have been obtained from the outer clothing worn by the deceased. That clothing is now drying and will be sent on to the Forensic Science Service for a full forensic examination. Photographs have been taken of both the scene and the post mortem examination of the deceased. There will be albums available for viewing tomorrow morning.'

'Thanks, Tim. The post mortem has revealed the cause of death to be a single blow to the top of the head. This blow was administered using an unknown metal instrument, possibly an ice axe or similar. It caused a massive brain injury and subsequently death. Prior to this fatal blow, this man has sustained a prolonged and savage beating. He's also been burned with a cigarette on his face no fewer than fifteen times. He's been tortured and beaten before his death. Bear that in mind when we're looking at possible motives for his murder.'

He paused to let that significant fact sink in, then continued, 'Found in the dead man's clothing was a receipt for the

Brambles Guest House on Woodhouse Road, here in Mansfield.'

Danny turned and said directly to Rob, 'As soon as this briefing's over, I want a team ready to visit this guest house. If this man's been a resident there, I want a full search of the room he's occupied and any other property he has there. This is a top priority and needs doing tonight. It could lead to a huge breakthrough in his identification.'

Rob said, 'I'll get that organised.'

Danny looked for Tim Donnelly again. When he saw him standing near the back, he said, 'Tim, can you also have a team on standby, please. If the guest house enquiry is positive, I'd like to have a scenes of crime team on site as soon as possible.'

'It will mean overtime, boss. My team have all been on since early this morning.'

'Overtime's no problem, Tim. Organise a team to be on standby, please.'

'Will do, boss.'

Danny scanned the room until he saw Rachel Moore. 'How are you progressing with the pupils and staff from Holly Primary School?'

'We've interviewed most of the pupils, the teacher and parents who were supervising the children on their trip, and have obtained statements from the two boys who initially found the body.'

'That's one school trip these kids will always remember. Is there anything startling from any of their accounts?'

'Nothing that takes us any further forward, boss.'

'How many children have you still got to see?'

'Only three kids left to see. Their parents couldn't be

contacted until quite late. Arrangements have already been put in place to complete that enquiry tomorrow morning.'

'Good work.'

'Who interviewed the members of staff at Cresswell Crags?'

DC Singh and DC Blake stood up, and Jagvir said, 'That was me and Sam, boss. The two women arrived at the visitor centre at eight thirty this morning. They arrived a little earlier than normal as they knew they had the school trip booked in. The car park was deserted when they arrived, and neither witness saw anybody on foot.'

'Does the visitor centre have cameras?'

'There's a single camera that covers the front door of the premises. It gives no view whatsoever into the car park, or of the path that leads from the car park to the murder scene.'

'Have they noticed anyone acting suspiciously over the last few weeks?'

Jag shook his head. 'No.'

Danny was thoughtful for a moment, then he addressed the gathered detectives as a whole, 'This isn't like most of the murders we investigate. There are no witnesses, there are no nearby residential areas to carry out house-to-house enquiries, and very little forensic evidence at the scene. Hopefully, the visit to the guest house this evening will yield some much-needed information that can take the enquiry forward. In the meantime, there are things we can do. I'll organise a press appeal in the morning, and as soon as the inquiries at Holly Primary School have been completed, I'd like a vehicle check point organised on the road adjacent to the entrance to Cresswell Crags, to search for any possible witnesses.

'Does anybody have any other ideas or questions?'

The room remained silent.

Danny said, 'Rob, as soon as you've organised a team to visit the guest house, let me know. I'll come with you.'

'Will do, boss.'

6

6.00pm, 16 February 1989
Brambles Guest House, Woodhouse Road, Mansfield

The line of CID vehicles and the white scenes of crime van were parked on a side street, just off Woodhouse Road. Danny spoke into the radio, 'DCI Flint to all units. Remain in your cars. I'll go in with DI Buxton and speak to the management. There's no point in all of us going straight in. Stand by here and await further instructions.'

Rob drove the car into the car park of the guest house. There were four other cars already parked, unattended.

Danny said, 'Have you got the receipt and the key?'

Rob nodded. 'Right here.'

The two detectives walked into the gloomy foyer of the guest house. The only light was from street lights that filtered in through the stained glass windows of the front door, and a dim table lamp that was on the reception desk.

The man sitting behind the desk looked dishevelled and disinterested by his visitors. He eventually tore his gaze away from the sleazy magazine he was reading. 'Have you booked a room?'

Danny held out his identification. 'I'm Detective Chief Inspector Flint and this is Detective Inspector Buxton from the MCIU. Are you the manager?'

'No. My wife runs the place. I'm just the hired help around here.'

'Is your wife here?'

'She's in the back, restocking the bar. Follow me.'

Sighing heavily, the man put the magazine back in the desk drawer, dragged himself from behind the desk and slouched along a corridor, with the detectives following. He opened a heavy fire door into the bar area.

A middle-aged, heavyset woman was stacking bottles from a crate onto the shelves of the bar. She had permed brunette hair and wore garish red lipstick and blue eye shadow that she'd probably been applying in the same way since the seventies. An unlit cigarette hung from her lips as she worked.

Hearing the men in the bar, she stopped what she was doing and looked over the counter. The man said, 'Lisa, these men are detectives. They want to speak to the manager.'

The woman removed the cigarette from her mouth, tutted loudly and said, 'Bloody hell, Clive. You know how busy I am. Couldn't you have dealt with this?'

The man shrugged and said sarcastically, 'You're the boss,' as he walked out of the room.

She muttered under her breath, 'That bloody man's useless,' then painted on a forced smile for the detectives. 'Lisa Hargreaves. I'm the manager. What can I do for you?'

Rob held out the clear exhibit bag containing the Yale key on the small wooden fob. 'Does this key belong to your guest house?'

Lisa took the bag and examined the key. She saw the small acorn motif on the piece of wood and said, 'Yes, it's the key for the Acorn Room. How did you get it?'

'Can you tell us who's staying in that room?'

'He's a businessman from Scotland. His details will be in the register on reception. I'll go and grab the book. Can I get you a drink while you're waiting?'

Danny said, 'No, thanks. Just the register will be fine.'

Lisa Hargreaves hurried out of the room, returning seconds later clutching a large black book. She flicked through the pages. 'Let me see. Here he is, Ian Drake. He's given his home address as 64, Blackskye Avenue, Kilmarnock, Scotland. His car's the red Vauxhall Astra in the car park.'

'Is he in his room?'

'He could be. I haven't seen him since last night. He went out for a meeting yesterday evening, and he wasn't down for breakfast today. Is something wrong?'

Ignoring the woman's question, Danny asked, 'When did Mr Drake arrive?'

'He booked in on the twelfth, four days ago. He booked the room for a week but said he may need to stay longer. He paid for seven nights in advance. That's why I was surprised when he didn't come down for breakfast. I mean, he's paid for it, after all.'

'Was anybody staying with him?'

'No, he's on his own. He didn't have much luggage.'

'Has he had any visitors?'

'No. He didn't talk to the other guests much either. Not that we're very busy at the minute.'

'Could we see if he's in his room?'

'Do you want to use that key or shall I get the spare?'

Rob said, 'Better if we use the spare key.'

'No problem. Follow me.'

The Acorn Room was on the first floor, at the front of the building, overlooking the car park and Woodhouse Road. The door was made of hardwood and had a small carving of an acorn on it that matched the motif on the key fob.

Lisa rapped on the door. 'Mr Drake, are you in there?'

There was no response, so she tried again.

When there was still no response, Danny said, 'Open it, please.'

Using the Yale key, she opened the door and stood to one side as the two detectives entered the room. The room was neat and tidy and there were no signs of a struggle. It was obvious the bed hadn't been slept in. There was a single brown suitcase at the foot of the bed, and a matching brown leather briefcase on the chest of drawers. On the bedside table, beneath the lamp, there was a set of car keys that also had a mortice key on the fob. The keys were sat on top of a leather-bound Filofax.

Danny turned to Lisa. 'Did he say where he was going last night?'

'He told me he had a meeting and asked me to arrange for a taxi to pick him up at six o'clock.'

'Which taxi firm did you call?'

'I have an arrangement with ACE Taxis. I would have called them.'

Rob said, 'Is that the firm on Carter Lane?'

'That's the one. They give me special rates, so I always pass any business from here onto them.'

Danny said, 'Mrs Hargreaves, I have a polaroid photograph of a man who could be your missing resident. If I show it to you, do you think you'd recognise him?'

'I don't like the sound of this, but yeah, I'd recognise him. I've spoken to him a few times while he's been staying here.'

'I'm warning you, there are some unusual marks on the man's face.'

She looked worried but said, 'I'll have a look.'

Danny took out the polaroid photo that had been taken at the mortuary, and held it out for Lisa to look at. She gasped and said, 'That's him, that's Ian Drake. What are all those marks? Is he all right?'

'Ian Drake was found dead this morning, Lisa. We're treating his death as suspicious and will need to search this room. Will that cause you or your other guests any issues?'

'How long will it take?'

'We'll get it done as soon as we can. The sooner we start, the sooner we'll be finished and out of your way.'

'Do whatever you've got to do. Do you think any of my other guests could be in danger?'

'There's nothing to make us think that. If that changes, you'll be the first to know. I'm going to tell my men to come in now, so we can get started.'

Danny spoke on the radio, ordering his detectives to enter the guest house.

Andy Wills was the first to enter the room and Danny said to him, 'I want Tim Donnelly and his scenes of crime staff in here first to do a thorough forensic sweep. Once that's done, I want everything that belongs to the deceased bagged and tagged. I want statements from Lisa Hargreaves, the manager, and her husband. I want all the other guests speaking to as well. Our victim may have been in conversation with one of them about why he was staying here. I'm going with Rob to ACE Taxis' office, on Carter Lane. Our deceased used one of their cabs last night. I want to speak to the driver and establish where he took our man, and if he met anybody. Have you got enough staff here?'

'Plenty.'

Danny turned to Rob. 'Grab the Filofax and the car keys. Let's have a look at the car.'

Slipping on a pair of latex gloves, Rob picked up the Filofax and the keys.

As more detectives entered the guest house, Lisa looked increasingly worried. Danny said, 'Mrs Hargreaves, why don't you wait downstairs in reception? I expect some of your other guests will want to know what's happening and they may need your reassuring words.'

'If you think that's best.'

Danny nodded and Lisa followed the two detectives back down to reception. They were passed on the stairs by white-suited scenes of crime staff making their way up.

Lisa looked at them wide eyed. 'Bloody hell, it's like being in a programme on the TV.'

Rob reassured her, 'It won't take long.'

'Will the newspapers get wind of what's happening and come sniffing around?'

'They may do.'

'What do I tell them?'

'If I were you, I'd just say the police were here to search a room. If you don't give them any details, they'll soon lose interest. You don't want any adverse publicity for the guest house, do you?'

She shook her head. 'No, I bloody don't. Things are dire enough already. What a bloody carry-on.'

Danny and Rob walked back outside into the car park and saw Tim Donnelly standing next to the white scenes of crime van.

Rob went to the CID car and used the radio to request a police national computer check on the registration number of the Vauxhall Astra.

Danny walked over to Tim. 'We think the red Astra belongs to our deceased. We've got the keys, but I want a full lift arranging to the forensic bay at headquarters so it can be given a thorough examination.'

Rob approached them. 'The PNC search shows the Astra's registered to Ian Drake, same address as the one he's given in the guest house register. This is his motor all right.'

Tim said, 'I'll arrange for the full lift. Do you want to leave me the keys?'

'Will do. Let me sort out an exhibit label for continuity first.'

Danny said, 'Andy's already upstairs. I want you to work the scene with him, please, Tim. There'll be a debrief at ten o'clock tonight.'

'Okay, boss.'

Rob returned and handed a completed exhibit bag containing the Vauxhall Astra key to Tim.

Danny and Rob then got back in their CID car. As Rob turned on the ignition, Danny said, 'Back to the office first. I want to give this Filofax to Helen Bailey so she can start researching Ian Drake. I'm conscious that we've just been given a massive boost in this enquiry. The sooner we know everything there is to know about Ian Drake, the closer we'll be to catching his killer.'

7

7.00pm, 16 February 1989
ACE Taxis, Carter Lane, Mansfield, Nottinghamshire

The two detectives had been waiting at the taxi office for ten minutes, the battered sofa they were sitting on becoming ever more uncomfortable by the second. The despatcher had told them the driver they needed to speak to, Les Williams, was making a drop at Mansfield Woodhouse and wouldn't be long.

Danny muttered to Rob, 'How long does it take to drive back from Woodhouse? What's the bloody hold-up?'

Rob shrugged. 'He can't be much longer.'

Headlights suddenly illuminated the office as a car pulled up in front. The despatcher looked over the counter at the detectives. 'That'll be Les back now. He's not going to be happy.'

The door opened and a short, stocky man with long,

greasy hair tied back in a ponytail walked in. His worn leather jacket was cut off at the sleeves and had a motorcycle gang emblem on the back. He strode purposefully up to the counter and yelled at the despatcher, 'What's so bloody urgent that you've dragged me back in here? I'm losing time and money not being on the rank. It's getting busy out there.'

Without looking up, the despatcher snarled back, 'These two cops want a word.'

Les Williams spun around and for the first time saw the two detectives in the foyer.

Danny stood up. 'I heard what you said about losing time and money. We've got a few questions to ask you about a fare you picked up from the Brambles Guest House at six o'clock yesterday evening. Depending on how cooperative you feel like being, we can either do that quickly and painlessly here, or take our time back at the station; it's entirely up to you.'

The taxi driver sat down on the sofa. 'We can talk here. I remember that fare from Brambles. Middle-aged bloke going to some sort of business meeting. He was very excited about it. He told me he was going to make a small fortune as soon as he signed the contract.'

Danny said, 'Where did you take him?'

'I dropped him off in the car park outside the Young Vanish pub at Glapwell.'

'Did you see him talking to anybody in the car park?'

'No. He paid me the exact fare, no tip. I turned my cab round and saw him walking across the car park towards the restaurant part of the pub. I didn't see him with anybody else. I only remember seeing him walking because I was calling him a tight bastard under my breath as I drove out of the car park.'

Rob said, 'Was the car park busy?'

'It was rammed. I can remember thinking they must have had some sort of do on, as it was packed and still early. That's why I had to drop him at the very top of the car park. It was the only space left to turn round.'

'What time was it when you dropped him off?'

'I picked him up at bang on six o'clock. It's only a fifteen-minute run to Glapwell, so I would have got him there no later than six twenty. He told me he was in plenty of time, as his meeting wasn't until six thirty.'

'Is this the first time you've picked this man up from the guest house?'

'Yep. I've never seen the guy, before or since. Is that everything? I really do need to get back out on the rank.'

Danny said, 'Did he say what this new opportunity was all about? What the contract was for?'

Growing impatient, Les Williams replied, 'He was babbling on about sales and marketing. Most of it was going right over my head. I was listening but not listening, if you know what I mean. Some passengers are just boring sods; he was one of those. All I remember him saying was that he was meeting both the company directors that night.'

'One last question and then you can crack on and earn some cash. Did the fare take anything with him to the meeting?'

'No. He wasn't carrying a briefcase, or anything like that. He did look smart, though, all suited and booted.'

'Okay, Mr Williams, thanks. We'll need to get a witness statement from you, but we can do that when you're not working. What time do you finish your shift?'

'I'm working until three o'clock tomorrow morning. After having some shuteye, I'll be getting up around ten-ish.

I can get into the police station for eleven o'clock, if that's okay?'

'That's fine. Ask to speak to a detective from the MCIU. Thanks for your help tonight, and don't make us come looking for you to make that statement.'

'I'll be there. I appreciate you letting me work now. I need to earn tonight, fellas, that's all. It won't be a problem tomorrow.'

Williams walked straight out of the office, jumped in his cab and drove away at speed.

Rob said, 'The Young Vanish?'

Danny nodded. 'Let's go.'

8

10.00pm, 16 February 1989
MCIU Offices, Mansfield, Nottinghamshire

The briefing room was heavy with smoke. There was a hum of noise as the gathered detectives spoke about the various enquiries they had been carrying out.

Danny and Rob walked in, and the room fell silent.

Danny said, 'I appreciate this has already been a long day, so let's crack on and get through this as quickly as we can. Andy and Tim, can you bring us all up to speed on the search at Brambles Guest House.'

Tim Donnelly spoke first. 'As far as forensics go, we've taken several fingerprint lifts that we'll be comparing with those of the deceased and the hotel staff. There were no signs of any struggle inside the room and no forensic issues have been found. There's no blood spatter or staining evident in the room.'

Danny said, 'Thanks, Tim. Have you made a start on the Vauxhall Astra?'

'The car's been lifted to the forensic bay at headquarters and will be the top priority in the morning. I had a cursory look inside the glove box and the boot. There was nothing useful in either. I'll be in touch as soon as we complete the full forensic examination tomorrow.'

'Thanks, Tim. Andy?'

'A thorough search of the Acorn Room has been carried out, and all of Ian Drake's property has been seized, bagged and exhibited. There were a few documents in his briefcase that will warrant further examination and enquiries. His clothing has also been seized.'

'Come and see me after the briefing about the documents that need more work. How did we do statement-wise?'

'Lisa and Clive Hargreaves have both made written statements. All the other guests have been spoken to and none of them recall having a conversation with our deceased. I've obtained negative statements from them anyway.'

'Good work, Andy. Are you satisfied there's nothing more, evidentially, to be obtained from Brambles?'

Andy nodded. 'Everything's been done, boss.'

Danny searched the room for DC Helen Bailey. 'Helen, how did you get on researching our deceased?'

'That Filofax is a goldmine of information. Ian Drake is a married man, born and bred in this area but now resident in Kilmarnock, Scotland. His wife is Irene Drake. They've been married ten years and have no children. It looks like he was an insurance salesman. There are a lot of references to Pearl Assurance Limited.'

'Was there anything in the Filofax that could shed light on why he's in this area?'

'There are references to various business contacts he's had while he's been down here, but details are sketchy. I'm still trying to put a little flesh on those bones.'

'I know it's early days, Helen. What else do we know about Ian Drake?'

'I ran his name and details through the Police National Computer and our own criminal records office. Ian Drake is known to the police but has a relatively small criminal record. Two convictions for shop theft and one for a minor assault, all committed when he was still a juvenile. However, in 1974, when he was thirty-four, he was arrested on suspicion of murder.'

Danny let out a low whistle. 'That's a bit of a leap. From shop theft and minor assault to murder. What were the circumstances?'

'Ian Drake was previously married to Melanie Drake. She disappeared in suspicious circumstances in 1974. He was arrested and questioned about his wife's disappearance, but no charges were ever brought. He left the area shortly after that.'

'Do we know who investigated Melanie Drake's disappearance?'

'I'll be able to obtain more detail on that tomorrow morning, boss.'

Danny addressed the room, 'Okay. We've got plenty of work to get through. A priority enquiry tomorrow morning will be to establish all the details of Ian Drake's involvement in the Melanie Drake enquiry. I also want as much detail as we can find on these business contacts Drake's had while he's been in this area. We know he was due to meet two people at The Young Vanish in Glapwell on the night he disappeared. Unfortunately, none of the staff at the pub can recall seeing Drake that night. The restaurant was extremely busy, as it was hosting a twenty-first birthday party as well as the usual customers wanting evening meals. Right now, we have no idea whom Ian Drake met there. What we do know is that he was last seen alive by the taxi driver who dropped him off in the car park at six twenty that evening.'

Andy Wills said, 'Are you happy with the taxi driver's account?'

'Les Williams seems a genuine bloke. He's due in to make a full written statement tomorrow morning at eleven o'clock. I don't think he's involved.'

'Any CCTV at the pub?'

'None that's working. They do have cameras covering all the entrances and the car park, but the entire system is awaiting an overhaul. The manager told us they're currently unable to store any recorded images. Tomorrow morning, I want all available staff tracing guests of that party. We need to find a sighting of Ian Drake inside the pub.'

He paused before continuing, 'Rachel, who's finishing off the inquiries at Holly Primary School?'

'DC Bailey and DC Baxter have made the appointments with the parents of the three outstanding schoolkids.'

'Good. In that case, I want you and Jane to drive to Scotland tomorrow morning. I've already arranged for the police in Kilmarnock to deliver the death message tonight. By the time you arrive, Mrs Drake will be aware of her husband's death and will know you're coming. I want you to visit Ian Drake's home address and speak to his wife as a top priority. I want you to establish everything you can about his current relationship. I want to know if his present wife was aware that Drake had been married previously. Where was he working? If his wife knew why he was in the Mansfield area. You're probably going to need at least a couple of days in Kilmarnock to carry out these inquiries. Does that cause either of you any problems?'

The two detectives shook their heads and Rachel said, 'It's not a problem, boss.'

Danny addressed the room, 'Finish up what you're doing. I want everybody back on duty tomorrow morning at six o'clock.'

9

10.00am, 17 February 1989
Nottinghamshire Police Headquarters

Danny knocked once and waited for Detective Chief Superintendent Potter to call him in before walking into his office.

Adrian Potter motioned impatiently for Danny to take a seat, then said, 'I understand you've got a new murder to investigate.'

Without waiting for an acknowledgement to his statement, Potter continued, 'I hope this new investigation isn't going to hamper any progress you're making on the Margaret White and Florence King murders. Those two inquiries will remain your top priority. Is that understood, Chief Inspector?'

Danny had been expecting this from Potter, and he gave his well-rehearsed response, 'I appreciate the situation, sir. I still have a full team of detectives working around the clock, carrying out enquiries with all the major oil companies and recruitment agencies that supply the oil industry. I'm still confident that we'll achieve a breakthrough in the very near future.'

Unimpressed, Potter said, 'And how exactly will that breakthrough manifest itself?'

'As you know, we have strong forensic evidence to suggest the person who committed both murders either currently works or has worked in the crude oil industry in some capacity. We also have a very unusual time frame between the murders being committed. I believe the killer works away from the area and then kills on his return, in between contracts. Detectives are working through the companies I mentioned, searching for men who fit those contract parameters. It's labour intensive but I'm convinced it's the way forward. DI Cartwright is supervising the inquiry. I'm sure she won't allow the pace to slacken.'

Danny wasn't convinced about what he was saying, but in the absence of any other meaningful inquiries, it was better to give Potter something rather than nothing.

Potter sat back in his chair, folded his arms and said, 'Do you genuinely believe that, Chief Inspector? Or are you just telling me what you think I want to hear?'

'I do believe that, but only time will tell, sir. I'm hopeful the detectives working on the inquiry will find what they're searching for.'

'I don't think I need to remind you that the chief constable is paying close attention to these two murder cases.'

Danny was aware of the huge political pressures being heaped on the chief constable. Richard White, son of the murdered Margaret White, was the current chairman of Nottinghamshire County Council Police Authority. Understandably, he demanded constant updates on any progress being made in the hunt for his mother's killer.

Leaning forward, Potter picked up his pen and said, 'Tell me about the body found at Cresswell Crags.'

Danny began meticulously working his way through the details of the Ian Drake murder as Potter made notes. He ended by outlining the inquiries he had planned to move the investigation forward.

'How long do you anticipate your two detectives will need to spend in Scotland? I don't want them ripping the arse out of the expenses pot.'

Slightly annoyed at the inference, Danny snapped back, 'Two days, three max. They'll only claim the usual overnight expenses. DS Moore isn't one to take liberties, as you know.'

Potter made a grunting sound before saying, 'Keep me informed of all developments. I want regular updates from either yourself or DI Cartwright. We need to show Richard White that we're making genuine progress.'

Danny stood and left the office. He understood about the pressure being applied to the chief constable, but still felt aggrieved that he was being ordered to pay special attention to one murder inquiry to the possible detriment of another.

He would do what he always did when it came to the politics, bite his lip and continue to maintain maximum effort in all inquiries he and his team carried out. The standard of effort put in by him and his team would not hinge on how well connected and powerful the deceased's family may be.

10

10.00am, 17 February 1989
Piper Delta One Oil Platform, North Sea

The man stretched out on his bunk and tried to get comfortable. It wasn't easy, as he was wearing a full survival suit and boots. The storm that had battered the oil platform for the last sixteen hours still showed no sign of abating. Towering waves slammed into the solid metal structure causing it to vibrate, the metal beams screeching in protest at the raw power of the elements.

It was the worst storm he'd experienced during his time working offshore. All the men on the platform were praying the storm would blow through soon. The rig was a hard enough environment without being confined to bunks for hours.

The noise of the storm meant there was no chance of

getting any sleep. He had instead spent the time staring at the date circled on the calendar hanging on the wall. The 19th of March was the day he would finally board the helicopter and get off this hunk of metal in the middle of the North Sea.

With thoughts of home uppermost in his mind, he gradually began to be haunted by events in his recent past. It didn't matter how hard he tried to shut out the whispering voice inside his head, it was impossible to cut it out completely. It was like having someone constantly murmuring in his ear, competing against the raging tempest outside.

That soft but demanding voice filled his head with dark, malicious thoughts, constantly urging him to kill again.

While he was working and occupied, the voice remained in the background. Life as a rigger on an offshore oil platform was hard, dangerous work, and there was never much downtime. This storm had proved an unwanted pause in his work life that had allowed the voice to gain a foothold.

His thoughts were now constantly consumed by the murders he had committed, and even more troubling, of murders he knew he would commit upon his return.

He knew killing was the only way he could quieten the voice, and he stared at the calendar again.

11

11.30am, 17 February 1989
64, Blackskye Avenue, Kilmarnock, Scotland

Jane Pope eased the vehicle to a stop directly outside the smart semi-detached house. The two detectives had shared the driving during the five-and-a-half-hour journey, and both were feeling tired.

They took a moment to compose themselves before getting out of the car. Jane said, 'Did Kilmarnock police confirm they delivered the death message?'

Rachel replied, 'It was confirmed to our control room at eleven o'clock last night. Mrs Drake's aware of her husband's death.'

As the two detectives got out of the car, Jane said, 'I wonder how she took that news.'

Rachel didn't answer the rhetorical question. Instead,

she opened the picket gate and walked purposefully down the garden path.

She waited for Jane to join her before using the letterbox knocker to rap on the door. After a couple of minutes, the door was opened by a woman who looked to be in her mid-forties. Her short, blond hair was unbrushed and her face looked drawn, devoid of any make-up. Rachel could see the woman's eyes were bloodshot, and the rims red. It was obvious she'd been crying recently and had probably been awake most of the night.

Rachel held out her identification. 'I'm Detective Sergeant Moore and this is Detective Constable Pope, from Nottingham CID. We're here to see Irene Drake?'

The woman tightened the belt of her dressing gown. 'The police who came last night told me detectives would be coming today. You'd better come in.'

The two detectives stepped inside and followed Irene Drake into the living room. She pointed to the settee. 'Please, take a seat. You must be tired after such a long drive. Can I get either of you a drink?'

Jane Pope said, 'We're fine, but you look exhausted. Why don't you point me towards the kitchen and I'll make us all a cup of tea.'

'I'm sorry. After the two coppers told me what had happened to Ian, I couldn't sleep a wink.'

Irene Drake sat down heavily in the armchair and continued, 'The kitchen's just through there, love. You'll find everything you need.'

As Jane walked out of the lounge, Irene dabbed at her already bloodshot eyes with a tissue. She looked close to tears again, so Rachel said gently, 'I know this is hard to take in right now, and I'm sorry that we've got to be here asking questions. We'll go at your pace. When you feel like you've had enough, just tell me, and we'll take a break. Any information you can give us will be a massive help in finding whoever did this, but there's no rush.'

'I understand, and I really do want to help, but this has all been such a massive shock. I feel like I'm still asleep, existing in my own nightmare. This was supposed to be our year. New year, new job, and a new life away from here.'

'How was it going to be new?'

'Ian was down south because he had the chance of a new job. He'd been headhunted by some company to be their new head of sales and marketing. We were both hoping it would mean a move back down south, to England. Neither of us like Kilmarnock that much.'

'Do you know the name of the company that approached him?'

'There's a letter here somewhere. I'll find it for you. Ian was so excited about the opportunity. He'd always loved being in sales and marketing but was so bored selling life insurance every day.'

Irene stood up and left the room, passing Jane as she walked back into the living room carrying a tray with three steaming mugs of tea.

Irene said, 'Sit yourself down, love. I'll be back in a minute.'

A few minutes later she returned clutching an envelope. She took the letter out and said, 'The company's called Diamond Foster Investments (Nottm).'

'May I see the letter?'

Rachel read the brief letter, which was an invitation for Ian Drake to be interviewed at the company's head office for the head of marketing and sales post. There was a PO Box number to reply to, if he was interested. It was signed, J Smith.

'How did this company know about Ian?'

Irene shrugged. 'I've no idea, but Ian was overjoyed at the prospect. I don't think he could quite believe his luck. The job at Pearl Assurance was okay and the money was decent, but there were no prospects for promotion. I know he found the Pearl work boring, and we both wanted a move back to England. This opportunity had come at the perfect time for us.'

'Do you have any other correspondence from this company?'

'No. After Ian wrote back to the PO Box number giving them his personal details, he was always contacted by telephone.'

'Why was he staying in Mansfield?'

'He knows the Mansfield area better than Nottingham, so he booked into a guest house for a week while everything was being finalised.'

'Have you spoken to him while he was at the guest house?'

'We spoke three nights ago. It was the fourteenth and Ian wanted to wish me a happy Valentine's Day. He was so excited and happy. He'd arranged to meet the company's directors the next evening to sign the contract. He told me he'd been offered the job and that the money was fantastic, almost double what he was earning here. It looked like the new start we'd both dreamed about was really happening.'

'Did he talk about any previous meetings he'd had with the company?'

'I don't think there were any other meetings. Ian told me everything had been negotiated over the telephone. He couldn't believe the deal he was being offered. It was just a matter of meeting the directors over a meal to sign contracts. He told me he'd be home on the sixteenth, and that we could crack open a bottle of champagne to celebrate.'

The tears started to flow again, and Rachel stayed quiet.

Irene quickly wiped her eyes and picked up her mug of tea, taking a long drink of the warm, sweet liquid.

She put the mug down and said, 'I'm sorry. It comes over me in waves. I'll be okay.'

Jane said, 'Does the name on the letter, J Smith, mean anything to you?'

Irene shook her head. 'No, it doesn't, and Ian never said anything about it.'

After a pause, Jane said, 'How did you and Ian meet?'

Irene half-smiled at the memory. 'We met on the coach travelling up to Kilmarnock. He had been visiting his sister in Nottingham, and I was trying to get a job as a secretary here. I was feeling nervous about the interview and Ian calmed me down. We had a right laugh on that coach journey, and arranged to meet for a drink in a few days' time. I'll be honest, I never expected to be offered the job, so I thought I'd be catching the bus back to Doncaster that night and I'd never see him again. Anyway, long story short, I got the job and ended up staying in Kilmarnock. We met up for that drink and started dating a few weeks later, when I moved to Kilmarnock permanently. After seeing each other for a year, we got married. That was ten years ago. Neither of us wanted kids, so it's just been the two of us ever since.'

'You married quite late in life.'

Irene picked up on the inference. 'We'd both been married before. My marriage had been a disaster. I was married to an abusive bully, but I managed to escape his clutches after six months and got divorced.'

'What about Ian?'

'He'd been married before. He told me his wife had walked out on him, and they got divorced. He also told me that after the divorce his wife had disappeared, and that the police have never traced her.'

'Didn't you think that was odd?'

'I know it happens. Ian was very open about everything. We didn't have any secrets. He told me the police had arrested and questioned him as though he'd murdered his wife.'

'What did you think?'

'I know Ian—' She swallowed hard before continuing, 'Sorry, I knew Ian wasn't like that. He wouldn't harm a fly. He was the epitome of a gentle man. He told me he wasn't involved in his wife's disappearance, and I believed him.'

'Did Ian ever say what he thought had happened to his ex-wife?'

'He once told me that he thought she'd gone to live abroad somewhere. He said she was a bit of a hippy, and a free spirit. He thought she was probably living in some hippy commune in Spain, or in a student squat in Paris.'

'That must have made things difficult when you wanted to get married.'

'Not really. As I said, he'd been granted a divorce some time before his wife went missing. They weren't living together by then, so we were able to marry.'

Rachel said, 'You mentioned Ian had a sister in Nottingham, back then. Is she still in Nottingham?'

'Yes. She lives in a village called Ravenshead, just outside Nottingham. They never got on well, but I tried to maintain contact. In fact, I spoke to Beth this morning. I informed her of what's happened to her brother. I'm going to stay with her for a few days. I've just got to organise the bus or the train, as I don't drive.'

'We'll be travelling back to Nottingham sometime tomorrow, so we could take you to your sister-in-law's, if it helps?'

'That would be a huge help. Thank you.'

'We've got some other enquiries to carry out here in Kilmarnock first, but if they go okay, we'll pick you up tomorrow. I'll let you know a time.'

'That's great.'

'One question, Irene. If Ian still has a sister living in Ravenshead, why did he book to stay at a guest house in Mansfield? Why not stay at his sister's?'

'Like I said, they didn't get on. They haven't spoken to each other in over seven years. I speak to Beth on the odd occasion, and she phones me once in a blue moon. You know what families can be like.'

'I suppose. Is there anything else you think we should know about Ian? Does he have any enemies around here? Any threats he's received lately?'

'No. There's nothing like that. We've always kept ourselves to ourselves. Neither of us were ever bothered about going out, meeting people. We were happy just being us.'

As the tears welled in the woman's eyes again, the two detectives stood up and Rachel said, 'Try and get some rest, Irene. We'll see you tomorrow.'

12

6.35pm, 17 February 1989
MCIU Offices, Mansfield, Nottinghamshire

The debrief had just finished in the main office and Danny was sitting with his supervisors discussing the day's progress.

'The inquiries we've completed so far at the Young Vanish are starting to worry me. None of the waiting staff or the people attending the twenty-first birthday bash recall seeing Ian Drake inside the premises. The bar staff have all been seen now, and none of them recalls seeing him either. Bar staff are the ones who usually remember faces.'

Andy Wills said, 'Do you want us to have a closer look at the taxi driver who dropped him there?'

'No. I'm satisfied with his account. I've read the statement he made earlier. It's consistent with what he told us at the office. It's making me think that Ian Drake never made it inside the pub at all. I think he was met by his killer, or killers, outside.'

'If that's the case, it means he was deliberately lured to that location, solely to abduct and kill him. Why would anybody want to do that to an insurance salesman from Kilmarnock?'

'That's the million dollar question. We need to concentrate our efforts on Ian Drake. Somebody obviously had a reason to do this, and it's down to us to find that reason.'

Rob Buxton said, 'Glen's already researching Ian Drake. I'll put Jeff and Sam with him. The three of them working together on his background are bound to turn something up.'

'Good. Because I think that's where the key to solving this case lies. There's something in Ian Drake's past that's now come back to bite him.'

Rob nodded. 'I agree. I'll get that organised tonight. I spoke to Helen Bailey just prior to the debrief. She's finally managed to contact the senior investigating officer who dealt with the disappearance of Melanie Drake in 1974. Retired Detective Chief Inspector Ted Harper had been in hospital for tests but he's home now and will be available to be seen tomorrow morning.'

'What's his address?'

'He lives at 12, Curzon Street, Gotham, Nottinghamshire.'

'If you're free tomorrow, Rob, we'll go and speak to him ourselves. Everyone else has inquiries already allocated.'

'No problem. Any news from Rachel in Kilmarnock?'

'I spoke to her earlier. They've completed their inquiries with Irene Drake, and with his work colleagues at Pearl

Assurance. They're travelling back tomorrow, and they're bringing Irene Drake with them. Ian Drake has a sister, Beth Richardson, who lives in Ravenshead. Rachel's dropping her off there.'

'That's good. They'll have plenty of time to talk to the wife on the journey. That could prove very useful.'

'My thoughts exactly. People always say more when they don't think they're being questioned. Having said that, it did raise a red flag with me about the victimology inquiries we've carried out so far. How come we didn't know about this sister living at Ravenshead? We really need to do better looking at Ian Drake.'

'I'll keep on top of that, boss.'

'Thanks. Rachel also gave details of the company that Ian Drake was looking to join. He was in this area, meeting with representatives of a company called Diamond Foster Investments (Nottm). I've told Rachel that I want her and Jane Pope to thoroughly investigate the company on their return. Apparently, all they've got so far is a PO Box number and a name on an introductory letter.'

Rob looked thoughtful and then said, 'It's a long time since I looked at company law, but I think a PO Box number can only be issued to a limited company if they provide Companies House with a full, physical postal address. If Companies House have a record of a postal address, that will be a good place for Rachel and Jane to start. I'll check that I've got that right, then speak to Rachel when she gets back.'

Danny glanced at his watch. 'I'm sorry, I need to get going. I'm already late for a meeting with Sue and our childminder. Tina, we'll talk first thing tomorrow morning about the oil company inquiries.'

Tina nodded. 'No problem. There's been no great breakthroughs and progress is generally slow. I can fill you in tomorrow morning. I hope the issues with the childminder can be resolved. Finding good childcare can be such a nightmare.'

13

10.00am, 18 February 1989
12, Curzon Street, Gotham, Nottinghamshire

Rob drove into the tiny village of Gotham. 'Nice place to retire.'

Danny said, 'Depends what you want out of retirement. This place looks like death to me.'

'Yeah, but you know me—anything for a quiet life. I would love to retire to a sleepy little village like this. One pub, one shop, and I'd be sorted.'

'Yeah. I can just see you as the squire of some little hamlet. Walking your three dogs to the pub every day.'

Rob laughed. 'Every other day. You can have too much of a good thing. Is that the cottage?'

As Rob slowed the car to a stop, Danny nodded. 'That's it. Very nice.'

'When did Ted Harper retire?'

'He left the force in '76 as a DCI. Let's see what he can tell us about Ian Drake.'

Danny waited patiently after knocking on the door. After a long wait it was opened by a man using a Zimmer frame to assist his walking. He said, 'You must be the detectives. Sorry for the wait, gents. It takes me a while to get to the door these days. Come in.'

Danny and Rob both held out their identification cards and Danny said, 'I'm DCI Flint and this is DI Buxton. It's good of you to see us today. I understand you've been in hospital. How are you feeling this morning?'

'I'm fine. It was just for tests. The docs are worried my kidneys are packing up. I'm seventy-three now, so I suppose I've got to get used to things not working the way they once did.'

In the living room, Ted Harper manoeuvred himself from the Zimmer frame into a high-backed armchair and gestured for Danny and Rob to sit on the settee opposite. 'Now then, gents. What did you want to know?'

Danny said, 'I'm investigating the murder of Ian Drake. I know you looked at him as a suspect when his ex-wife disappeared in 1974.'

'His ex-wife being Melanie Drake. I always remember that job, because I was never happy about shutting it down. My gut instinct was that she hadn't just gone missing. I always thought she'd been murdered. And now he's been killed. All sounds a bit bizarre.'

'Why did you think Ian Drake had a hand in his ex-wife's disappearance?'

'He was the obvious choice, I suppose. They'd been through an acrimonious divorce six months earlier, and he was still feeling bitter about having to sell the house they had previously shared. He couldn't afford to run it after she walked out.'

Rob said, 'So she left him?'

'Yes. I never met the woman but, by all accounts, she was a strange person. A bit of a hippie chick, but with a nasty, spiteful core. Our enquiries revealed it was Melanie who ruled the roost in their home. She was a little older than Ian and, by all accounts, led him a bit of a dog's life. He would often turn up for work with bruises on his face.'

'Inflicted by her?'

'He would never admit that, but that was the inference. I don't think he ever said anything because of his male pride and the kids.'

A surprised Danny said, 'I didn't know they had children.'

'Ian and Melanie were foster parents. They used to foster kids on short-term placements for the social services.'

'How long did they do that for?'

'A few years, but then the complaints started.'

'Complaints?'

'During our enquiries into Melanie's disappearance, we learned that some of the foster kids had made complaints of abuse.'

'Sexual abuse?'

'No, physical abuse. From what we could gather, which wasn't much, it was more Melanie than him. More evidence of that vicious streak people spoke about.'

Rob said, 'I don't understand. Why couldn't you gather much information on those allegations?'

'The assault allegations were all dealt with by uniform. It was never passed to the CID. No action was ever taken by the police, and no arrests were ever made. Six weeks prior to the couple's divorce, and less than a month after the police investigation, Melanie and Ian Drake were removed from the foster register by the social services. Read into that what you will, but as the old saying goes, there's never any smoke without fire.'

'Why didn't the police do anything about the allegations?'

'I can't give you a definitive answer to that, as I wasn't part of the investigation. What you've got to understand is this all happened in the seventies. It was very different back then. Some matters weren't investigated as thoroughly as they should have been. And the other significant reason, I suppose, was the kids making those allegations were almost feral. They led the uniform police officers a merry dance back then, nicking cars, stealing anything that wasn't nailed down. They were the proverbial pain in the arse. I can understand why the investigating officers didn't fully accept what these kids were saying. I'm not excusing that outlook, but I can understand it.'

Danny said, 'Did you get any assistance at all from the social services? Did they give you an explanation why they had removed them from the register?'

'Not to our enquiry, they didn't. I suppose they might be a little more forthcoming these days.'

'We'll investigate it and ask the question again. You said you always felt Melanie had been killed. Why was that?'

'Just the circumstances of her disappearance. The night she went missing she'd been to an art class in Mansfield and never made it back to the house in Mansfield Woodhouse where she was renting a room. It was as though she had just vanished into thin air. There was a lot of talk about her running off to live on the South Bank in Paris, or one of the hippy communes in Mojacar, Spain. I thought that was all fanciful nonsense spouted by some of her hippy friends. All her belongings—not that she had a lot—were still at her rented place. Even hippies with a free spirit don't leave like that.'

'Apart from Ian Drake, were there any other suspects?'

'Not that we found. That's why the bosses wound down the enquiry. As they were quick to point out to me, I couldn't run a murder enquiry without a body. It left a bad taste in my mouth when I retired, because I'd always believed Melanie Drake was murdered. I was that convinced she was dead, I took the trouble to find out who her dentist was, so if we found an unidentified body later, I'd have that information to hand already.'

Rob said, 'What about the abused foster kids? Did you ever investigate any of them?'

'We did a cursory enquiry into all of them. But for me, their age was against them. Their ages ranged from eleven to sixteen, so I felt kids that young couldn't murder a grown woman, especially one with a vicious streak.'

'During your enquiries, did the social services provide you with a full list of the names of the children fostered by the Drakes?'

'Yes. All that information should still be in the file.'

Danny asked, 'One last question, Ted. Do you think Ian Drake murdered his ex-wife?'

The old man was thoughtful for a long time, then he shook his head. 'No. I didn't back then, and I still don't today. He was too weak. Physically, he was capable, but mentally he was a pathetic individual. He wept openly when we questioned him, begging us to believe him. He had a cast iron alibi for the night Melanie went missing, and there was never any physical evidence to support a murder charge, so he was released. Nothing has ever come to light since, to suggest I got it wrong back then. I'm satisfied he didn't kill Melanie. Which has always begged the question, if she is dead, and he didn't kill her, then who did?'

14

6.00pm, 18 February 1989
Laburnum House, Milton Street, Ravenshead,
Nottinghamshire

Rachel and Jane stood on the doorstep of the palatial detached house in the beautiful village of Ravenshead. Rachel let out a low whistle. 'My God, this place is a mansion. Why on earth did Ian Drake stay in that dingy guest house when he could have stayed here?'

Irene Drake, standing just behind the two detectives, said, 'I told you, Ian and his sister never got on.'

Jane said, 'Why was that?'

Before Irene could answer, a tall, elegant woman opened the carved oak door. Her long dark hair had been put up into a neat bun, and her make-up was minimal but perfectly applied. Dressed in a navy blue trouser suit, she was obviously casual but still impeccably smart and fashionable. It was clear from the woman's appearance and the house and grounds that money was no object.

Rachel said, 'I'm Detective Sergeant Moore and this is DC Pope. We're looking for Beth Richardson.'

The woman ignored the introduction and strode forward to greet Irene Drake. 'Irene, it's good to see you, but why are you here with the police?'

'They came to see me in Scotland, and kindly offered to drive me down.'

For the first time Beth Richardson acknowledged the presence of the two detectives. 'That was very kind, thank you.'

Rachel said, 'It's no problem. We were driving back down to Nottinghamshire anyway, and it's helped Irene out. May we have a moment of your time, Mrs Richardson? There are a few questions we'd like to ask you about your brother.'

'Yes, of course. Come inside. You must all be ready for a drink after the journey.'

'Thank you, a cuppa would be great.'

Ten minutes later and the two detectives were in the sitting room, nursing a cup of tea in a bone china cup and saucer.

Irene had refused a drink, saying she had a headache and needed to lie down. After showing her to one of the guest rooms, Beth Richardson had returned to the sitting room.

She sat down opposite the detectives. 'You said you had questions about my brother?'

Rachel placed her cup and saucer on the walnut coffee table and said, 'Were you aware that Ian had been staying in Mansfield recently?'

'Not until Irene called me and told me about his death. I had no idea prior to that.'

'Why did he stay in a guest house rather than here, with his own sister?'

'Families can be strange things, Detective. My brother and I haven't spoken for such a long time. If Irene didn't take the time and effort to call me every now and then, it would have been easy for me to forget I even had a brother.'

'What caused such a deep rift between you two?'

'Relationships.'

'In what way?'

'When he married that dreadful woman, Melanie, it caused a massive tension between us. I'm slightly older than Ian, and because our parents both died when we were young, I've always felt an obligation to look out for him. I could see that she was no good for my brother, but he was besotted. When I tried to intervene, he said some awful things about my husband that I could never forgive.'

'Like what?'

'My husband, Douglas, is a very wealthy man. He's an overseas property developer who's made a lot of money building holiday homes on the Spanish Costas. Ian always referred to him as "the crook". Nothing could be further from the truth; Dougie has always worked bloody hard for his money. I think Ian had always been a little jealous of his success. So, when he lashed out at what he saw as my interference in his relationship with Melanie, he was very spiteful with his comments about my husband.'

'Why were you so convinced that Melanie was wrong for your brother?'

'Ian was a gentle soul, weak physically and mentally. Melanie was older than him and I could see that she was a manipulative, strong woman who easily controlled my brother. I also witnessed a vicious, cruel streak in her one day that really troubled me.'

'Can you tell us what you saw?'

'I was visiting their house a couple of weeks before they were due to get married, and I walked in on them arguing.'

She paused before continuing. 'Well, I say arguing... It wasn't really an argument. She was screaming in his face, and he was cowering away from her. I saw her punch my brother, hard, in the face twice. She only stopped because she realised I was standing there.'

'What happened?'

'She stormed out, leaving me alone with my brother. I asked him what the argument was about, and he just shrugged. I was so angry at his pathetic acceptance of this woman's physical aggression. I told him he was a weak fool if he married her, and that I wouldn't be going to the wedding.'

'Have you had any contact since?'

'I did contact him when I found out he'd got a divorce from her, but he wasn't really interested. I tried again when I learned he'd been arrested by the police over Melanie's disappearance.'

'What happened that time?'

'By the time I tried to talk to him, he'd already arranged to go and live in Scotland. I told him he was an idiot to run away and that everyone would think he had something to do with whatever had happened to Melanie. He said he didn't care what people thought. That was the last proper conversation we had.'

Jane said, 'How did contact with Irene come about?'

'Irene is a sweet, loving woman. When she got together with Ian, she was keen to reconcile her husband with his sister. Despite her best efforts, Ian was having none of it. Understandably, my husband still isn't keen on Ian either, so there was no will or inclination, from either side, to make a reconciliation happen. Irene and I have stayed in touch. We speak on the telephone, infrequently. I've never visited my brother's house in Scotland, and this is the first time Irene has ever been here. I thought inviting her to stay here for a few days was the right thing to do, given the circumstances. The last thing she needs is to be left all alone in Scotland.'

Rachel said, 'That's very kind of you.'

She paused before continuing, 'You said earlier that people would think Ian had some involvement in Melanie's disappearance. Is that what you thought?'

'Not at all. Ian was a timid man. There's no way he would ever harm another living thing. It's just not in his nature.'

'Thanks for being so open, Mrs Richardson. I know it's not easy talking about family matters. Have you any idea how long Irene will be staying with you?'

'I made the invitation open ended; she can stay here as long as she needs to.'

'Is your husband around today? We'd like to talk to him about his brother-in-law as well.'

'Dougie is in London. He spends a lot of time down there on business. I'll tell him you want to talk to him. I'm sure he'll get in touch when he's home. Now could you answer a question for me, please?'

'If I can.'

'I understand from a friend who works for the police that there could be a long delay in releasing my brother's body for the funeral. Is that right?'

'I'll speak to my boss, DCI Flint, and find out for you.

There can sometimes be quite lengthy delays, but that's not always the case. As I say, I'll find out and get in touch.'

'Thank you. I'll show you out. Thanks again for bringing Irene down. The poor woman's obviously still in shock.'

As the two detectives walked back to their car, Rachel said, 'What did you make of the sister?'

'She's hard to read. There's something about her that's a little strange. I can't quite put my finger on what, though.'

'I think there's a cold, calculating edge to her that doesn't quite sit with her genteel, friendly manner.'

'Never mind the sister, Ian Drake's first wife sounds a right nasty piece of work. The boss is going to be very interested in finding out what Melanie Drake was like.'

15

6.35pm, 18 February 1989
MCIU Offices, Mansfield, Nottinghamshire

Tina Cartwright knocked once on Danny's office door, then walked in. He put his pen down and said, 'Everything okay?'

'I think we've finally got something from this oil company inquiry.'

'Go on.'

'Jag's been talking to a company based in Birmingham today. Global Fossil Energy Exploration are a company who specialise in the recruitment of engineers and other trades required by the oil industry.'

'What makes them different to the other companies you've already spoken to?'

'As their name suggests, they recruit workers from the UK to work on oil and gas exploration worldwide. Because they're involved mainly with the overseas market, they provide both long- and short-term contracts. The obstacle has always been trying to find a company that provides contracts for longer than two years. This company provide workers with contracts up to five years.'

'Are they willing to help us?'

'Jag's been speaking with them off and on all day. He says they're extremely cooperative. They're currently checking their employee records to find workers who have been employed overseas on contracts that match our criteria.'

'That does sound promising. How soon can they let us have some details?'

'This is the downside. They've promised to get back to Jag with a definitive list in the next four weeks.'

'Why four weeks? That seems a long time to check a few employment records.'

'Unfortunately, it's not that simple. This company have thousands of contracted workers. They're having to check each name on their books to ascertain the length of contract. There's no quick way to search their records. The computer they have cannot search on contract duration, so they're having to do it manually. Surprisingly, they're still happy to do that, even though it's going to be a time-consuming exercise for them.'

'It's good they're willing to do that for us. Jag must have been very persuasive.'

'I heard him telling the chief executive of the company some of the details of the two murders we're investigating. By the time he'd finished talking, the guy couldn't do enough to help.'

'That's clever work. Tell Jag to keep pushing the company. If we can get that information any quicker than four weeks, that would be a massive help. We need to find something from these oil company inquiries, and this looks like our best bet so far.'

'I'll speak to Jag and tell him to keep the pressure on.'

'Thanks, Tina. Keep pushing. Sounds like you're getting closer to the breakthrough we all need. It's going to be a tough few months running two separate murder inquiries that are both short on positive leads. We need that breakthrough.'

16

8.00pm, 18 February 1989
MCIU Offices, Mansfield, Nottinghamshire

Danny was just about to leave for home when he saw Rachel and Jane walk back into the office.

'How did you get on in Kilmarnock?'

'We did everything we needed to. There was nothing of note from Ian Drake's previous employees. Pearl Assurance knew nothing about his plans to leave the company. His bosses described him as a quiet man who kept himself to himself. He didn't socialise with colleagues, just did his job and went home. They were very shocked to hear what had happened to him. We're a little late getting back because we spoke to Drake's sister when we dropped Irene off at her home in Ravenshead.'

'I know you gave me your thoughts about Irene last

night, but did she offer anything different during the journey south?'

'Nothing that would shed any light on what happened to her husband at Cresswell Crags. They seemed to be an ordinary couple going about their lives. No enemies, not even a disagreement with a neighbour.'

'What about Drake's sister? What was she like?'

'Beth Richardson's a confident middle-aged woman who's married to Douglas Richardson. He's an extremely successful overseas property developer. They live in what can only be described as a mansion, just off the Mansfield Road at Ravenshead. The house stands in at least a couple of acres of land that backs onto the Newstead Abbey estate.'

'What did she have to say?'

'She was quite open about the non-relationship she had with her brother. They haven't spoken to each other for several years, over an incident that occurred just before Ian was due to marry Melanie.'

'What incident?'

'She walked in on a vicious argument between her brother and his fiancée. During that confrontation she witnessed Melanie physically punch Ian in the face twice.'

'Did he protest?'

'No. And it was his subservient attitude and acceptance of his fiancée's physical violence and aggression that caused Beth to fall out with her brother.'

There was a brief pause before Rachel continued, 'Beth Richardson has some very strong views about her ex-sister-in-law. To say she dislikes the woman would be an understatement. She described her to us as being a manipulative, uncaring woman with a vicious, spiteful streak. She tried to persuade her brother not to marry Melanie, and that's what caused the friction between the two of them. Heated words were exchanged that have never been taken back.'

'Did she say anything about her brother's death?'

'She had been unaware he was in Mansfield. It was only when Irene contacted her on the telephone to let her know what had happened to him that she knew he'd been staying in the area.'

'How long is Irene staying with her sister-in-law?'

'Beth Richardson said she could stay for as long as she needed to. She has the funeral to arrange. Speaking of which, they've both asked when Drake's body can be released.'

'I'll speak to Seamus Carter and then make a decision on that.'

Danny paused before continuing, 'I want you and Jane to follow up on the PO Box number registered to Diamond Foster Investments (Nottm). Rob did some digging last night, and to have a PO Box number issued, the company must provide a genuine postal address to Companies House. The address given to Companies House for Diamond Foster Investments is Arnott House, St. George's Drive, The Meadows, Nottingham. Visit the address tomorrow morning and speak to the person responsible for recruitment into the company. We need to establish who contacted Ian Drake about this career opportunity. I also want you to research Beth and Douglas Richardson. See if you can ascertain exactly what level of animosity there was between Beth and Melanie Drake, and between Douglas and Ian Drake.'

17

9.15am, 19 February 1989
Arnott House, St George's Drive, The Meadows, Nottingham.

Jane Pope leant against the CID car and said, 'This is the place. Arnott House.'

'Doesn't look like a successful advertising and marketing hub to me.'

The building they were both staring at was a huge warehouse-type structure which had once been a thriving hosiery mill. After that business had gone to the wall, the mill had fallen into disrepair before being converted into several small business units. There was a large board outside displaying the names of the various businesses, all housed under the same roof.

Jane Pope studied the board. 'There's no sign for Diamond Foster Investments (Nottm).'

Rachel could see spaces on the board where nameplates had once been attached. 'Perhaps they've moved to better premises. Let's see if we can find someone inside who's responsible for the admin of the building.'

The two detectives walked through the double doors into what would have once been a fancy reception area. It was now showing signs of decay. Paint was peeling and the decorative plaster covings were crumbling. At one end of the foyer was a chipboard door with a sign saying 'Private'.

Rachel knocked loudly on the door and could hear movement inside.

Impatiently, she knocked again. This time a voice from within shouted, 'Just a second. I'm coming.'

The door was flung open by an overweight, sweating man wearing an ill-fitting suit and scuffed, unpolished shoes. His hair was lank and greasy, and he wore glasses with the thickest lenses Rachel had ever seen.

Rachel said, 'Are you who we need to speak to about renting office space here?'

Behind the spectacles, the man's eyes lit up at the prospect of money to be made. He said, 'What size unit are you interested in? You're in luck, ladies. We've recently had a couple of offices become available.'

Now she knew she was dealing with the right person, Rachel held out her identification card and said, 'Police. I'm Detective Sergeant Moore and this is DC Pope. We understand a company called Diamond Foster Investments (Nottm) rents office space here. We'd like to see it.'

The fat man's mood changed instantly, and he snarled, 'Do you have a warrant?'

'I can come back with a warrant, if you think I need one. I can also come back with the Fire Prevention Team and the

Health and Safety Executive. Then we can see exactly how long it takes them to shut down this little enterprise. I've already seen one fire door secured with a padlock. It's your choice. Do I need to get a warrant?'

The man scowled and stared hard at Rachel before saying, 'Okay, okay. You don't need a warrant. That company rented an office on the third floor. I'll show you.'

'Thank you, Mr... I'm sorry, I didn't catch your name.'

'Peter Hill. I manage letting out the individual units. I collect the rents and carry out any repairs needed. The building is owned by a consortium of Asian men. I report directly to a guy called Asif Iqbal.'

Jane asked, 'Don't you keep a fire safety log for people visiting the premises?'

'Yes. It's on the counter there.'

'Who supervises people signing in?'

Hill shrugged. 'Everyone is told to make sure they sign the register when they are on the premises.'

'But you don't ensure they do?'

With an exasperated tone, Hill replied, 'That would be impossible. There's only me here. I can't watch the front door all day.'

Jane picked up the heavy book and flicked through the pages. There were no visits logged for Diamond Foster Investments (Nottm).

As they walked up the crumbling staircase, Rachel said, 'You said they rented an office, not they rent an office. Aren't they here anymore?'

'I don't know if they ever were here, if you know what I mean. I only ever saw one man. He arranged the let in the first place, and then came back to hand the keys in. They were the only two times I saw him. I stuck my head inside the door once, when he wasn't there. All that was in the office was a chair and a telephone. This is the one.'

Hill took out a bunch of keys, struggling to find the right one. Eventually, he unlocked the door and stepped to one side to allow the detectives inside.

The room was as Hill had described it. There was a single chair in the centre of the room, but the telephone had been removed.

Rachel said, 'When did you last see the man who rented the office?'

'At the beginning of the month, when he returned the keys. I told him the rent was due. He paid the rent he owed in cash, and said he no longer needed the premises. It was all a bit weird.'

'How long did he rent the office?'

'Just over a month. I can get the exact dates if you need them, but I'm pretty sure it was from the first week in January.'

'How did he pay the rent?'

'Always cash. He paid the deposit and a month's rent up front when I first met him.'

'How much was the rent?'

'It was an initial down payment of two hundred pounds, then a hundred a week.'

'So, he paid you six hundred pounds in cash when he first rented the office?'

'Yes.'

'Has anybody rented the office since?'

'No.'

'I'm going to arrange for our scenes of crime people to fingerprint the office. Have you touched anything inside?'

'No. This is the first time I've been inside since they left.

How long will it take them to fingerprint? I need to get this office rented out as soon as I can.'

'Don't panic, Mr Hill. I'll get them here this afternoon. They'll only need a couple of hours. Now, what can you tell me about the man who rented the office?'

'Not much. He told me his name was John Smith.'

'Did he produce any identification?'

Hill shook his head.

'Did he give you an address?'

'It was somewhere in Leeds, I think. I can find out for you; I'll have made a note of it.'

'The address sounds like it'll be as genuine as his name. What kind of operation are you running here? Are any of these offices rented by genuine businesses?'

An indignant Hill said, 'Of course they are. I told you I thought this guy was a bit weird.'

'Did you ever ask him why he wanted the office?'

'Yes. He said he wanted a short-term rental to evaluate the strengths and weaknesses of an innovative marketing venture he'd thought up. It obviously wasn't viable, or he would've stayed longer.'

With more than a hint of sarcasm in her voice, Rachel said, 'Obviously.'

Rachel turned to Jane. 'Go back to the car, arrange for scenes of crime to visit asap, and get some statement paper. We'll need to take a statement from Mr Hill.'

Hill tutted and said, 'Bloody hell. How long will that take?'

Rachel snapped back, 'It will take as long as it takes. I'm not at all happy with how you're managing this operation, so I suggest you cooperate. Do we understand each other?'

Hill nodded, locked the office door, and handed the key to Rachel.

As they walked down the stairs, Rachel said, 'What did this John Smith look like?'

'Ordinary. I don't know.'

'Try harder.'

'He was white, mid-forties. Dark, greying hair, clean shaven. Whenever I saw him he was wearing the same grey suit and a black Crombie coat. He looked like an ordinary bloke.'

'Would you recognise him again?'

The reply was as short as it was emphatic, 'No chance.'

18

3.00pm, 19 February 1989
MCIU Offices, Mansfield, Nottinghamshire

Rachel Moore sought out Danny as soon as she returned to the MCIU office. It was important he understood the reality of Diamond Foster Investments (Nottm).

She had tasked Jane Pope with contacting Companies House, to see what other information could be gleaned from them about the bogus company, and also asked her to check with West Yorkshire Police the validity of the address in Leeds supplied by John Smith to Peter Hill.

She knocked once and walked into his office.

Danny looked up from the statement he was reading. 'How did you get on at Arnott House? Did you manage to speak to anybody from Diamond Foster Investments?'

'The company's bogus, boss. Arnott House is a huge

building that's been subdivided into small business premises. You can rent a single room as an office; it's one of those setups.'

'Did you speak to anyone who arranges the lets?'

'Yes. We've obtained a statement from the manager of the operation, a man by the name of Peter Hill. He told us that a single office was rented by a man under the company name of Diamond Foster Investments (Nottm). Hill told us he'd looked in the office one day, and the only furniture was a chair and a telephone.'

'Who rented the office?'

'A man named John Smith. He gave Hill what I believe are obviously false details—the name John Smith, and an address in Leeds. Jane's checking with West Yorkshire Police on the Leeds address. I fully expect them to come back and say John Smith isn't known at that address, if it exists at all.'

'Could Hill describe the man who rented the property?'

'Vaguely, and he says he wouldn't recognise him again. Hill isn't the most cooperative of witnesses.'

'Any CCTV cameras covering this building?'

'There's nothing so sophisticated in that flea pit, boss. I've got scenes of crime examining the rented office for fingerprints this afternoon, but I'm not hopeful. Whoever set this up has been very careful so far. I can't see them making such a basic error as leaving a fingerprint.'

'It's still worth a try. Looks like we're back to square one then. Are you free the rest of the afternoon? I could do with your input on the press appeal I'm doing at four o'clock. I was going to ask for any information on the movements of Ian Drake, in particular any sightings of either him or his red Vauxhall Astra around the Cresswell Crags area between the tenth and the fourteenth of February. I think we should also add a request for any information on a company called Diamond Foster Investments (Nottm).'

'No problem. I'll give you whatever information I can on the company, such as it is.'

There was a knock on the door and Jane Pope walked in. 'West Yorkshire have just got back to me. That address in Leeds doesn't exist. I've also spoken to Companies House. The only details they have for Diamond Foster Investments is the Arnott House address and a company director named as John Smith. No other details listed.'

'No filed accounts? No company secretary? No accountant details?'

'Nothing, boss. They're obliged to list the company for twelve months. If nothing is filed, the company will be removed from the register.'

Danny was thoughtful before saying, 'Good work. Somebody's gone to an awful lot of trouble, and expense, to lure Ian Drake back to this area. We need to find out why. What's he done in the past to make someone that desperate to get even?'

19

6.35pm, 19 February 1989
Rochester Close, Kilton, Worksop, Nottinghamshire

Mike Molloy was eating his fish and chip supper straight out of the paper, the greasy wrappers resting on a tray on his lap. The television in the corner of the flat was on, and the local news bulletin for the East Midlands region had just started.

As a self-employed private detective, Molloy liked to keep abreast of local current affairs. Business was slow, so anything that could give him an advantage when it came to snaring clients was important. He had realised quickly, when he set up his private investigation business, that clients liked to believe he was a smart, intelligent man. A good knowledge of current affairs was important for that image.

He used his already greasy fingers to scoop up another chunk of fried cod before shovelling it in his mouth. He would finish his supper, watch the news, then make his way to the French Horn pub for a couple of beers. Molloy was a creature of habit, and this was his nightly routine.

He put the last few chips in his mouth, then began sucking the vinegary grease from his fingers, one by one. As he did so, a news article spiked his attention. A detective was making a press appeal about the murder of Ian Drake. A shiver ran down the spine of Mike Molloy as he heard the name. Could it be the same Ian Drake he'd been paid handsomely to track down?

When the detective went on to request any information on a company called Diamond Foster Investments, Molloy knew it had to be the same Ian Drake.

Wiping the remaining grease from his fingers on the arm of the settee, he reached into his jacket pocket and grabbed a pen and note pad. He hastily jotted down the telephone number for the incident room.

He had some thinking to do. He would do that over a couple of pints.

First and foremost, he'd been hired to trace Ian Drake. Once he'd achieved that and passed on the information, he was then asked to rent office space in Nottingham, using the name Diamond Foster Investments (Nottm). He was to set up a telephone line in the company name.

He'd been paid handsomely for the information but had no idea who had employed him. Whoever it was had always paid in cash, the envelopes posted to his office in Worksop. It wasn't an unusual scenario for him to have no physical contact with clients. In a lot of instances, he totally understood that need for anonymity.

He knew setting up the office in Nottingham was dodgy,

so to cover his tracks he'd provided false details to the lettings manager.

Once the office and telephone had been set up, he again passed on the details to his anonymous client. Once again, he'd been rewarded handsomely. He never asked the question of why the office was needed. He figured the less he knew about the details, the better.

That said, a man he'd been instrumental in tracing had now been murdered.

As he saw it, he had a simple decision to make. He could ignore what he had heard on the news, or he could go to the police and get ahead of what looked like a nasty business by telling them what his involvement had been.

The only problem with the latter option was that he could give no information to the police about the people who had hired him. All he had was the telephone number he'd used to contact the client and pass on the information. He knew that lack of information would make his position precarious.

He grabbed his coat and hoped a couple of pints of Heineken would aid his decision making.

20

8.00am, 20 February 1989
MCIU Offices, Mansfield, Nottinghamshire

The morning briefing had almost finished. The last item on the agenda was the results, if any, from the previous evening's press appeal.

DC Nigel Singleton looked tired. He'd worked a quick turnaround and hadn't finished his previous shift until midnight. He stood up and said, 'I worked the late turn answering the phones. I took a call just before eleven o'clock from a man who gave his name as Mike Molloy. He sounded a little drunk on the phone, but basically, he said he had information about Ian Drake.'

Danny said, 'Did he give any details about the kind of information he had?'

'No, he was deliberately vague. All he said was, he'd been hired to trace a man called Ian Drake.'

'Hired?'

'Yeah. He wouldn't stay on the phone to talk, but I managed to get his full name and an address in Worksop out of him before he hung up.'

'And?'

'And I did some digging last night, and then again first thing this morning. The address he gave me was false. I thought the name would be bogus as well but there is a Mike Molloy in the Worksop area. He's an ex-cop who served with the South Yorkshire force. Since retiring, he and another retired colleague have set up a private investigation agency.'

'That would tie in with the 'being hired' comment. What's the name of this private investigation agency?'

'The agency's called Sentinel Investigations Agency. They've got office premises on Hardy Street, in Worksop town centre.'

'Good work, Nigel. Anything else?'

'Like I said, the home address he gave last night is false. The road doesn't exist.'

'Why do you think he gave a false address?'

Nigel shrugged. 'He did sound undecided about wanting to talk to me on the phone. He sounded like he'd had a good drink. I wondered if he changed his mind half way through our conversation, but by that time he'd already given me his real name.'

Nigel paused and then continued, 'Anyway, I contacted South Yorkshire Police this morning and had them fax over the last warrant card photograph they had for Mike Molloy. I've shown the photo to DS Moore, and Molloy loosely fits the description of the man who rented the office at Arnott House.'

'What did South Yorkshire Police have to say about Molloy? I'm sure you asked the question.'

'I did. Molloy retired on an ill health pension after suffering a back injury in a car crash on duty. He was a traffic cop for most of his service and was involved in a nasty pile-up while pursuing a stolen vehicle. The cop I spoke to wouldn't go into too much detail, but apparently Molloy was fortunate not to be prosecuted for dangerous driving. Reading between the lines, it sounds like the force were glad to get rid of him on a medical pension. He served just over twenty years and retired as a uniform constable.'

Danny was thoughtful for a moment, then said to DS Wills, 'Andy, I want you and Nigel to visit Sentinel Investigations. Let's see if it was this Mike Molloy who phoned the incident room last night.'

He turned to Nigel. 'Do you think you'd recognise his voice?'

'I think so. He was slurring his words a little, but he had quite a pronounced South Yorkshire accent.'

'If you're happy it's the same man, treat him as a witness to start with, but if the only way you can get him to engage with you properly about his involvement with Ian Drake and Diamond Foster Investments is to arrest him, then do it. We need to get into his ribs and establish exactly who hired him to trace Drake, and why. I think Mr Molloy's going to have some difficult questions to answer.'

21

9.30am, 20 February 1989
Sentinel Investigations Agency, Worksop,
Nottinghamshire

Sentinel Investigations Agency office was on the first floor of Byron House. The building had seen better days, and the treads and risers creaked as the two detectives climbed the wooden staircase to the first floor.

The office door was a dark brown varnish, and in fancy gold lettering was the name Sentinel Investigations Agency.

Andy looked at Nigel and said, 'This is all a bit Perry Mason. I bet the receptionist's a cheroot-smoking blonde with red lipstick and killer heels.'

Nigel shook his head. 'Nah. No receptionist. Nothing that classy in this dump.'

Andy rapped on the wooden door and waited.

He heard footsteps approaching the door.

It was opened by a man the two detectives instantly recognised as Mike Molloy. He hadn't changed much from the photograph used on his last South Yorkshire Police warrant card.

Andy held out his own warrant card and said, 'I'm DS Wills and this is DC Singleton. We're from the Major Crime Investigation Unit and want to speak to Mike Molloy.'

Molloy stared at the warrant card through bloodshot, tired eyes. He rubbed the stubble on his chin and said, 'That's me. Why do you want to talk to me?'

Nigel Singleton said, 'Because you called our incident room late last night and said you had information about Ian Drake.'

'I didn't call anybody last night. There's been a mistake, or somebody's deliberately given you my name.'

'When you phoned in last night, it was me you spoke to. I know it was you who called in; I recognise your voice. You were obviously in two minds what to do, and that's why you gave me a duff address. Unfortunately for you, that was after you'd already let slip your real name. Why don't we all go inside and have a proper chat.'

The detective stared at Molloy and continued, 'Something's obviously bothering you about all this, or you wouldn't have made the phone call. And I know it was you who made that call.'

A now very worried Molloy said, 'Okay. I did make the call last night, but I've had a think about things and I've got nothing to say.'

Andy said, 'Can we come in?'

Molloy pushed the door wide open, turned and walked back to his desk. The two detectives followed and sat on chairs in front of the desk.

Nigel said, 'Last night you told me you had information about Ian Drake. What can you tell us?'

It was obvious to the two detectives that Molloy was still fighting some inner conflict, but after a long pause he finally said, 'All right, all right. I was contacted by a client who wanted to remain anonymous. They paid me to trace Ian Drake.'

'And did you?'

'Yes. It was a simple job and the money being offered was too good to turn down. I did the usual checks—health, employment, social security. It was no trouble locating him.'

'Then what did you do?'

'I passed on that information to the client.'

'How?'

'By telephone. I called them and told them where he was.'

'You keep saying they or them. When you spoke to the person on the telephone, was it a man or a woman?'

'A man.'

'Did he tell you why he wanted to trace Ian Drake?'

'All he said was that he was an old business partner and that he had set up an amazing new business and he wanted to involve Ian Drake for old times' sake.'

'Why did he want to remain anonymous?'

Molloy shrugged. 'I couldn't tell you. Most of my clients do. That's nothing unusual.'

Nigel said, 'Do you still have the contact telephone number?'

'Yes, but that's all I've got for you. I never saw the client at all.'

'How were you paid?'

'Cash posted in an envelope to the office.'

'How much?'

'I was paid five hundred pounds to trace him.'

'Had you any idea who Ian Drake was before being asked to trace him?'

'No.'

There was a pause, and then Andy said, 'Was that your entire involvement?'

Molloy reached for his cigarette packet and lit one. He took a deep drag on the cigarette and as he exhaled the blue smoke, he shook his head.

'What else did you do?'

'I was asked by the client to set up a temporary business premises and install a land line. I was to use the name Diamond Foster Investments (Nottm).'

'And did you?'

Molloy nodded. 'I knew a place in Nottingham that rents office space with no questions asked.'

'Where?'

'A place called Arnott House in The Meadows.'

'What did you do?'

'I sorted it with the bloke who organises the lettings. I paid him the going rate and a little sweetener so he wouldn't get too nosey. Then I arranged for the telephone line to be connected. I'd sorted it in a day. I paid the advance and rent in cash and gave the bloke a false name and address so there would be no comeback on me.'

Nigel said, 'Why did you feel the need to cover your tracks? Were alarm bells starting to ring?'

'I just wasn't sure. I'm used to dealing with anonymous clients, but I couldn't work out why he wanted me to set up this bogus company. It all sounded dodgy.'

'So why do it?'

'The money was too good to turn down. I've been struggling of late. My partner in the business pulled out and I'm finding it difficult to meet all the overheads on this place by myself.'

'What were you paid?'

'Five hundred pounds to set up the office and then another five hundred when I returned the keys.'

'Did you give the office keys to your client?'

'Yes.'

'How?'

Molloy looked up at the ceiling. 'This is going to sound so wrong.'

He paused, took a deep breath and said, 'When I contacted the client and told him I had the keys and asked how he wanted me to get them to him, he gave me instructions to drop them off.'

'What do you mean?'

'I was told to put the keys in a brown envelope and put them in a telephone box in Worksop town centre late at night.'

'Which telephone box and what time?'

'The drop was arranged for two o'clock in the morning, at the telephone box at the junction of Bessecar Road and Jasmine Street.'

'Did you see anybody or any vehicles in the area when you dropped them off?'

'That junction's in the middle of a housing estate. Nobody was about, but there were plenty of cars parked up.'

'How were the keys returned?'

'They came in the envelope with my final payment, through the post.'

Andy said, 'Do you have the client's contact number here?'

Molloy opened a drawer, took out a screwed-up sheet of notepaper that had a telephone number scribbled on it and passed it to Andy.

'Is that all the documentation you have for this job?'

Molloy cradled his head in his hands and said, 'This is why I bottled it when I phoned last night. When the last payment arrived in the post, I was instructed by the client to destroy all the paperwork I'd generated. I know how that makes me look, especially now this Drake bloke's been murdered. I've been stupid and naïve, but I'm not involved in this man's death.'

'Why keep the phone number?'

'After I'd burnt the file, I realised I still had the contact number, as it had been in my desk drawer and not in the file. I screwed it up once and threw it in the bin, but then I decided to keep it. I think it suddenly dawned on me that I may have become mixed up in something that could go seriously bad. If it had been kept in the file, I would have destroyed it with everything else.'

'So, more by luck than judgement then.'

Molloy lit another cigarette. 'I suppose so, but at least you have it now. Will you be able to trace the client from the number?'

'Let's hope so. Now, what can you tell me about your client's voice?'

'Not much. It was always the same man I spoke to. There was no strong accent. He sounded like he was from down south. Not a broad cockney. But well spoken. He was obviously well educated and not short of cash. Money never seemed to be an issue.'

'Are you prepared to make a statement about your involvement?'

'Yes, of course. Am I in any trouble?'

'What you've done certainly isn't ethical, but we'll have to establish whether you've broken any laws. The best thing you can do now is to cooperate fully with our investigation. No more holding back information or giving false details. Understood?'

Molloy nodded, and as he reached for yet another cigarette, he muttered, 'Yes,' under his breath.

22

4.30pm, 20 February 1989
MCIU Offices, Mansfield, Nottinghamshire

It had been another long day. Danny was holding a debrief with his supervisors to assess the progress on the day's inquiries.

Andy Wills had just finished detailing the extent of the involvement of private investigator Mike Molloy.

Danny let out an exasperated sigh and said, 'What the hell was he thinking? And he's an ex-cop? I want you to look very closely at what he's done. If anything crosses the line into illegality, I want him prosecuting. Understood?'

'Yes, boss. He's made a full statement and is cooperating fully with our investigation.'

Danny could feel his temper rising. 'That's all well and good. But it's becoming blatantly obvious that Ian Drake was lured back to Nottinghamshire to be killed, and this idiot has played a fundamental part in facilitating that.'

Andy nodded. 'I'll examine his actions and see if any charges are appropriate. Nigel's currently working on the contact telephone number. Hopefully we'll be able to trace the anonymous client through that.'

Danny calmed down a little and realised he shouldn't be taking his frustration out on his sergeant. 'Good work today, Andy. Ignore my frustrations; they're aimed at Molloy, not you. Let me know as soon as Nigel gets anything from the phone number. I want more research into Drake's background. There must be a reason why he was enticed back here just to be killed. Look for any possible local connections. I want to know why here. Why Mansfield? Why Cresswell Crags?'

He paused, then turned to Rachel. 'Rachel, I want you to concentrate on these unfounded allegations of cruelty from the time when Drake and his first wife were foster parents. Contact the social services and obtain as much detail as you can. We've got the list of children fostered by the Drakes in the seventies. I want you to trace those children, who will now all be adults. Let's find out everything we can about them. Obviously, prioritise those children who made the allegations and then work through the others on the list.'

'No problem. Any news on releasing Ian Drake's body to the family?'

'The coroner has declined their request for now. Can you contact the sister, give her my sincere apologies, and inform her that the coroner's unable to release her brother's body for burial or cremation yet, and we'll contact her as soon as that situation changes. Did you and Jane find anything else out about the sister and her husband?'

'The sister seems to be no problem, but Jane has turned up some very interesting things about her husband. To say that Douglas Richardson sails close to the wind in some of his business dealings would be putting it mildly. He has some rather unsavoury business associates, who have strong links with criminal gangs from London.'

'That's interesting. Ask Jane to keep digging. Don't forget to tell Mrs Richardson the coroner's decision.'

'Will do, boss.'

'Thanks, Rachel. I know that's never an easy message to pass on to relatives.'

There was a pause and then Danny said, 'Rob, I want you to find out what you can about the PO Box number that was on the letter sent to Ian Drake. Is there any way we can trace who established the PO Box? How was any correspondence collected or forwarded on? There must be a way we can trace who set up the PO Box in the first place.'

'Okay.'

There was a knock on the door and Nigel Singleton walked in. 'Sorry to interrupt the briefing, sir. I've just got a result on the telephone number.'

Danny said, 'Go on.'

'That number relates to a public telephone. It's located in the British Library in London.'

Danny let out a long sigh. 'Great. Have you contacted the library?'

'Yes, sir. The place is huge. There are forty public telephone booths within the library. These telephones are all payphones, so there are no records kept of calls made in or out.'

'Marvellous. So we're back to square one. This is one

slippery, crafty sod. You all know what needs doing. Get cracking.'

23

10.00am, 1 March 1989
Pleasley Vale, Mansfield, Nottinghamshire

Steve and Jenny Cowan were chatting happily as he drove their battered Ford Escort van along the rutted unmade road towards the derelict cottage. The pit electrician was looking forward to doing more renovation work on the property he'd bought for a song from the farmer at Wren Hall Farm.

The farm labourer's cottage had stood empty for over fifty years and the farmer had been amazed when Steve approached him with an offer to buy the property. He'd been reluctant to sell at first, but after his wife had pointed out that it would be nice for her to have some female company close by, and that it would cause the farm no inconvenience if the cottage was occupied, he had agreed to the sale.

Bill and Beryl Oakes had instantly taken a shine to the

pleasant, hardworking young couple who were soon to be their closest neighbours.

Jenny Cowen was expecting their first child and Steve felt he needed to get his family a roof of their own. Since marrying, the young couple had lived in a single room at his parents' house. He appreciated everything his parents had done for them, but now there was a little one on the way, he felt the time was right to strike out on their own.

As a skilled electrician at Clipstone Colliery, he wasn't daunted by the amount of work it would take to make the cottage in the woods fit to live in. He had plenty of friends who worked in the building trade and who would offer their skills and labour at mates' rates.

All the work done so far had been on the outside of the property. The roof had now been repaired. The timber beams had been sound but most of the slate tiles had needed to be replaced. New windows and doors had been fitted and the cottage was now secure and, more importantly, watertight. He was excited, because it meant he could finally start work on renovating the interior of the property. His plan today was to fully inspect all the wiring in the cottage. He suspected that a complete rewire would be necessary to make the property safe. The power had been reconnected the day before, so theoretically, there was now an electricity supply to the cottage. The water, gas and sewage services wouldn't be connected for another week. If there was power at the cottage, he could do everything he wanted to do today. Jenny had been up early that morning making flasks of coffee and sandwiches. Being six months pregnant, she knew she wouldn't be able to do much to help, but she wanted to measure the new windows and start planning for the curtains.

Steve brought the van to a stop outside the cottage. It looked so much better already, with its new slate roof and pristine, hardwood-framed windows. Once the stone walls had been cleaned of graffiti, it would look stunning.

Steve started to unload the tools he would need and said, 'Don't expect too much inside, babe. It's still a mess in there. It needs a good sweep-out before I start checking the wiring. Why don't you wait in the van for a bit? It's going to get dusty.'

'Just let me have a peek inside first. The outside looks wonderful.'

Feeling a surge of pride in the work he'd already completed, Steve unlocked the front door and placed his toolboxes in the hallway. He put a light bulb into the existing ceiling fitment, said a small prayer and flicked the switch. As light flooded the hallway, he punched the air and exclaimed, 'And God said, let there be light!'

With a broad smile on his face, he stepped back outside and said to Jenny, 'Come inside and have a quick look then.'

Jenny handed him a beaker full of hot coffee. 'Get this coffee down you while I have a look around.'

He took the coffee. 'Thanks, babe. Be careful where you put your feet. The leaking roof has let a lot of water in over the years. Some of the floorboards are totally rotten.'

Jenny tiptoed her way through the cottage, taking care not to trip on the rubble-strewn floors.

Steve stepped into a room at the rear of the cottage and said, 'I think this could be the master bedroom. What do you reckon?'

'I love it. All that dappled light coming in through the trees looks amazing.'

Taken by the moment, without looking at the floor, Jenny

stepped across the centre of the room towards the window, to get a better look outside. There was a creaking sound and then her right foot disappeared through a rotten floorboard. She stumbled forward but didn't fall completely. Instantly, Steve grabbed her and held her upright. 'Are you okay?'

He helped her extricate the trapped foot by ripping up the floorboards around her leg. As soon as her foot was freed, he sat her down and inspected the damage. Her tights had ripped, and she had a two-inch gash on her shin, which was bleeding profusely.

'Stay here. I'll fetch the first aid kit from the van so I can clean that cut. I think you need to go to the hospital. Looks like you're going to need a couple of stitches in that cut.'

Steve had just reached the van when he heard his young wife let out a bloodcurdling scream. All thoughts of cleaning the cut vanished and he raced back inside the cottage to see what had alarmed his heavily pregnant wife.

Jenny had backed herself into a corner, away from the hole in the centre of the floor. She had her hands clamped over her face and was crying.

He rushed to her side. 'What happened?'

Without taking her hands from her face Jenny said, 'Look in the hole.'

Steve stepped over and looked inside the hole he'd made as he'd ripped out the floorboards.

What he saw took his breath away.

There was a body under the floorboards. The skeletal face grinned up at him. Horrified and fascinated in equal measure, he bent forward for a closer look. He could see long, fair hair and what looked like women's clothes on the human remains.

He'd seen enough.

He helped Jenny to her feet and helped her walk back outside to the van.

As he drove the van back towards Wren Hall Farm, Jenny said, 'What are you going to do?'

'Call the police and get them out here. I'll see if Beryl will drive you to the hospital to get your leg seen to while I go back and wait for the cops to arrive.'

Steve was trying to remain calm in front of his young wife but inside he was panicking. His head was full of questions. *Who was that woman? How long has she been there? Will my young bride ever want to live in the cottage now?*

The questions vanished as he drove into the farmyard. 'Wait here. I don't want you walking unless you've got to. I'm worried about the baby after the shock you've had. I'll go and ask Bill if I can use their phone to call the police.'

Through tearful eyes, Jenny looked up and spluttered, 'Don't be long. I'm frightened.'

24

11.30am, 1 March 1989
Pleasley Vale, Mansfield, Nottinghamshire

Danny and Rob stood inside the cottage, staring down into the hole in the floor. Scenes of crime technicians, under the supervision of Tim Donnelly, had carefully removed further rotten floorboards, fully exposing the skeletal remains.

Squatting next to the body, Seamus Carter closely examined the now fully visible skeleton. He looked up at Danny. 'My best guess is that these are the remains of a Caucasian female, approximately thirty to forty years of age. I need to get the remains back to the mortuary, remove the clothing, and have a proper look. We'll need to be extremely careful how we get the remains out of the hole. If we're not, all I'll have to examine will be a jumble of bones.'

Rob said, 'The undertakers are waiting outside. They'll work to your instruction. Do you need anything else?'

'Some better lighting would be good. One dim light bulb isn't at all adequate for what we've got to do.'

Tim Donnelly said, 'The portable lighting is on its way from headquarters. It should be here anytime.'

The big pathologist straightened up. 'I don't want any attempt to move her until I can properly see what I'm doing. Let's wait outside and I'll tell you my thoughts on what I've seen so far.'

The two detectives followed Seamus outside into the fresh air.

Danny said, 'How long do you think she's been there?'

'Hard to say. I'm no fashion expert, but looking at the clothes, I'd say she was dumped there sometime in the seventies. How long's the cottage been derelict?'

'I've got people with the farmer now. Apparently, the cottage had stood empty for over fifty years. The young man who found the body, Steve Cowan, bought it off him three months ago. Can you tell us anything else about the body?'

'From my cursory examination in the gloom, I could see that her hands were tied behind her back. I didn't want to move the remains too much, but I could just make out binding around the wrists. There's also evidence of a large fracture to the top of the skull. Again, I'll be able to tell you more at the post mortem under proper lighting.'

'Of course. But in your opinion, we're looking at foul play?'

'One hundred percent. This person was bound and struck about the head, before being interred beneath the floorboards of a derelict building.'

From the far end of the unmade track came the rumble

of a diesel engine as the scenes of crime mobile generator arrived.

Rob said, 'That'll be the portable lighting. It will take Tim and his team at least fifteen minutes to set it up.'

Seamus added, 'And a good hour for me to extract the body.'

Danny looked at him. 'Will you be ready for the post mortem at two o'clock?'

Seamus stroked his bushy beard. 'Let's say three o'clock, to be on the safe side. This is going to be very tricky, and I know Tim will want everything photographing under decent lighting before we start the removal.'

'Three o'clock it is. I'll see you at Kings Mill Hospital mortuary.'

Danny turned to Rob. 'Stay here and work the scene with Seamus and Tim. Who's at Wren Hall Farm?'

'Rachel and Helen are getting statements from Steve Cowan and Mr and Mrs Oakes. Jenny Cowan is still being checked over at the hospital, but arrangements are in place to obtain her statement as soon as she's well enough.'

'Good. As soon as the body's moved, I want a team from the Special Operations Unit here to search the cottage and the surrounding area. For all we know, there could be other bodies under the floors in that cottage. I want every floorboard ripping up, until we're satisfied there's nothing else.'

'Got it.'

'I'm going back to the office to get the immediate enquiries organised and get everything in place for the briefing at six o'clock this evening. I'll see you at the mortuary at three.'

25

2.45pm, 1 March 1989
Kings Mill Hospital Mortuary, Mansfield,
Nottinghamshire

Danny had arrived early at the mortuary. He had travelled to the hospital with DC Nigel Singleton, who would be acting as exhibits officer for the post mortem examination.

When he walked into the brightly lit examination room the remains found under the floorboards at the cottage in Pleasley Vale woods were already on the stainless steel examination table. Tim Donnelly and two of his technicians were carefully removing the clothing from the remains.

Seamus Carter was supervising the operation. Every so often his loud Irish voice would boom out, 'You're going to have to cut that. Don't try to remove that.'

The two detectives quickly donned forensic suits and gloves and walked across the room to join DI Buxton.

As the individual garments were removed from the body by the technicians, they were photographed and handed to DC Singleton, so he could bag them and complete the exhibit labels. The thin nylon cord that had bound the wrists was carefully cut away, leaving the knot intact. Several precious metal rings were removed from the skeletal fingers, and a necklace of large wooden beads was removed from around her neck.

As he took the garments from the technicians, Nigel Singleton carefully went through the pockets, removing any articles he found and exhibiting them separately.

Rob said to Danny, 'Special Ops are still searching the cottage. They'd already ripped up all the floorboards before we left. There's nothing else in the cottage. They still had to check the chimney and do the surrounding areas, but it doesn't look like we've got a mass-disposal site.'

A wave of relief swept over Danny as he thought back to another woodland clearing that had recently yielded the four victims of mass murderer Sam Morgan.

'Thank God for that', he muttered under his breath.

Nigel Singleton walked over and said, 'I think you need to see this, boss.'

Danny and Rob followed the young detective to the bench where he'd laid out the completed exhibits. Nigel pointed to the cord that had been removed from the woman's wrists. 'It's a bowline knot.'

Rob said, 'The same knot that was used to bind the hands of Ian Drake?'

'Yes, boss.'

Danny asked, 'Anything from inside the clothing?'

'There's some unusual-looking jewellery she was wearing that may be identifiable, and she had a paperback library book in her coat pocket.'

Danny picked up the book. It was a hackneyed copy of a Jane Austen novel. Danny opened the book and saw that it was from Mansfield Woodhouse Library. The date stamp said, 27/10/74.

Danny showed the stamp to Rob. 'We need to ascertain who took this book out and never returned it.'

'I don't know if the library records will go that far back, but I'm on it. That's going to be one hell of a fine, after all this time.'

'It certainly narrows down our date parameters when we're trying to establish who this woman was.'

Seamus Carter's voice echoed around the stark room, 'I'm ready to start now, Danny.'

Danny turned and looked at the now naked remains on the stainless steel table. The woman's body was virtually a skeleton covered in places by parchment-thin strips of flesh that had been underneath clothing and hadn't completely rotted.

Seamus spoke into a Dictaphone as he commenced his examination with a visual description, 'The body is that of a white female, age approximately thirty-five to forty-five years of age. Five feet three inches in height. Judging by the size of the clothes she was wearing, I would say she was a slim woman in life, who probably weighed around eight or nine stones.'

He moved to the top of the table and bent forward to examine the skull. He removed the thin film of flesh that still anchored the woman's long blonde hair until he could see the exposed bone beneath.

'Danny, come and see this.'

Danny stepped over to the table and Seamus pointed at the top of the woman's skull. 'Can you see the small hole that has fractures running from it? That look like a spider's legs?'

'Yes.'

'That would have been your cause of death. This woman has been struck on the head with a heavy object that had a spike attached. That spike would have penetrated the brain. Death would have been quick.'

'Isn't that similar to how Ian Drake was killed?'

'A very different object, but a penetrating wound to the top of the skull nonetheless.'

'What could have caused that wound?'

'Looking at the small diameter of the hole, a nail or something similar. It's too small to be a screwdriver. And a screwdriver wouldn't have caused the fractures emanating off it. My best guess would be a heavy piece of wood that had a large nail protruding from it. But without the actual weapon, it's only an educated guess.'

'Thanks.' Danny then turned to Rob. 'That's two similarities to how Ian Drake was murdered.'

Rob said, 'The floorboards in that room were all nailed to the joists by six-inch nails. Could she have been struck with one of those?'

Seamus shrugged. 'It's possible, but without the actual nail to examine, I couldn't say.'

'The floorboards have all been ripped up now, so if one of them was used, we've already lost it as potential evidence.'

Seamus then began the post mortem examination

proper, taking samples as he methodically went about his grisly business.

Almost two hours later the examination was complete.

Seamus said, 'The good news is that her teeth were still intact. There's evidence of a lot of dental work having been done, so there should be a dental record of this woman somewhere. Bad news is, there's no way I can get any fingerprints or any viable samples for a DNA comparison.'

'Did you find anything else that could have caused her death or are you satisfied with the head wound theory?' asked Danny.

'There's nothing else. The only injury I could find was the wound to the skull.'

Rob said, 'Did she have any other injuries that may help us with an identification?'

'The flesh, what there is, is too degraded to establish any scar tissue, and there were no healed fractures of the skeleton that I could see. I'm afraid all you've got are the dental records.'

'When can you let me have your report?'

'I'll get it over to you tomorrow afternoon at the latest.'

'Thanks, Seamus.'

Danny took one last look at the remains on the stainless steel table. His thoughts turned to his next immediate priority—how to identify this woman.

Only once he had established that could he then start the colossal task of trying to find her killer.

Something about the circumstances surrounding the deaths of these last two murder victims was gnawing at him. This unknown female and Ian Drake had obviously been killed years apart, but there were a couple of similarities in their deaths. The way they'd both been bound using the same knot. The single catastrophic blow to the head that had killed them both.

The two questions nagging at Danny were simple.

Were the similarities weird coincidences?

Or were the two bodies somehow tied in death?

26

6.00pm, 1 March 1989
MCIU Offices, Mansfield, Nottinghamshire

The gathered detectives fell silent as Danny and Rob entered the briefing room. Most of them had spent the day at Pleasley Vale, working the scene at the remote cottage. They were tired and hungry.

Danny recognised the mood and said, 'I can see you're all shattered, so let's make this quick, but let's make it thorough too. Okay?'

He waited for nods and murmurs of approval before continuing, 'The victim is a white female, aged between twenty-five and thirty-five years of age. She was killed by a single penetrative blow to the top of her head. That same blow not only penetrated the brain, causing fatal injuries, but was also powerful enough to cause multiple fractures to the skull. We're investigating another murder, which now means as well as the ongoing inquiries into the deaths of Florence King, Margaret White and Ian Drake, we have this inquiry. This means we're all going to be working long hours for the foreseeable future. With that in mind, as of now all annual leave and rest days are cancelled. We're going to have our work cut out to progress all these separate inquiries. If this causes anybody any major difficulties, come and see me after this briefing.'

He paused to let that sink in before saying, 'Our top priority is to identify this woman as soon as we can. Forensic evidence is negligible due mainly to the length of time the body has been in situ, but there are still several ways we can achieve an identification.'

Danny looked at Rob. 'DI Buxton will now go through the clothing and other items found on the victim.'

Rob said, 'The victim was found fully clothed, having been secreted beneath floorboards of a derelict building. As you know, that building has been derelict for over fifty years. The pathologist has estimated the body has been there for between fifteen and twenty-five years. I know it's a massive time parameter but that's the best he could do. However, the clothing the deceased was wearing is quite distinctive and looks to be from the seventies. Photographs have been taken of each garment as well as the other items found on the body. Those individual items will all be stored in the forensic exhibit store upstairs. Some of you will be given a single garment to research tomorrow morning. See your individual supervisors to find out what you've been allocated after this briefing. There were also several items of jewellery found with the body. These will also be researched in the same way. Is everyone clear so far?'

He paused, waiting for any comment. When there was

none, he pressed on, 'DS Moore and DC Pope, I want you to research the book that was found in the pocket of the victim's coat. It's a library book that was taken out of Mansfield Woodhouse Library. The last date stamp inside the book is 27/10/74. I want you at that library tomorrow morning, as soon as it opens. The book itself is in the exhibit store upstairs, having been ninhydrin-tested for any fingerprints. I've no idea how long the library would keep a record of overdue books, but this is possibly our best chance of getting an early identification of the deceased.'

Rachel said, 'No problem. We'll be there when the doors open in the morning.'

Danny looked for the scenes of crime supervisor. 'Tim, can you give us all an update on the work carried out at the scene, please?'

Tim Donnelly nodded. 'The Special Operations Unit have completed their search of the cottage and the surrounding area. We've lifted several prints from inside the cottage. Tomorrow morning we'll be making comparisons with the new owners and anybody we know who has carried out renovation work at the cottage recently. We've also carried out fibre lifts on all the clothing recovered and these will be stored for future comparison. We've lifted smudged prints from the library book after the nin test. Unfortunately, they're not good enough for any comparison work. Apart from those few fingerprints and the fibre lifts, there's nothing else to report forensically. Seamus Carter has completed the X-rays of the victim's teeth, so they are now available for dental records comparison. There'll be a full album of photographs from both the scene and the post mortem available tomorrow morning. There will also be larger photographs available of the individual garments removed from the body.'

'Thanks, Tim. Priority enquiries for tomorrow are all geared to achieve an early identification. Two of you will be tasked with trawling through missing persons reports made during the time parameters given by the pathologist. DS Wills, I would like you to supervise that enquiry. Depending on how many MFH files there are, we'll adjust the staffing level. I'm hoping two detectives will be adequate for now.'

Andy Wills said, 'Okay. I'll come and see you tomorrow when I know what we're looking at.'

'Have we completed the statements from everyone at Wren Hall Farm?'

Rachel Moore answered, 'Yes. Statements have been obtained from Bill and Beryl Oates, and from Steve and Jenny Cowan. I've put them on your desk.'

'Good work. How was Jenny Cowan when you saw her?'

'Still shook up, but she and the baby are both fine. The leg injury required a few stitches but isn't serious.'

'That's good news. Right, everyone, finish up what you're doing and go home. I want everyone back here at six o'clock tomorrow morning, ready to be allocated your research assignments. It's been a long day already, so don't be late getting away tonight.'

Danny walked back into his office, followed by Rob. He closed the door and said, 'We need that identification. Without that we've got nowhere to start.'

'Let's see what tomorrow brings. I'm feeling confident that we'll turn something up. You've got good people out there.'

Danny nodded. 'I know. I just feel the pressure early on. That doubt always manifests itself the same way. There's a sense of hopelessness to begin with, but then as enquiries are made and things develop my optimism returns. I'll be fine in the morning when I've slept on it.'

'Don't beat yourself up, Danny. It's that very feeling of doubt that drives you to work harder. Don't think you're the only one who feels it. We all do.'

'Thanks, Rob.'

Danny scribbled the words 'press appeal' into his logbook, and said, 'I want you to talk to Tim Donnelly tomorrow morning and arrange for the clothing we recovered to be dressed on a shop mannequin and photographed, ready for a press appeal, if we don't achieve an identification ourselves.'

'Will do.'

Rob left the office, leaving Danny alone with his thoughts. He hadn't mentioned it in the briefing, but he was still troubled by the coincidences between this murder and the murder of Ian Drake.

He had a nagging feeling that although separated by many years, the two killings were somehow connected.

27

8.45am, 2 March 1989
Mansfield Woodhouse Library, Nottinghamshire

From their car parked across the street, Rachel and Jane watched the woman approaching the front doors of the library.

Rachel said, 'This looks promising. Come on.'

As the two detectives walked towards the woman standing outside the library doors, they could see her rummaging in her handbag for something. Eventually, she pulled out a set of keys and began to unlock the main door.

Rachel took out her identification and said, 'Excuse me. I'm Detective Sergeant Moore and this is DC Pope from the CID. We need to access the library records as a matter of urgency.'

'Sorry, duck, you'll have to wait for Maria, the librarian, to do that. I'm only here to do the cleaning. It's a bit chilly out here. Do you want to come inside and wait? Maria shouldn't be long; she's usually here bang on nine o'clock.'

'That would be great, thanks. What's Maria's last name?'

'Hennessey. I'm going to have a brew before I start cleaning. Would you like one?'

'If you're putting the kettle on anyway, why not? A coffee would be great, thanks. Neither of us take sugar.'

'Just grab a seat here in the reception area. I'll bring them out to you.'

At exactly nine o'clock, the library door opened and a young woman in her late twenties walked in. She had short, mousy-brown hair and wore a navy blue business suit and stylish spectacles. She was a little taken aback to see the two women sitting in the reception area, drinking coffee. Recovering her composure quickly, she said, 'Can I help you?'

Rachel and Jane both stood, and Rachel said, 'I'm Detective Sergeant Moore and this is DC Pope. We're here to see Maria Hennessey.'

'I'm Maria Hennessey. What's the problem? Has the library been burgled? Is Mrs Jenkins all right?'

Rachel said quietly, 'Don't be alarmed, it's nothing like that. If Mrs Jenkins is your cleaner, she's fine. She let us in and, as you can see by the coffee cups, made us very welcome.'

Having reassured the librarian, Rachel continued, 'The reason we're here is because we need to access the library records as a matter of urgency. We're in possession of a book that was taken out of this library in 1974 and obviously never returned. We need to establish who borrowed the book back then. Would your records on overdue books cover that far back?'

With a sense of relief washing over her, Maria said, 'Do you have the book with you?'

DC Pope handed over the Jane Austen novel. 'This is it. It's been fingerprinted—that's why the pages are a strange colour now. It's okay for you to touch it.'

The librarian flicked open the sleeve of the book and inspected the date stamps and the reference number of the book.

She said, 'The library has just had all its records updated onto a computer system. The new system is only geared up to store records for five years. You're in luck, though, as we haven't had time to destroy all the old card indexes. They're still being stored in the attic.'

Rachel said, 'Are there many?'

'Thousands. You'd be amazed how many books are taken out of the library and never returned.'

Rachel must have shown her disappointment at the number mentioned, because the young librarian said, 'Don't worry, the record cards were all stored in boxes marked by the year, so it shouldn't be too difficult a task to locate the box, or boxes, that relate to 1974. I'll go up into the attic and have a look for you.'

'Do you need any help?'

'No, it's fine, I'll manage. Stay here and finish your coffees. I won't be long.'

Ten minutes later, Maria Hennessey returned with a large cardboard box. She put the heavy box down on the table and said, 'There's one more box to bring down. Seventy-four must have been a bad year for returns. The box is open. You can start going through the cards whenever you're ready.'

As Maria walked away to retrieve the second box, Rachel

lifted the lid and saw rows of envelope-sized cards containing details of library customers. She took out the first one. The surname began with the letter A.

She looked at Jane and said, 'Bloody hell. They've been stored alphabetically. I was hoping they'd be in date or reference number order. We're going to have to physically check each card for the reference number on our Jane Austen novel.'

Jane Pope grinned. 'Best get started then, Sarge. The good news is that our mystery woman's name is in here somewhere.'

Rachel grabbed the next card and said, 'Are you always this bloody cheerful?'

28

11.15am, 2 March 1989
MCIU Offices, Mansfield, Nottinghamshire

Danny walked into the main office searching for Rob Buxton. As soon as he saw him talking to Fran Jefferies, he shouted, 'Rob, bring all the paperwork we have from the investigation into Melanie Drake's disappearance into my office.'

A few minutes later, Rob walked in carrying the two large manila folders that contained the documents. With a quizzical look on his face, he asked, 'What's up?'

'I've just had a phone call from Rachel, at Mansfield Woodhouse Library. The library still had all the old card records, and she's found the name of the person who took the book out of the library back in '74.'

'And?'

'It was Melanie Drake, ex-wife of Ian Drake. She gave her

address back then as 114, Vale Road, Mansfield Woodhouse. Those similarities have been playing on my mind all night. I should have spotted this connection earlier. I've read through this documentation a couple of times already, and I'm sure that somewhere in the statements, one of the witnesses from the art school mentions a distinctive kaftan coat Melanie Drake was wearing.'

'Like the one our dead woman was wearing?'

'Exactly. I want you to help me go through all this paperwork and see if we can find anything else.'

'No problem. Didn't Ted Harper say that he had obtained details of her dentist, in case they found a body later?'

'Yes, he did. Hopefully, that information will also be in these files. Locating her dentist will save us a stack of time.'

'What are Rachel and Jane doing now?'

'Visiting the address shown on the library records to ascertain if anybody there can remember Melanie Drake.'

'Pass me half the paperwork. We'll soon get through it.'

29

11.30am, 2 March 1989
Vale Road, Mansfield Woodhouse, Nottinghamshire

Rachel and Jane stood on the doorstep of the mid-terrace house on Vale Road. There was a sign in the front window that said, 'Rooms to Rent'. Jane said, 'It doesn't look big enough to be able to rent rooms.'

'These houses are deceptive; they go back for ever.'

Rachel banged on the front door again, and this time her knocking was answered with a bellowed response, 'I heard you the first time!'

The door was opened by a red-faced, middle-aged woman who had her hair in curlers. She was wearing a garish, turquoise-colour housecoat, and yellow marigold gloves.

She looked the two detectives up and down and snarled,

'You'd better not be Jehovah's Witness, dragging me down here. I've got bloody work to do.'

Rachel took out her identification and said, 'Not Jehovah's. We're from the CID. I'm DS Moore and this is DC Pope. We need to ask you some questions about Melanie Drake.'

'Who?'

'Melanie Drake. Apparently, she was staying here when she went missing in 1974.'

'Oh, her. I remember now. The police were crawling all over this place back then. Bloody hell, duck, that was fifteen years ago. I told your lot everything I knew back then; I even made a written statement.'

Jane Pope said, 'I know it's a long shot, but is there anything still here that belonged to Melanie? Something she may have asked you to keep safe for her?'

'No, nothing like that. The detectives who were looking for her back then took everything from her room.'

Rachel said, 'How long had she been staying here before she went missing?'

'I'm not sure.'

Noticing the detective's disapproving look, the woman shook her head and said tersely, 'I'm not being awkward. It's just so long ago. I really can't remember anything about the woman. I'm sorry I can't help you.'

There was another pause before she continued, 'Look, ladies, I'm extremely busy this morning. Do you mind if I get on? I've got two guests arriving in a couple of hours, and I've still got their rooms to fettle.'

Rachel could see she wasn't going to get any cooperation. 'Okay, no problem. Give me your details so I can find the statement you made to the enquiry back then.'

'My name's Hilda. Hilda Blackstock.'

With that, the woman slammed the door, leaving the detectives on the doorstep.

With a sarcastic edge to her voice, Jane said, 'Thanks for everything, Hilda.'

'Come on. Let's get back to the office and see if we can find her original statement.'

30

5.00pm, 2 March 1989
MCIU Offices, Mansfield, Nottinghamshire

As soon as the dental records confirmed the woman found dead at Pleasley Vale was Melanie Drake, Danny had called an immediate briefing to update the entire team.

It had taken longer than anticipated to confirm the identification, as the original dentist who treated Melanie Drake in the past had retired. It had taken Rob another hour or so to locate the dentist who currently held the dental records for Drake.

Once located, it was a simple matter of comparing the X-rays obtained by Seamus Carter to the existing dental record.

He called the gathered detectives to fall silent and said, 'I've called you all back in because we've made significant progress and we now have a positive identification on the dead woman. Melanie Drake was reported missing in 1974. She was the estranged wife of Ian Drake, the murder victim found at Cresswell Crags.'

He paused to let the information register before continuing, 'So that leaves us with some very interesting questions. Why were these two people targeted? What lurks in their past that would cause someone to want to kill them? Why were they murdered in an almost identical fashion, but fifteen years apart?'

He waited until the gathered detectives had finished making notes before continuing, 'All future enquiries will be geared towards delving into their past, to try and find some of those answers. I've already briefed your supervisors on the enquiries that need doing as a matter of urgency. Finish off what you're doing now and go home. We start again tomorrow morning at eight o'clock.'

Danny looked for Rachel. 'Rachel, can I see you in my office, please.'

Rachel followed Danny into his office. As he sat down, he said, 'Close the door. I know you were side-tracked this morning with the library book inquiry. I need to know how you're getting on with the inquiry to trace the foster children that were in the Drakes' care.'

'Even before this morning's delay, it's been slow going. I'm getting zero cooperation from the social services. I've been chasing them for their files on the children fostered by the Drakes for days, with no response.'

'Who is your point of contact at social services?'

'Jill Friar. She's the office manager at Mansfield.'

'First thing tomorrow, I want you to visit her in person

and demand action. Let me know if you have any problems. We need those files.'

'Will do.'

'Good work at the library today. Jane told me how many cards you had to wade through.'

'Yeah, they'd been stored alphabetically. Thank God her name was Drake, and not Williams or Yates, or we'd both still be there.'

31

9.00pm, 9 March 1989
The Bell Inn, Sheffield, South Yorkshire

Mike Molloy sat alone in a booth in the smoke-filled pub. In between taking sips of lager, he constantly glanced at the entrance door. Nervously, he glanced at his watch. His ex-colleague from the Traffic Wing, Ray Sykes, had promised to meet him at eight thirty. He was already half an hour late.

Just as he was thinking it was going to be a no-show, he saw the door open, and a worried-looking Ray Sykes walk in.

Mike walked over, shook Ray's hand and said, 'Thanks for meeting me. I was starting to think you weren't coming. What you having to drink?'

'I shouldn't be here, Mike. We both know this could cost me my fucking job.'

'Don't be daft, mate. Who's going to know? You know I won't say anything, don't you? Now what are you having?'

'Do I? Fuck it, get me a pint of bitter.'

Ignoring the barbed response, Mike paid for the beer and both men returned to the booth. As they sat down, Mike said, 'There's no need to look so worried, Ray. I know you're doing me a massive favour, and I really appreciate it.'

'I don't want to know any of the gory details. I just want some reassurance that you don't need this information for anything dodgy.'

'It's only a car registration check, for Christ's sake. How dodgy can it be?'

'I know what it is, and we both know that misuse of the police computer can get me fired, so don't give me any of that bollocks.'

Molloy raised both his hands in a gesture of appeasement. 'Okay, okay. I'm sorry. Look, I promise you, it isn't for anything dodgy. This is a one-off. I'll never ask again, okay?'

'Too right it's a one-off, and don't bother asking again.'

There was an awkward silence for a few minutes until Mike said, 'Well? Who owns the bloody car?'

Ray took another long drink. 'The number you gave me was for a grey Range Rover. It's registered to Douglas Richardson, Laburnum House, Milton Street, Ravenshead, Notts.'

'That's brilliant. Thanks, mate.'

Ray drained the remaining beer from his glass and said, 'Don't make me regret this, Mike. I'm off.'

As Sykes stood to leave, Mike said, 'Don't rush off. Stay and have another beer. We can have a proper session and talk about the old days when we were on patrol together.'

'No, thanks. I meant what I said. This meeting never happened. Got it?'

Mike again held up both hands as an apology and through tight lips said, 'All right, I get it. Go on, then, fuck off. Don't let me keep you.'

Ray Sykes walked away and muttered, 'You always were an insufferable prick, Molloy.'

'That's probably true, but I never mentioned to your wife about your little indiscretions, did I, Raymondo? We both know why you did this vehicle check for me, so don't take the moral high ground, you arsehole.'

Ray heard the comment, chose to ignore it, and stormed out.

Mike walked to the bar and ordered another pint of lager. He'd taken a gamble not telling the detectives that he had the registration number.

It had been worth the long wait in the shadows to get a glimpse of the driver of a grey Range Rover as he approached the telephone box where he'd left the keys for the bogus office. He knew something about the whole setup was wrong, and he wanted some insurance. The registration plate of the Range Rover was that insurance, and thanks to the fact that Ray Sykes had never been able to resist a bit of skirt, he now knew who his mystery client was. He took a long swig of the cold lager and smiled. He wondered just how much Douglas Richardson would be prepared to pay to keep his anonymity.

32

10.00am, 10 March 1989
Nottinghamshire Police Headquarters

It was with a real sense of trepidation that Danny approached the office of Chief Superintendent Potter. He'd received a call at home the previous night and been instructed to be at headquarters at ten o'clock for a meeting with Potter.

Eight days had passed since the euphoria of identifying Melanie Drake. Since then, progress on all the current cases being investigated by the MCIU had slowed to a crawl. He knew Potter would be demanding answers in relation to the progress being made on those individual murders. Unfortunately for Danny, there was very little progress to report on. As he approached the office door, he suddenly felt the full pressure of the responsibility he was under.

He knocked once and waited for the now familiar reedy voice to yell, 'Enter!'

Potter pointed to the seat in front of his desk. 'Sit down, Chief Inspector. First things first. What progress has been made on the Margaret White murder?'

Danny wasn't surprised this was Potter's first question. He was fully aware of the pressure being exerted from above to get results on that inquiry.

'I'm hopeful that we'll hear back from Fossil Energy Exploration in the next week or so.'

Potter sat back in his chair and let out a heavy sigh. 'Is that the best you can do? I've been hearing that same promise for weeks now. We need to start seeing some action, and soon.'

'The inquiry team are in constant liaison with the chief executive of the company. He's cooperating fully with us, but his staff have a hell of a lot of work to get through. They are bending over backwards to help us. What you must understand is, this company are a huge recruitment agency. They have clients across the world and thousands of contractors on their books.'

'I appreciate everything you're saying. God knows I've heard it enough times. I just hope, for your sake, that this inquiry doesn't turn out to be some wild goose chase.'

'I still believe it's our best chance of tracking down the person responsible for the deaths of not only Margaret White but also Florence King. Let's not forget about her, sir.'

Danny could feel himself becoming angry, and he fought to control his emotions.

'Chase them. The next time you're sitting here, I want you to be telling me about the names they've provided—nothing else. No more lame excuses. Understood?'

'Sir, I appreciate the pressure you're under—God knows I'm feeling it myself—but I cannot push them any more than we already are. If we push too hard, there's a real risk of the company withdrawing their support, and then we'll end up with nothing. I need you to show a little more patience.'

Potter made a tutting sound before saying, 'Talk to me about the murders of Ian and Melanie Drake. Any progress on those enquiries?'

Danny could hear the heavy sarcasm in Potter's voice but chose to ignore it. Instead, he outlined exactly where his teams investigation had taken them so far. It didn't take long; there wasn't much progress to report on.

Potter removed his wire-framed spectacles from his face and stared hard at Danny. 'I know we haven't always seen eye to eye, Danny. But understand I'm telling you this now as a friend. The chief constable is seriously considering the viability of the MCIU. As you know, up to this point, he's always been your biggest supporter. I was all for disbanding the unit when I first arrived, as I didn't see it as value for money. Over time I've seen the worth of having a dedicated unit to investigate the most serious crimes. But you and your unit need to find the person who killed Margaret White, or I fear it's only a matter of time before her son Richard decides that you aren't fit for purpose. Don't underestimate the power of the police authority. They're the people who control the purse strings and can seriously influence a chief constable in his decision making. Jack Renshaw will continue to fight your corner, as will I, but not for much longer.'

Danny wasn't shocked.

He knew all about County Councillor Richard White and the pressure he was exerting on the chief constable.

He stood up and said, 'I'll continue to do my best, and if Jack Renshaw decides that's not good enough, then so be it.'

'Forget the dramatic statements and just get a result.'

33

9.00pm, 10 March 1989
Mansfield, Nottinghamshire

Sue walked into the lounge and flopped on the sofa next to Danny. 'She's settled again now. Something had disturbed her but she's snoring her little head off again.'

Without looking at his wife, Danny muttered, 'That's good.'

'Didn't you want the TV on?'

'Not really.'

'What's wrong? You've been distant ever since you got home.'

Finally, Danny turned to face his wife. 'I'm sorry. Got a lot on my mind, that's all.'

'Work?'

Danny nodded.

Sue pressed, 'Spill the beans, mister. I'm not having you moping about like this for days. What's happened?'

'I had a meeting with Potter this morning. I think the days of the MCIU could be numbered.'

'Why? I thought you said he was coming round and you were starting to feel better about working with him.'

'That's just it. It's not Potter who's the problem this time, it's Jack Renshaw.'

'What's the chief's problem?'

'It's because I'm getting nowhere on the murder investigation of Margaret White. Her son's a county councillor who sits on the police authority. He's bringing pressure to bear on the chief constable, and that pressure inevitably falls on my shoulders.'

Sue's expression turned to one of indignation. 'That's so unfair. You've always said to me, "You can't find what isn't there". Does the chief really think that an alternative to the MCIU could solve this woman's murder any faster?'

'I don't know what he thinks. Potter intimated to me this morning that unless I get a result, and soon, the MCIU could be history.'

Sue remained tight-lipped for a couple of minutes before saying, 'So what are you going to do about the situation?'

'What?'

'Well, are you going to sit and sulk like some moody schoolkid, or fight back?'

Danny smiled inside. It was only when his wife got angry that her American accent came to the fore. He looked at her and could see the passion burning in her ice-blue eyes.

He placed his hand gently on her cheek and said, 'I'll do what I always do. I'll suffer the stress and strain for a day or so while I assess the situation, and then I'll come out swinging. I know I'm on the right track to catch this man, but it's taking too long to make significant progress, and time is the one commodity I'm running out of.'

Sue leaned forward and kissed him long and hard on the mouth.

'Just keep doing what you're doing, Danny. Always remember this: Potter and Jack Renshaw are damn lucky to have such a good man on the job.'

34

9.00am, 12 March 1989
MCIU Offices, Mansfield, Nottinghamshire

Rachel Moore knocked once and then walked into Danny's office. 'It's finally arrived. It's been like pulling teeth, but I've now got the complete list of every child fostered by Ian and Melanie Drake. And I now know which of those children made formal complaints about their treatment while in their foster care.'

'Good God! What's been the hold-up?'

'Like I told you, social services just haven't wanted to part with any information. I've either been on the phone to Jill-bloody-Friar, or seen her in person, every day since we last spoke. It's still taken until this morning to finally get everything sent through.'

'But you're satisfied you've got everything you need now?'

'I think so, yes. I just hope we don't turn anything else up that needs their cooperation.'

'How many children are we talking about?'

'There were eighteen altogether, various age groups and a mixture of sexes.'

'How many made complaints about their treatment?'

'There were five complainants in all. We already knew their names from the files created by DI Harper when he was investigating Melanie Drake's disappearance; we just didn't know anything about them. I'm guessing that social services were as reticent about handing over information back then as they are today.'

'I've already arranged a meeting, scheduled for this afternoon, with Daphne Henshaw, the head of Nottinghamshire Social Services. I don't want this failure to share information to become a recurring problem. There's every chance that during your investigations you'll need to go back to Jill Friar for more information. I'm going to hopefully grease those wheels this afternoon with Henshaw.'

'That would be great. It's a pity you couldn't do it ten days ago.'

'It wasn't for the want of trying. The day after we had our conversation, I tried to arrange a meeting but she's been on annual leave. It's her first day back in the office today.'

'Typical. Who takes annual leave in March?'

Danny shrugged. 'Not me or you, that's for sure. Who's going to be working through the list with you?'

'I've briefed Jane Pope, Helen Bailey and Glen Lorimar to work with me on the names. It's not going to be a simple task. All the information we have on them is from when they were children. These people are all adults now and will, no doubt, have led very different lives. They could be anywhere, doing anything.'

'Did you ever establish why the Drakes were removed from the list of foster parents?'

'I've asked Jill Friar that question every time we've had a conversation, and I'm still none the wiser.'

Danny could see the frustration in Rachel's face. He grinned. 'You really must work on your communication skills, Sergeant.'

Rachel allowed herself the faintest of smiles and said, 'Yeah, right. You haven't met the bloody woman. She's so evasive it's enough to make a saint swear.'

'I'll endeavour to get a definitive answer to that question from Daphne Henshaw this afternoon. Leave me the times and dates of all your conversations with Jill Friar. I'll get this issue sorted today. I need regular updates from you, how your team are progressing with the names. Concentrate your efforts on the five complainants to start with.'

'Will do, boss. Good luck with Daphne Henshaw.'

35

2.00pm, 12 March 1989
Nottinghamshire County Council Offices, Trent Embankment

Danny had been impressed by the punctuality of Daphne Henshaw. At precisely two o'clock she had beckoned him into her office on the third floor of County Hall.

'Take a seat, Chief Inspector. How can I help you?'

'I'm currently investigating the suspicious deaths of Ian and Melanie Drake. They were both murdered in a very similar way, but fifteen years separate the two offences. One line of enquiry we're currently following involves the complaints made against the couple by five children whom the social services had placed in their foster care in the mid-seventies.'

The director of social services looked puzzled. 'I don't

exactly see how I can assist those enquiries. None of that would come under my remit.'

'I need your assistance because we're being met with zero cooperation by certain people at your Mansfield office, where all the information on the children that made those complaints is held.'

Daphne Henshaw was thoughtful for a few moments and then said, 'What information have you requested?'

'We wanted sight of every piece of information you hold. I want to track these people down and question them now, to ascertain if they have any involvement in either of these crimes. It's quite possible that one of these children was abused in such a way by these two people that they decided to take the law into their own hands.'

'Do you honestly believe that's possible?'

'Yes, I do, and it's my job to investigate any such possibility. I would appreciate a little more cooperation from your staff at Mansfield in that task.'

'Quite so. Whom have you spoken to at the Mansfield office?'

'The problem seems to be with the office manager there, Jill Friar. For some reason, she's reluctant to disclose any information held in your records to the police.'

Henshaw scribbled down the name on her pad. 'Is there any information you need as a matter of urgency?'

'My detective sergeant running that inquiry has assured me that she has everything she needs for now, but it's been a long time coming and there's every chance she may need to go back to Jill Friar in the future for more information.'

'And you don't want the same stalled response to any requests?'

'Exactly that.'

'I'll speak with Jill Friar immediately after this meeting and ensure she understands both the seriousness and the urgency of your investigations. I'll explain to her that she's to cooperate fully with your sergeant in the future. What's the sergeant's name, by the way?'

'Detective Sergeant Rachel Moore.'

Again, Henshaw scribbled the name on her pad.

'Is there anything else, Chief Inspector?'

'There's one question we haven't yet received a satisfactory answer for. Why were the Drakes removed from the foster care register?'

'Now that's a question I can help you with. I do remember this case. I had just started the role of assistant director back then. As you know, none of the allegations of cruelty made by those children were ever substantiated, and no charges were ever brought by the police. However, other whispers began to surface—nothing concrete; just murmurings from social workers that were enough to cause the then-director a problem. He took the decision to remove the Drakes from the foster care register. I supposed he based his decision on the old *"no smoke without fire"* adage. I must admit, I was surprised when they were removed, as nothing had ever been proven against them.'

'Do you think it was the wrong decision?'

'That, we'll never know. Hopefully your investigations may give us that answer. Is there anything else you need from me?'

'No, thanks. Thank you for your time today. I look forward to a greater spirit of cooperation in the future.'

'Indeed. Leave it with me.'

36

10.00am, 15 March 1989
MCIU Offices, Mansfield, Nottinghamshire

Rachel knocked once on Danny's office door and walked in.

'Just an update for you, boss. Jane and I have completed researching the names of all the foster kids looked after by Ian and Melanie Drake. We now have current addresses for all the kids who were in their care. Obviously, they're adults now, so it's taken some doing.'

'Good work. Have you identified the kids who made the complaints to the police?'

'Yes. As you know, there were five complainants back then. We've concentrated our research on those five.'

'Good. I want you to see them first. They would have the biggest axe to grind against the Drakes, especially if they felt let down by the police at the time.'

'Will do, boss.'

'Take Glen Lorimar and Helen Baxter with you and split the names between the four of you. I want those five interviewing sooner rather than later. It will be interesting to see if they can shed any light on how the Drakes interacted with each other, as well as how they treated the children in their care.'

There was a loud knock on the door and Danny shouted, 'Come in.'

Tina looked round the door and said, 'Sorry to interrupt your meeting, but I think we may have a problem, boss.'

Rachel said, 'I'll keep you informed how the interviews go.'

'Thanks, Rachel. What's the problem, Tina?'

'I've just had a long telephone conversation with the chief executive of Fossil Energy Exploration.'

'This doesn't sound good.'

'His staff have completed the trawl through their files, and they now have all the information we need.'

'I sense a but coming.'

'But he has concerns over the amount of personal information on their contracted staff that's contained within those files. Basically, he wants some reassurances on how we're going to use that information and how we're going to dispose of any information we don't use.'

'Would it help if I spoke to him personally?'

'I hope so. I've taken the liberty to book us an appointment to see him tomorrow morning at their head office in Birmingham. I thought you'd want to get this matter sorted as quickly as possible. I know how badly we need that information.'

Danny flicked open his diary. 'What time tomorrow?'

'Ten o'clock. We'll be back here by one o'clock at the latest. I hope it isn't a problem.'

'No problem. I'm clear all day tomorrow. Unless something comes in overnight, it shouldn't be an issue.'

37

10.15am, 15 March 1989
Laburnum House, Milton Street, Ravenshead,
Nottinghamshire

Douglas Richardson spoke in hushed tones, but the anger and venom were clear in his voice. 'I asked you a question, Beth. Why is that bloody woman still here?'

'She's not doing any harm. I've told her she can stay until the funeral.'

'And how long's that likely to be? Do you have any idea at all?'

'No, but I don't see why it's a problem.'

'I don't care if you see why it's a problem or not. I just want that woman out of my house. God only knows why you invited her down here anyway.'

'Because she's grieving the loss of her husband, my brother. I thought it was the right thing to do. Why are you so dead set against her being here?'

'I don't appreciate being quizzed by the police in my own home, and that's what her presence here has meant. At any time, those nosey fucking detectives could be back here, asking more bloody questions just because she's still here. I want her gone.'

Beth's voice rose a little as she said, 'I'm not happy about this at all. At the end of the day Ian was my brother, as well as her husband.'

In a mocking tone, he replied, 'Oh yeah. Your precious brother who you had nothing to do with, and who couldn't stand us. We had nothing to do with them when he was alive, and that's how I'd prefer it now that he's dead.'

He could see the tears welling in his wife's eyes as she said, 'Stop being so fucking spiteful. That's my brother you're talking about.'

'Spare me the crocodile tears. You always told him he was weak and useless when he was alive. Don't pretend you have any feelings for him now.'

She glared at him and spat out a single word, 'Bastard!'

He grabbed a handful of her hair and pulled her face close to his own. 'I've got to go back to London tonight. By the time I get back, I want her back in Scotland. Understood?'

She squirmed, trying to release his grip on her hair. He tightened his grip and repeated, 'Back in Scotland. Is that understood?'

She gasped at the pain and spluttered, 'Yes, yes. I'll tell her to leave today.'

He released her hair and shoved her backwards into the kitchen worktop. 'When will you ever learn it doesn't pay to defy me? Get out of my sight.'

38

9.45am, 16 March 1989
Fossil Energy Exploration, Birmingham, West Midlands

The offices of Fossil Energy Exploration were in the heart of the fashionable Jewellery Quarter in the centre of Birmingham. Danny parked the car in one of the visitors' bays outside the main reception.

He turned to Tina and said, 'I always knew there was a lot of money in the oil industry, but these offices look amazing. Who is it we're seeing?'

'The chief executive, Robert McCloud.'

The two detectives made their way into the huge marble-floored reception area. The receptionist stood to meet them. 'Can I help you?'

Tina said, 'I'm Detective Inspector Cartwright and this is Detective Chief Inspector Flint. We're here to see Robert McCloud.'

The young woman glanced at the diary in front of her and said, 'Yes, he's expecting you. Would you follow me, please.'

She led the detectives to a lift and hit the button for the top floor. The lift doors opened onto another reception area. This one had luxurious walnut panelling on all the walls, a huge picture window that afforded panoramic views across the city, and the same marble flooring as downstairs. There was a desk situated outside one of the two double doors that led off this reception area.

An older woman sitting at the desk stood to greet the receptionist, who said, 'Ms Hamilton, these are the detectives from Nottingham.'

'Thanks, Fiona. That will be all.'

The young woman stepped back in the lift and closed the doors. The secretary said, 'May I see some identification, please?'

Danny and Tina took out their warrant cards and Danny said, 'We appreciate Mr McCloud seeing us today. His company's already been a massive help to us.'

She gestured to the cream leather sofa. 'Take a seat, please. I'll let Robert know you're here. He's still with his nine o'clock appointment, but I'm sure he won't be much longer. Would you like any refreshments?'

'No, thank you, we're fine.'

At exactly ten o'clock the double doors opened and two men emerged. They shook hands and the shorter of the two said, 'That's great. I look forward to hearing from you soon.' He made his way to the lift doors and pressed the button. The doors opened and he stepped inside.

The other man, who looked to be in his mid-fifties, stepped towards Danny and Tina. 'Good morning, Detectives. I'm Bob McCloud. Thank you for agreeing to see me this morning. I'm sure we can iron these few issues out.'

The accent was from one of the southern states, probably Texas, thought Danny. Tina hadn't mentioned that Robert McCloud was an American. The chief executive was a tall, gaunt man with a sun-damaged, weather-beaten face and a shock of snow-white hair that looked at odds with the impeccable charcoal-grey, pinstripe suit he wore. He had the sort of face that would have looked more at home if he were wearing oil-stained overalls on a rig, somewhere in the desert.

Danny stood and said, 'No, thank you for seeing us. I'm Detective Chief Inspector Flint and this is Detective Inspector Cartwright. She's informed me that your company's been of great assistance to us already.'

'Come through and we'll get this little problem sorted. I really want to help in every way possible if I can.'

He closed the double doors and gestured for Danny and Tina to sit in the leather chairs opposite the huge desk that dominated the room.

He walked around the desk and sat down. Leaning back in his chair, he said, 'When my staff approached me with the request from you guys, they told me a little of the murders you are investigating. They sounded so horrendous that I told them to pull out all the stops and prepare the list you'd asked for as soon as possible. Although it was very labour intensive and took my guys plenty of hours, that was never a problem.'

He paused, choosing his words carefully. 'I personally, and F.E.E. as a company, always want to assist law enforcement wherever I can. As I explained to Inspector Cartwright yesterday, the only issue I have is with the amount of personal client information contained in the documents you're asking us to disclose.'

There was another pause before McCloud continued, 'All I want are some assurances from you guys. I need to know how you intend to use this information. I'll also need to have an agreement in place that covers the subsequent destruction of all the material you don't use. If we can deal with those two issues, I still very much want to help.'

Danny was thoughtful for a minute or so. 'The only problem there could be is with the destruction of the unused records. If we're fortunate enough to make an arrest after trawling through all the data provided by your company, under the Police and Criminal Evidence Act I'll be obligated to disclose all that documentation to the defence lawyers, even if that material is unused in the subsequent trial.'

The tall American steepled his fingers and said, 'Is there a way you could limit or control that disclosure?'

Tina said, 'I could make an application through the trial judge that any such documentation is returned to the prosecution after initial disclosure to the defence. This would prevent them from leaking any of that information, because if they did, they would then be in breach of the judge's order.'

'How difficult would it be to get the judge to make such an order?'

'It wouldn't be easy. They don't like doing anything that could prevent full disclosure. It's possible in a case such as this, where much of the documentation we will have to go through to potentially find our killer would be immaterial.'

There was a long pause before the chief executive said, 'Okay. It goes a little against my better judgement, but because of the awful nature of these crimes, I'm prepared to trust you and go the extra mile. I'll release the data to you, but I'm relying on you to ensure the personal details of thousands of this company's clients don't find themselves in the hands of the media or any other outside agencies. Is that clear?'

Danny said, 'Thank you. What I can guarantee from the outset is the integrity of your files while my team are carrying out the investigation. Both myself and Tina will do our utmost to protect that confidentiality, should we be fortunate enough to bring the guilty party to trial.'

'And if you don't find what you're looking for in these records, Chief Inspector, what then?'

It was a question Danny hadn't allowed himself to even think about. If this turned out to be another dead end, it would be a disaster. He'd effectively pinned all his hopes on this inquiry.

He said, 'If that's the case, we'll return all your files back to you, and that will be the end of your company's involvement.'

'Good enough.'

McCloud stood, walked around the desk and extended his hand towards Danny. The two men shook hands and McCloud said, 'I'll arrange for the documentation to be shipped over to your offices tomorrow morning. It will need to be signed for and kept somewhere secure. I warn you now, the documentation we have for you will probably fill a Ford Transit van.'

A beaming Danny shook McCloud's hand and said, 'Thank you. We'll be waiting for it in the morning. Inspector Cartwright will be responsible for the documentation's safe keeping and will remain in regular contact with you.'

'I'll send over Jimmy Matheson with the files tomorrow.

He's one of our best HR guys. He'll be able to explain the complexities of the various contracts and aid your search. He can work with you for as long as you need him.'

Very shrewd, thought Danny. *You're prepared to release the files but you will have somebody keeping a very close eye on them.*

Danny smiled. 'That would be a massive help. Mr Matheson will be made very welcome and can work alongside Inspector Cartwright.'

McCloud turned to Tina, shook her hand and said, 'I'm relying on you to keep this data secure, Inspector. I genuinely hope you can find the son of a bitch you're looking for in those records.'

McCloud opened the double doors and walked with the detectives to the lift. As they waited for the doors to open, he said, 'Please let me know when the shipment arrives tomorrow and, if you can, I'd appreciate being kept in the loop of any major developments.'

Danny said, 'Mr McCloud, you've been a massive help already. I'll personally inform you of any developments. Thanks again.'

The tall American gave a half smile and said, 'As we say back home, good hunting, Detective.'

39

10.00am, 16 March 1989
High Peak Outward Bound Centre, Derbyshire

Jane Pope steered the CID car down the narrow lane towards the courtyard of the High Peak Outward Bound Centre.

The centre was hidden away in the picturesque village of Youlgreave. A group of half a dozen youngsters dressed in waterproof clothing and carrying hard hats and lifejackets were milling around in the yard.

Sitting in the passenger seat, Rachel Moore said, 'Looks like we're just in time. They're obviously going somewhere.'

As Jane parked the car, she could see there were two adult instructors standing with the children, one male and one female. The two detectives got out and approached the female instructor.

Rachel said, 'Good morning. We're looking for Kevin Briar. Is he around?'

The young woman said, 'The boss will be out in a second. Is it something I can help with?'

Before Rachel could answer, the door to the reception area opened and a man dressed in dark green waterproofs walked towards them. Rachel studied him as he approached. He appeared to be in his thirties and had a muscular, stocky frame that was accentuated by his lack of height. He had a suntanned, weather-beaten complexion that spoke of a life lived outdoors.

He gave a warm smile and said, 'Can I help you?'

Rachel said, 'We're from the police. We'd like to speak to Kevin Briar.'

'That's me. What do we need to talk about?'

'We need to ask you a few questions about the time you spent in foster care in the seventies.'

He laughed. 'Bloody hell, ladies, I've been to bed since then. I can't remember anything about that. It's all so long ago, and to be honest it's a part of my life I try not to think about. Besides which, now isn't a good time. We're about to take these kids canoeing in Matlock.'

Not one to be easily put off, Rachel stepped closer to Briar and said quietly, 'This is a murder enquiry and I need to speak to you right now. You can join your colleagues later. I won't keep you long, but you do need to answer my questions.'

There was something in the detective's tone of voice that made Briar realise this wasn't a discussion he was going to win. He turned to the female instructor and said, 'You and Mike take the kids into Matlock and go through all the safety drills with them. I'll join you shortly. Nobody goes in the water until I get there, understood?'

'Understood, boss.'

She turned to the youngsters and shouted, 'Get in the Land Rover, kids!'

With cries of excitement, the youngsters clambered into the back of the Land Rover, stepping over the towbar for the trailer that held the nine fibreglass canoes.

As the Land Rover and trailer disappeared up the lane, Briar said, 'You'd better come inside, but I'm going to need to see some ID before we talk.'

Once inside the small office, and with the introductions done, Rachel said, 'This really won't take long, but I need to know what you remember about being fostered by Ian and Melanie Drake.'

'Just a second. Out there you said this was a murder enquiry. Who's been killed?'

'They have. The Drakes. Both of them.'

'What? That's crazy. What happened?'

Ignoring his question, Rachel said, 'How old were you when they took you into foster care?'

A still stunned Briar said, 'About fourteen, I suppose.'

'How long were you with them?'

'Until I was just over fifteen. The social services moved me back into a care home after I made the complaint against the Drakes. What a waste of time that was, but at least it got me out of there.'

Jane Pope asked, 'Was it that bad?'

'They were both a bloody nightmare. She was a vicious cow, and he was a perv.'

'In what way, vicious?'

'She was cruel. She liked to hurt us. Do you want to see

for yourselves?'

Briar removed his waterproof jacket and stripped off the t-shirt he was wearing underneath. He turned his back towards the two detectives. 'They're fading now, but look across my shoulders and the back of my neck—you can still see the scars.'

The two detectives could see countless round marks dotted across the man's shoulders.

Jane said, 'What caused the scars?'

'Melanie Drake's party trick was to wait until I was in the bath. There was never a lock on the door, so she could just walk in on me. If she had her cigarettes and lighter with her, I knew I was in for it. She had this expression she liked to say, "I'm going to use my favourite ashtray". That favourite ashtray was me. She'd have a drag on her cigarette, then place the tip on my back. The pain was horrendous, but I never once yelled out or cried. I wouldn't give that bitch the satisfaction. She was one evil cow.'

'How often did this happen?'

'Regularly. It was always the same routine. I was never allowed to take a bath on my own. One of them would always come in to watch me. Usually, it was just Ian Drake, the perv. He would just sit there staring at me as I washed. Dirty bastard.'

'Did he ever touch you?'

'No, it was never like that. He just liked to look. And then the bitch would come in and start bollocking me for all the stuff I'd been up to that week.'

'Stuff?'

'I'm not going to lie; I was a little shit back then. I was into everything. I'd steal cars for joyriding, nick from shops and sheds. I was into all sorts of shit, but I never broke into anyone's house. The cops hated me, and to be fair I hated them too.'

Rachel said, 'And Melanie Drake used to question you about what offences you'd committed?'

'It wasn't questioning. She would just shout and bawl at me while I was naked in the bath. She often made me sit there until the water was stone cold and I was shivering. That's when she burnt me with the fags.'

'Was Ian Drake there when she did that?'

'Every time.'

'What made you eventually complain to the police about them?'

'That, I can't really remember. I know I wasn't that bothered about making a complaint, because I knew the cops wouldn't be arsed about doing anything for me. I just thought nothing would happen. I was right, wasn't I? Nothing did happen to them.'

'So, nobody persuaded you to complain?'

'One of the social workers may have said something; I really don't remember.'

He was silent for a moment, then said, 'I do remember other kids were going to complain at the same time, so I may have just gone along with them.'

'Who else was in foster care at the Drakes' house while you were there?'

'Different kids would come and go all the time, boys and girls. Some stayed longer than others.'

'Were you friends with any of them?'

'I was friends with all of them. It was hard enough being in care without falling out with the other kids.'

Jane said, 'Were you close with any of them?'

'Not really. The one I used to get in trouble with all the

time was Dom. I suppose he was my best mate. He used to get exactly the same treatment as me from that evil cow.'

'Who's Dom?'

'Dominic Finch. We lost touch shortly after we went back into the care home. Just before our sixteenth birthdays he got moved to new foster parents down south somewhere.'

'Have you kept in touch with him or any of the other kids from back then?'

'No. Like I said, it's a period of my life I've tried hard to forget. I've got a good business here and I enjoy my life. I concentrate on that. Talking of which, have you about finished? I've a group of excited kids in Matlock, waiting to go canoeing for the first time.'

Rachel said, 'We're done, thanks. We may need to speak to you again, though. Any holidays booked?'

'Look around you, Detective. Every day's a holiday here. I've no plans to go away anywhere.'

'Okay. Thanks for your time this morning and enjoy your day.'

'Will do. I'm still in shock. I can't believe that the Drakes have been murdered. Bloody hell, there really is such a thing as karma.'

As Rachel and Jane walked back to their car, Rachel said, 'What do you think?'

'Silly comment about karma when two people have been killed. He came over a little strange, and he didn't look all that shocked to me. The look of surprise looked a bit false.'

'My thoughts exactly. Quite a strange character. I think we'll need to speak to him again at some stage. Who's next on the list?'

'Lyndsey Collins. She's now a hairdresser working in a salon at Mansfield.'

40

10.00am, 16 March 1989
Rainworth, Nottinghamshire

The two detectives waited at the side of the site hut and watched the man-mountain approach. His muscular arms were covered in tattoos that were semi-hidden beneath layers of dried cement and sand.

Glen Lorimar said, 'Owen Crawley?'

'That's me. The foreman said you were cops and wanted to speak to me. Is something wrong?'

'Nothing's wrong, Owen. We need to ask you a few questions from your time in foster care and the complaint you made against Melanie and Ian Drake.'

There was a look of astonishment on the young bricklayer's face. 'You're having a laugh. How am I supposed to remember stuff that happened when I was a kid?'

Helen Bailey said, 'We'll try and jog your memory. It

must have been quite a big deal back then, talking to the police about what had happened.'

'I suppose I can remember bits of it.'

'Like what?'

'I still remember what a total bitch that woman was. I don't remember anything about him. It was always her.'

'What about her?'

'She was the one I complained to my social worker about. That woman used to slap me about and pull my hair all the time. If I did the least thing wrong, or forgot to do something, it was always the same response from her. She'd slap me around the face. I remember one day she hit the side of my head so hard I thought she'd deafened me. I couldn't hear anything out of that ear for ages. Why are you asking me about this now? This all happened years ago.'

Glen said, 'It's something we're looking into again.'

'I'm not making any more statements. It was a waste of time back then, and it would be now. Nobody believed a word we said.'

'Why do you think that was?'

'I don't know. As soon as I made that statement to the police, I was moved out of their house and back into the care home. My social worker said that as I was out of it now, I should drop the complaint.'

'And did you?'

'Yeah. I knew others had complained. The social worker told me they didn't need my complaint as well.'

'So you knew other people had complained?'

'I knew there were other kids getting it far worse than me who had complained. I was only at the house for a couple of months, and I was still only eleven, so I didn't get it as bad as some of the older ones.'

Helen said, 'Can you remember who those others were who got it worse than you?'

The young bricklayer was thoughtful for a minute, then he said, 'There were two older lads. They were both around fourteen or fifteen, I think.'

'Can you remember their names?'

'One was Dom... something, and I can only remember the other one's nickname. Everyone called him "Patch".'

'Did you witness them getting worse treatment than you?'

'I never saw it but I heard them talking about it enough. It used to frighten me to death, thinking about what would happen if I stayed in that house.'

Helen looked at the huge man standing in front of her. It was hard to grasp how such a big, strong man could have been so terrified as a child, and by a woman.

She asked, 'What sort of child were you, Owen?'

'I was very small and timid. I was painfully shy back then. I was fostered again later by a couple who ran their own gym business. I got into weight training with them and it changed my life.'

'Would you say you were terrified of Melanie Drake?'

'Totally. I can remember crying myself to sleep every night. Dom and Patch would try and calm me down. They told me they'd look out for me and wouldn't let anything bad happen.'

'Did they say anything about what was happening to them?'

'They told me bits, but I think they didn't want to scare me even more than I already was. Dom always said he'd make her pay for what she was doing, and that he wouldn't be a kid forever.'

'What do you think he meant by that?'

Owen Crawley shrugged his huge shoulders. 'I don't know. You'll have to ask him that. Can I get back to work now? This little chat is costing me money and I can see the foreman glaring at me.'

Glen said, 'Yes. We're done. Thanks for talking to us. We may need to speak to you again.'

'No problem. Come and see me at home if you do, then I won't have to rush back to work. The foreman's got my home address.'

41

1.00pm, 16 March 1989
The Ivy, 1-5 West Street, London

Douglas Richardson sipped the brandy and allowed the spirit to lie on his tongue, savouring the myriad of flavours. He always liked to finish a fine meal with an expensive brandy, and the Remy Martin Louis XIII Rare Cask was one of the very best.

Sitting opposite him in The Ivy restaurant was Mason Connor. It was Connor who had made the reservation at the famous eatery in the centre of the city.

Connor was a brutish-looking man, short and stocky, with crew-cut hair and scar tissue above both eyebrows. He wore Savile Row suits, a gold Rolex Oyster watch, and several sovereign rings on his fat fingers. None of those refinements of wealth stopped him from looking exactly what he was. Mason Connor was a thug, a villain who had grown up in the mean streets of South London. He was a man of violence who had made a vast fortune from criminality, and he made Douglas Richardson nervous.

Connor fixed the property developer with a rattlesnake stare and said, 'Last time we spoke on the telephone, you said you had a problem that could involve me. I'll be honest, Dougie, that concerned me, because as you know, I don't do problems. What is it that's worrying you so much you feel you might need to bring my name into it?'

Delivered in a broad South London accent, Connor's husky voice made the question sound even more menacing.

Richardson could feel himself starting to sweat. He considered his response carefully. 'When you asked me to try and track down my brother-in-law, for a mutual acquaintance I did it as a favour, no questions asked, because we're friends. Now I'm being confronted with a ton of shit. I've had the police constantly sniffing round. They've been to my house twice already, asking awkward questions. My business doesn't need this scrutiny.'

Connor twirled the brandy around the large bowl glass that looked tiny in his huge hands and said, 'Let's get a couple of things straight. Firstly, you traced Drake not because we're friends doing each other a favour, but because I told you to do it as our mutual acquaintance needed that information. Secondly, we're not and never have been friends, you prick. I've made you a very wealthy man by giving you opportunities others would give their right arm for. Be under no illusion, Dougie boy, I can change all that in a heartbeat. If you've got a problem,' he emphasised the word *you've* and then paused before continuing, 'it's yours to deal with. Do we understand each other?'

'I know that. I'm just not sure how to deal with it.'

'That's a shame, because nobody else can deal with it for you. It's your problem, nobody else's. We had one unrecorded conversation that can never be traced back to me. If somebody was even thinking about mentioning that conversation to the wrong people, then I'd deal with that in my own way. I would ensure that problem disappeared altogether. Do you get me?'

Richardson totally understood the meaning of the not-so-veiled threat and hastily said, 'I would never say a word to anybody. Don't worry, I can deal with the heat. I'm sure that once the funeral's out the way, everything will get back to normal.'

'That's good. I'm glad we understand each other. I've always done business the same way. If a problem arises, you get rid of the problem. It's a very simple process. Are there any other problems you haven't mentioned?'

'I'm worried about our mutual acquaintance talking out of turn.'

The gangster smiled. 'That's somebody you don't have to worry about. That person has more to lose than anybody.'

'Can you tell me who it is?'

Connor snarled, 'There you go again with your stupid questions. Why the fuck do you need to know who it is?'

Richardson could feel beads of sweat standing out on his forehead. 'I don't, I don't. Sorry.'

'You need to get a grip of this situation, Dougie, and sort yourself out—before I do.'

'I'll sort it. It's just the pressure I'm getting from my wife as well. Drake was her brother, after all.'

'Are you telling me it's your lovely wife who's the problem? Because as I told you, I make problems that affect me disappear.'

'No, no. Of course not. She's just upset about her brother. Once the funeral's out the way, things will soon get back to normal.'

'Good. Because I don't want to hear the name Ian Drake again. Understood?'

Richardson looked at the tablecloth and nodded.

Connor said quietly, 'Any problems, you deal with them. Got it?'

'Got it. I'm sorry I brought it up. I won't mention it again.'

Connor stood and said, 'I'm glad we understand each other. Thanks for the lovely grub. You don't mind getting the bill, do you, Dougie?'

'Of course not. My pleasure. I'll sort the bill and I'll sort everything else.'

Connor leaned forward and playfully pinched Richardson's cheek. 'Good man. That's more like it. We've got some potentially huge deals coming up that will make us both a shitload of money. We don't need any crap to get in the way of business, do we?'

For the first time, Douglas Richardson allowed himself a smile. 'No, we don't. It's always business that counts.'

42

2.00pm, 16 March 1989
Cool Cuts, Harrop White Road, Mansfield,
Nottinghamshire

The two detectives glanced in the window of the hairdressers and were pleased to see no clients inside. The two members of staff were sipping coffee, obviously taking a break.

Rachel opened the door and walked in, followed by Jane. The older staff member stood in welcome. 'Hi, ladies. Have you got an appointment?'

Showing her identification, Rachel said, 'We're from the CID. I'm DS Moore and this is DC Pope. We need to speak to Lyndsey Collins.'

With a look of concern forming on her face, the woman said, 'I'm the manager. Lyndsey's on her lunch right now, but she'll be back any time. Can I ask what this is all about?'

Rachel held up her hand. 'There's absolutely nothing to worry about. Lyndsey's not in any trouble; we just need to ask her a few questions.'

Before the manager could say anything else, the door to the salon opened and an attractive, slim black girl walked in. As she began to take off her coat the manager turned to her. 'Lyndsey, these ladies are from the CID. They want to ask you some questions. Why don't you take them into my office so you can talk to them in private.'

There was a look of surprise and anxiety on the young woman's face as she approached the two detectives. 'What do you want to talk to me about? I haven't done anything wrong.'

Rachel said, 'Relax, you're not in any trouble, but we do need to talk to you. Let's talk in private.'

As Lyndsey ushered the two detectives into the office at the rear of the salon, the manager said, 'Don't forget you have Mrs Bainbridge's perm booked in at two thirty.'

As she closed the door, Lyndsey hissed back, 'I won't.'

Once the door to the manager's office was closed, Rachel said, 'It really is nothing to worry about and shouldn't take long. We want to talk to you about the time you were in foster care with Ian and Melanie Drake.'

A look of relief washed over the young woman's face. 'Is that all it is? God, you two had me terrified.'

Jane said, 'I'm sorry, that wasn't our intention. This enquiry is urgent so we wanted to see you as soon as we could; that's why we came here and not to your home address.'

'It doesn't matter. It was just a bit of a shock.' She half-smiled and continued, 'It will give them two in there something to gossip about anyway.'

Rachel said, 'What can you remember about your time with the Drakes?'

'I was very young when I stayed with them. I think I'd just had my eleventh birthday when I got sent to stay with them. I didn't stay with them long, thank God. It was the worst month of my childhood; they were so cruel.'

'How come you were only there for such a short time?'

'I didn't really understand back then but looking back now I think my social worker realised something was drastically wrong and she got me out of there. I remember crying buckets every time I met her. I never told her exactly what was going on, but she knew I was desperately unhappy at that place, so she got me moved. I ended up back in the children's home, but anywhere was better than being at that house.'

'Why was it so bad?'

'It was just awful. The woman was so cruel. For no reason, she'd make me sit in a cold bath for ages. Her husband would come in, sit on the toilet seat and watch me as I washed myself. If I started to shiver or cry, the woman would bellow in my ear.'

'Did she ever hit you?'

'No, she didn't, but she terrified me. I was just a kid and she used to get some sort of pleasure from bullying and ridiculing me in front of her husband.'

'Did he ever touch you?'

'No, he would just sit there watching. He never said a word against his wife. He just went along with whatever she told him to do.'

'Why didn't you tell your social worker what was happening?'

'Probably because back then I was just a terrified little girl.'

'Do you remember any of the other children who were at the house?'

'No. It was all so long ago, I can't remember.'

Jane said, 'We have a record of you making a complaint to the police about the behaviour of the Drakes. Can you remember doing that?'

'Vaguely. I do remember the police coming to the children's home and asking me a few questions about the Drakes. I told them about the cold baths and how they were towards me, but I never heard anything else. My social worker never mentioned it again after that one visit.'

'I know it was a long time ago, but can you remember how the Drakes were with each other?'

There was a pause and then Lyndsey said, 'The woman was the boss in that house. The husband just did whatever she told him to do. He never even dared to answer her back. I think that's another reason I found her so frightening, because she seemed to control her husband so easily. It made me wonder what she could do to me.'

'Anything else you remember?'

'That's it. It's a period of my life I've tried hard to forget.'

Rachel said, 'Thanks for your time today, Lyndsey. I know you've an appointment at two thirty, so we won't keep you any longer. We may need to see you again, but we'll contact you by phone next time.'

'No problem. I don't think there's anything else I can tell you though.'

There was a pause and then she said, 'Can I ask you something ? Why are you asking all these questions now?'

'We're investigating the suspicious deaths of Ian and

Melanie Drake and we're trying to build a picture of what they were like back then.'

A look of genuine surprise descended on the young woman's face.

Rachel said, 'We'll let you know if we need to talk to you again. Thanks, Lyndsey.'

'No problem. I'll show you out'.

As Lyndsey led the two detectives through the salon to the front door, she whispered under her breath, 'Bloody hell, I can't believe they're both dead.'

43

2.30pm, 16 March 1989
Ferndale Primary School, Bestwood, Nottingham

The deputy head introduced Sandra Mellor to the detectives waiting in his office, then excused himself saying, 'Just let the school secretary know when you leave, please.'

Glen Lorimar held out his identification and said, 'Ms Mellor, I'm DC Lorimar and this is DC Bailey. We need to ask you a few questions. It's nothing for you to be concerned about.'

'I know I haven't done anything that would necessitate a visit from the police. What I'm more concerned about is the fact that you deemed it urgent enough to come to my place of work to question me.'

The simmering anger and resentment, although held back, was obvious to the two detectives.

Helen Bailey said, 'Ordinarily, we would have been able to take our time, make further enquiries and find your current home address. We always prefer to speak to people at home. The fact is, we're currently investigating two murders, so time is of the essence. As soon as we had a location for you, we had to follow it up. I hope we've been courteous and discreet enough not to cause you any problems here.'

Still feeling disgruntled, Sandra said, 'Well, you're here now, so what's done is done. Why do you need to ask me questions about two murders?'

Glen said, 'The victims of those murders were Ian and Melanie Drake. Records show you were fostered by them, back in the seventies. We need to know what you can remember about that time, and about the Drakes themselves.'

A look of surprise crossed the teacher's face but was quickly replaced by one of indifference. She chose her words carefully. 'I'm sorry to hear that, but part of me isn't surprised.'

'What do you mean?'

'I can honestly say that Melanie and Ian Drake were two of the vilest people I've ever had the misfortune to meet. What is it they say, what goes around comes around?'

'What do you mean?'

'Look, Detective. I wouldn't have known either of those two people now if I passed them on the street. I haven't seen them since I left their house. The way they treated some of the children in their supposed care was disgraceful. That hateful woman was especially cruel. If you treat enough people that way throughout your life, I think eventually someone's bound to bite back. That's all I meant.'

Helen asked, 'How long were you fostered by the Drakes?'

'I was there for four months. I had just turned twelve when I was sent there. It was without doubt the worst four months of my life. Every time I met my social worker, I told her what was happening and begged her to get me somewhere else. Eventually, she moved me. The only good thing about that entire experience was that when I left, I was taken in by the foster parents I still live with. I went from the worst possible environment to a lovely stable home with two wonderful, caring people.'

'Why was it so bad at the Drakes'? What was happening?'

'Cruelty, both mental and physical, occurred on a daily basis.'

'What did they do to you?'

'I always seemed to get off lightly. I would just be shouted at or made to go without food. It was always for the least little thing. I was never physically abused, unlike like some of the others.'

'Did you witness some of this abuse?'

'Yes. It was terrifying. She would carry out the punishments, and he would watch and do nothing.'

'Punishments?'

'Physical violence.'

'And you told your social worker all this?'

'Some of it. I remember after I'd left I was visited by the police, who asked me a ton of questions about my time there, but then nothing happened. I just got on with my life, and because I was so happy with my new foster parents, I soon forgot about the Drakes.'

Glen said, 'You said, unlike some of the others. Who in particular?'

'There were two boys staying with them when I was there. They were both older than me—teenagers. They were always getting in trouble with the police. They always bore the brunt of her attentions.'

'Can you remember their names?'

'Dom Finch and Kev Briar. Kev was always referred to by his nickname, Patch.'

'What happened to them?'

'I often saw both boys getting slapped around by her. But there was worse done to them behind closed doors.'

'How do you know that?'

'The two lads would show me the scars the next day.'

'Scars?'

'They showed me where she'd burnt them with cigarettes. They showed me the fresh burn marks all over their backs.'

'Did you tell your social worker about these assaults?'

'To my eternal shame, I didn't. It was drummed into me by the two lads that if I said anything about the burns, she would start on me too. So I just kept quiet about it all. I did hear that not long after I left, the Drakes were stopped from fostering any other children.'

'Have you stayed in touch with any of the children who were at the Drakes' while you were there?'

There was a slight hesitation before she said, 'I stayed friends with Dom and Patch, because they looked after me while I was there. I think I dodged the worst of the abuse because of them. They were like my big brothers. They were so close back then they did everything together. Most of it was bad. They were always getting into trouble with the cops.'

'Are you still in touch with them?'

'No. We drifted apart. The boys went back into a care home in Nottingham, but then Dom was sent down south.'

There was another pause before she added, 'I haven't seen either of them for ages.'

Glen said, 'Apart from the cruelty you witnessed, what else can you remember about the Drakes?'

'Nothing much. I remember that she ruled the roost. He was like her lapdog and would do whatever she said. She was only a small woman, but when I was a child, she appeared terrifying. The way she controlled everything always made me feel so scared. I felt like I was never going to escape from the nightmare. That's why the two boys helped me so much.'

'Okay. That's all we need for now. Now we have your home address, if we need to talk again, we'll contact you at home. Once again, I'm sorry for any inconvenience we may have caused you.'

'No problem.'

'One last thing. Do you know if Dominic and Kevin stayed in touch after Dominic moved?'

'Sorry, no, I don't.'

44

6.00pm, 16 March 1989
MCIU Offices, Mansfield, Nottinghamshire

Danny walked into the briefing room and saw Rachel and Jane talking to Glen and Helen. They were comparing notes on the interviews they'd undertaken with the people fostered by the Drakes. He approached them.

'How did you get on?'

Rachel said, 'We saw four out of the five. Glen and I are driving to London tomorrow to interview the fifth.'

'Anything we need to look at closer?'

'We've just been comparing notes and they pretty much all say the same thing. Melanie Drake subjected the children in her care to systematic abuse.'

'Such as?'

'It ranges from slaps to beatings and worse.'

Danny waited to hear what worse meant.

After a brief pause, Rachel said, 'It seems that the main way she demonstrated this cruelty was to wait until the kids were in the bath and then burn them with cigarettes.'

Danny was aghast. 'What, all the kids were subjected to that?'

'No, not all. The two teenage boys were the main recipients of this special treatment.'

'The two on our list?'

'Yes. Kevin Briar and Dominic Finch.'

'It's interesting that she used a cigarette and there were all those cigarette burns on Ian Drake's body.'

'We were just saying the same thing.'

'And all the people you've interviewed today corroborate this.'

'They do. And we've seen for ourselves the scars on Kevin Briar. He was more than happy to remove his t-shirt and show us where she'd burned him. We'll see what Dominic Finch has to say about it all tomorrow.'

'So, if Melanie was the main instigator, what was Ian Drake's role in all of this?'

Glen Lorimar said, 'He was a passive observer. He was always present when the cruelty was being dished out by his wife, but he would just sit and watch. He never intervened or attempted to stop any of it happening.'

Rachel added, 'A lot of the abuse suffered by the kids was in the bathroom. There was no lock on the door, and they would be routinely subjected to cold baths. The cigarette burns always happened when the boys were sitting in the bath. Ian Drake would sit in the bathroom and watch what was happening to the kids.'

'The girls as well as the boys?'

'All the kids. The girls were very young, eleven or twelve, and he would sit there staring at them while they were naked in the bath getting shouted at by Melanie.'

'Bloody hell. I can't believe they were never prosecuted for any of this shit.'

'The kids told the social workers what was happening, but it seems they were never believed enough to warrant any action. A couple of the kids were moved by their social workers shortly after they were placed with the Drakes, but the police involvement was negligible. The kids all remember being questioned by the police, but the Drakes were never arrested and interviewed—just taken off the foster register.'

'What about Kevin Briar, the lad who was burned with the cigarettes? How did he come across?'

Rachel said, 'Jane and I spoke to him. Quite a strange character. He acted surprised when we told him that we were investigating the murders of Ian and Melanie Drake, but it was all a bit too forced and false. I don't think it came as any surprise to him at all, and he certainly detested them both.'

'Do you think he's capable of killing one or both of them?'

Rachel was thoughtful for a few seconds. 'I don't think we can afford to rule him out. I think we should have a close look at him. We may get a better idea when we've spoken to his best friend, Dominic Finch, tomorrow.'

'Good work today. Jane and Helen, I want you to start digging deeper into all these people, especially the two teenage lads. I want to know if any of them are still in touch with each other. I want full background checks doing on

Kevin Briar and Dominic Finch—finances, relationships, the works. Rachel, Glen, I want an update tomorrow as soon as you've spoken to Finch.'

'Yes, boss.'

45

6.00pm, 16 March 1989
Laburnum House, Milton Street, Ravenshead,
Nottinghamshire

Doug Richardson was in a foul mood. He had been ever since his meeting with Mason Connor. The gangster scared him, and it was an uncomfortable feeling for a man used to being in total control.

It had been a long, tiring drive from London. The traffic on the motorway had been horrendous and the two-and-a-half-hour journey had taken closer to four hours. He parked the Range Rover on the drive, grabbed his briefcase off the passenger seat and walked to the front door of his house.

As he approached, the door opened and he was greeted by his wife, Beth. 'Darling, you've been ages. Is everything okay?'

As he walked inside, he growled, 'Bloody traffic was a nightmare. I need a drink.'

His wife fussed around him. She took his coat and briefcase and said, 'You go and sit down, darling. I'll fix you a drink. Scotch on the rocks?'

He grunted a reply and walked into the lounge, kicking his shoes off as he did so. As he flopped into his favourite armchair, Beth returned with his drink and said, 'Dinner won't be long. How was London?'

He took a big gulp of the malt whisky and allowed the fiery liquid to burn his throat. He ignored his wife's question and said, 'Has the unwanted house guest returned to Scotland?'

Beth forced a smile. 'Irene left yesterday. I paid for her train ticket and drove her to the station. Ian's funeral has been delayed by the police, so she agreed there was no point in staying here.'

'Not before time. I don't know what possessed you to invite her here in the first place. It was bloody stupid.'

'I just thought she might need some help.'

'How many times have I got to tell you? Don't think. You're bloody dangerous when you start thinking.'

He could see that his wife had something else to say, but that she was reluctant to speak.

'What is it? I can see you've got something you want to tell me. Spit it out, woman.'

'The police were here again yesterday after Irene had left.'

'What did they want?'

'Two detectives came to give me some more details about Ian's death. They think he was lured here deliberately to be killed.'

'Why on earth would they think that? That's nonsense.'

'They asked me questions about you as well. They wanted to know how you got on with Ian now.'

'Why are they asking questions about me? This is bloody ridiculous. What did you say to them?'

'I told them that you were angry when Ian called you a crook.'

His face reddened and he shouted, 'For God's sake, woman! Why did you tell them that?'

'Because you're not a crook. I told them Ian had always been jealous of your success.'

'How can you be so stupid? You do realise that the police will be looking at my business dealings now.'

'Don't be silly, darling. Of course they won't.'

Enraged, he stared at his wife. He was just about to launch himself at her when she did what she always did when they were having cross words. She made herself scarce, saying, 'I'll go and finish preparing dinner. I've put all your mail in the study.'

He knew she would scuttle off to the kitchen, her little sanctuary. He would deal with her stupidity later. Right now, he needed another drink.

He made his way to the study, poured himself another large scotch and picked up the mail on his desk.

As he sat down, he flicked through the letters. One caught his eye. It was a brown envelope; his name and address had been handwritten and it had been posted using a second class stamp.

Intrigued, he grabbed his letter opener and slit the top of the envelope. It contained a short handwritten note from somebody demanding a meeting. The note explained that it would be in everyone's best interest for them to meet.

He quickly scanned to the bottom of the page and saw it had been signed, Mike Molloy. There was a telephone number to call.

As he thrust the letter into the bottom drawer of his desk, a sudden chill descended over him, and he felt the hairs on the back of his neck rise. Molloy was the private detective he'd hired to trace Ian Drake.

Worrying thoughts cascaded into his brain. *How has he found out where I live? What does he want? How the hell am I going to deal with this problem?*

The thought of it being a problem suddenly forced an image of a snarling Mason Connor into his brain. In that instant he knew precisely how he was going to deal with Mike Molloy.

The last thing he needed, with the police already sniffing around his private affairs, was a meddlesome, on the take private detective.

46

11.00am, 17 March 1989
Temple Place, London

Glen parked the car in the single visitor space available at the front of the impressive building.

Rachel said, 'It's a good job they reserved this space; there's nowhere to park for miles round here.'

Glen turned off the ignition. 'And Dominic Finch owns this building?'

'It's owned by Small Bird Finance, which is the company he set up eight years ago.'

'How did he make his money?'

'He provides finance for huge property developments abroad. SBF have provided the finance for many of the high-rise developments on the Spanish Costas.'

The two detectives got out of the car and walked into the reception area. Rachel approached the two women sitting behind the desk and said, 'DS Moore and DC Lorimar here to see Dominic Finch.'

The younger of the two turned to her colleague and whispered, 'Dominic's eleven o'clock. I'll take them up.'

The impeccably dressed young woman stepped from behind the desk, pointed towards a single elevator door and said, 'This way, please.'

She used a code to access the lift, and once inside she pressed the button for the top floor. As the doors closed, she said, 'Dominic's asked me to inform you that he doesn't have long this morning. He's got another appointment at eleven thirty that he simply cannot put off. He didn't want to cancel you at short notice but hopes you understand he won't have long to answer your questions.'

Rachel said, 'It's good of him to see us. Hopefully, this shouldn't take long at all.'

Nothing else was said. The elevator door opened directly into Dominic Finch's office. He was leaning on the grand desk that dominated the room. His arms were folded across his chest as he waited for them.

Behind the desk was a wall of glass and Rachel could see Blackfriars Bridge to the left, Waterloo Bridge to the right, and the famous landmark of Big Ben was just visible in the distance, also to the right.

The receptionist introduced them to her boss, then remained near the lift door.

Dominic Finch was a small, wiry man. His head was totally shaved, and he wore rimless spectacles that did little to mask his fiercely intense blue eyes.

He wasn't what Rachel had been expecting at all.

She had expected a high-powered executive in a power suit crafted by the finest Savile Row tailors. Instead, here was this small, ineffectual-looking man wearing faded jeans, a powder-blue Ben Sherman shirt and Adidas training shoes.

It was Finch who spoke first. 'Did Elizabeth explain I've a hectic schedule today and haven't got long? I understand from your phone call that you wanted to talk to me about my time in various care institutions when I was a kid. I'm curious why you would want to know about this now. Perhaps you can enlighten me, now we're face to face?'

Rachel said, 'We're interested in the time you spent in the foster care of Ian and Melanie Drake when you were fifteen.'

'I see. I was with the Drakes for about eighteen months. I had my fifteenth birthday at their bloody house.'

'What was your time like with them?'

'It was much the same as most of my experiences in the care system. It was shit. I still don't understand why you're here asking me about this now. Unless you provide me with some reasons, I'm going to call a halt to this conversation. This is all ancient history as far as I'm concerned.'

'We're investigating the suspicious deaths of Ian and Melanie Drake. That's why we're interested to know about your time with them and what they were like as a couple.'

Finch was thoughtful for a minute, before saying, 'I'll keep this brief for you so we're not wasting each other's time. Those people were vicious and cruel. They treated all the kids in their care terribly. I do recall complaints about their behaviour were raised with the police at the time and nothing was ever done about them. So I really don't feel inclined to waste any more of my time talking about them. I don't want to appear uncooperative, but I just haven't got time for this bullshit. I'll talk to my lawyer and provide you with a written testimony of my time with them if you like, but I'm done answering your questions today.'

Rachel was not easily put off. 'I will take you up on that offer of a written testimony. There's one question I'd like an answer for today. From our enquiries so far, it appears you had a close friendship with Kevin Briar while you were both fostered by the Drakes. Are you still in touch with him?'

Finch ignored Rachel's question, looked directly at his receptionist and said, 'Elizabeth, can you show the detectives out, please, and provide them with the name and contact details of my lawyer. Any future questions they have, they can direct through him.'

He walked back behind his desk and stared out of the window at the river eight stories below.

Elizabeth pressed the lift doors and as they opened, she said, 'This way, please.'

Knowing they would get nothing more from Finch, the two detectives stepped back inside the lift. The silence returning to the ground floor was oppressive, as nothing else was said.

It was only when the lift door finally opened that Elizabeth said, 'I'll get you the details of Dominic's lawyer.'

As they walked back to their car, Glen said, 'Well, he wasn't very forthcoming, was he?'

'Not at all. Was it just me, or did you think he already knew exactly why we were there?'

'It wasn't just you. I got that impression too. He was totally unmoved when you mentioned the deaths of the Drakes. I reckon he already knew they were dead.'

'I'm glad I wasn't imagining things. I think we need to have a much closer look at Dominic Finch.'

47

4.00pm, 17 March 1989
MCIU Offices, Mansfield, Nottinghamshire

Rachel and Glen had spent the last two hours researching Dominic Finch and they were now ready to take their findings to Danny.

Rachel knocked on his office door and walked in. Danny had been expecting an update on their visit to see Finch in London.

'How did you get on?'

Rachel said, 'Dominic Finch didn't want to answer any questions. He was uncooperative and told us to direct any questions we have in writing through his lawyer.'

'I see. What reason did he give for failing to cooperate?'

'He considered it all to be a waste of his valuable time. He told us it was ancient history and not something he wanted to waste time on now.'

'Did he answer any questions at all?'

'No. He totally ignored me when I asked if he was still in contact with Kevin Briar.'

'Okay. Well draw up a list of questions you think are relevant to this inquiry, send them to his lawyer, as directed, and let's see what responses we get. If nothing else, they'll be in writing and will be irrefutable later.'

'I've already started on that, boss. There was something else that we both agreed on after the meeting.'

'And what was that?'

'We both got the impression that Finch was fully aware that Ian and Melanie Drake were dead. There was no reaction at all from him when we told him about the murders.'

'Do you think we need to have a closer look at Finch?'

'That's what we've been doing since we got back from London. It's thrown up some very interesting points.'

Danny waited for Rachel to elaborate.

'There are concerns that Finch has ties with organised crime in the capital. There are reports that his finance company is being used to launder vast sums of money from these criminal gangs. He's on the Metropolitan Police Fraud Squad's watch list, but to date they haven't been able to tie him into anything illegal.'

'So, they think he's involved in criminality but haven't got the evidence to take things any further?'

'That's certainly the view of the Fraud Squad DI I've been speaking to in London. While he remains on the watch list, Finch is under permanent scrutiny by them.'

'Surveillance?'

'The DI informed me he's pushing for permanent surveillance on Finch, but that he's been unable to gain the relevant authorities yet. It's easier for them to get surveillance authorities on the organised crime figures he's linked with.'

'Are the Fraud Squad satisfied of those links with organised crime?'

'Finch has been seen, on several occasions, in meetings with various individuals connected with organised crime.'

'Does he live in London?'

'He has an expensive penthouse flat not far from his office that also overlooks the river, a holiday cottage in Derbyshire, and several properties abroad.'

'Okay. Send the list of questions to the lawyer, and let's see where that takes us. Come and see me when you get the responses.'

48

7.35pm, 19 March 1989
Rochester Close, Kilton, Worksop, Nottinghamshire

Doug Richardson had waited for Mike Molloy to leave his office in Worksop town centre. He had then followed the private detective to what appeared to be his home address on Rochester Close.

Molloy had parked his battered Ford Fiesta on the drive of the property and used a key to get inside. Richardson thought it safe to assume it was the man's home. He had then waited patiently at the end of the cul de sac, pondering his next move.

On two previous occasions, he'd dialled the telephone number in the handwritten note that had been posted to his own home. Both times had been from a pay phone and on both occasions, he'd hung up before the call was answered.

Something inside him told him that Molloy, armed with

the knowledge of his involvement in the suspicious death of Ian Drake, was going to attempt to extort large sums of money from him. He also believed the private detective wouldn't settle for just one payment.

He knew if he met him and paid him off, it would only be a matter of time before the slime ball would be back for more money.

At the same time, he couldn't afford to ignore the situation and do nothing. When he'd been ordered by the gangster, Mason Connor, to find someone who could trace Ian Drake, he had never dreamed he would find himself in the middle of this shitstorm. Drake was now dead, possibly murdered by the person who had approached Mason Connor for help in finding him. All the police knew was that Molloy had been hired to locate Drake. Right now, they didn't know who had hired the private detective. Richardson couldn't take the risk of that information getting out. He knew he was the only link between Mike Molloy and Mason Connor.

At their last meeting, Connor had made it clear that he wanted no comebacks and would act instantly if he thought there was a possibility of Richardson being compromised. The businessman knew exactly what that would mean. Connor would arrange for that link to be removed and would see to it that he was killed.

It left him with no choice.

He had to deal with Molloy in the same way Mason Connor would. He intended to remove the threat.

Quite how he was going to do it, he didn't know. He was a businessman, not a gangster.

As his problem seemed to be generating more questions than answers, he rubbed his eyes. When he removed his fingers, he saw that the front door of Molloy's house had opened.

He watched as the private detective stepped outside, closed and locked the door. He walked past his car on the drive and continued up the street.

Richardson gave him a good head start and then followed slowly in his Range Rover.

It was obviously a route known well by Molloy. He left the estate, then walked along a dimly lit stretch of road that had no pavements, just grass verges on either side. He could see Molloy up ahead walking carefully along the soft verges, and continued to follow at a safe distance in his car.

After two hundred yards, pavement appeared on one side of the road and Molloy crossed over to walk on the harder surface.

He continued to walk along the road for another five minutes, before walking into the car park of the French Horn public house. With an obvious familiarity, Molloy walked straight into the pub.

Richardson drove his car slowly into the car park and parked up in one of the many shadows. From his position he could see the main entrance to the pub.

The dimly lit stretch of road he had watched Molloy walk along had given him the glimmer of an idea for how he might solve his problem.

If Molloy walked home the same way, there was an easy opportunity for him to get rid of the private detective—make it look like an accident.

All he needed was for everything to be in his favour later. He had to ensure there were no witnesses.

Patience would be the key.

49

10.50pm, 19 March 1989
Archway Road, Old Clipstone, Nottinghamshire

The man was exhausted after his long drive from Aberdeen. The extra money he had paid to ensure his car was well maintained at the airport car park had been worth every penny.

The Ford Sierra RS Cosworth had started first time and had a full tank of fuel.

It had been a long, tiring journey that had begun on the North Sea oil rig at the crack of dawn. He had boarded the helicopter that would take him to Scatsta Airport on Shetland at seven thirty.

He'd had to endure a four-hour wait for his connecting flight from Scatsta to Aberdeen. It was then a gruelling seven-and-a-half-hour drive from Aberdeen back to Nottinghamshire. He had stopped once at the motorway services for a strong black coffee to help keep him awake.

Now, as he drove his car along Archway Road, he felt exhausted. He drove onto the driveway of the last house on the road, switched the engine off and remained in the car. He stared at the house in the darkness. There were no street lamps on this part of Archway Road.

He was glad to have finally arrived, but there was something about the house that always filled him with a sense of foreboding.

He hated the place.

It was one of the reasons he spent so long working away on the rigs. The desolate, secluded house held too many dark secrets. He could already feel the muscles in his back and neck starting to tense up at the thought of unloading the car and going inside.

As tiredness took over, he knew he had to get out of the car or risk falling asleep where he sat. He took all the bags from the boot of the car and piled them next to the front door. He could hear the engine of the high-powered car ticking loudly as it cooled down. He had driven it hard and fast on the empty motorway. It was a car designed to be driven fast, and he always drove it to the max.

He unlocked the front door of the house and pushed it open. Standing on the threshold, he took a deep breath. The house had been locked up for almost six months and the air inside smelled musty and a little damp.

With a sense of reluctance, he stepped inside and flicked on the hall light. Nothing had changed. The house looked exactly as it did when he had walked out months ago. He walked into the kitchen and lit the central heating boiler. He could hear the old house starting to creak and moan as the heat began to circulate through the radiators.

He felt too exhausted to unpack everything there and then. Leaving all the bags where they were in the hallway, he locked the front door and walked wearily upstairs to his bedroom.

He quickly undressed and got into bed. The sheets felt damp and cold to the touch, but he knew his body heat would soon warm them through.

As he closed his eyes to try and sleep, he could hear a familiar voice drifting into his head, filling it with the same evil thoughts. He desperately tried to block them out and hoped his exhausted state meant sleep would eventually come.

50

10.50pm, 19 March 1989
Kilton, Worksop, Nottinghamshire

From his position in the pub car park, Doug Richardson could see Mike Molloy standing in the doorway of the pub. It was a cold, frosty night but the windscreen of his Range Rover was clear. He could see Molloy talking to another man in the doorway of the pub. It was closing time and other customers had already left.

Both men were laughing and joking, and with the side window of his car slightly open Richardson could hear Molloy slurring his speech, talking in an overloud manner.

After five minutes, the other man turned and walked back inside.

Richardson could now hear the bolts on the pub door being dragged across as the landlord locked up for the night, leaving Molloy alone in the car park.

As Molloy started to walk away from the pub, he was swaying and stumbling along. Richardson smiled as he realised the private detective was drunk. He knew it would make his coming task that much easier.

He waited for Molloy to stagger down the road before starting the engine and driving slowly out of the car park. He passed Molloy and then parked his car on the unlit stretch of road, where there were no pavements.

Patiently, he waited for Molloy, who was making slow progress as he swayed from side to side. The private detective was walking in the middle of the road, not bothering to use the grass verges.

Richardson waited for Molloy to walk by, then he checked the vehicle's mirrors and looked ahead. There were no other vehicles, and no other people on the road.

It was time to remove the problem of Molloy.

He revved the engine of the powerful Range Rover and accelerated the vehicle directly towards the drunken man.

Molloy must have heard the vehicle approaching because Richardson saw him stagger onto the grass verge. With no hesitation, Richardson steered the vehicle onto the grass verge, smashing into Molloy. The Range Rover was half on and half off the verge at the point of impact.

The private investigator was knocked high into the air by the force of the collision. Richardson struggled to control the steering of the powerful vehicle, eventually bringing it to a skidding halt back on the road.

He looked in the rear-view mirror and could see the prone figure of Molloy, illuminated by the red brake lights, lying on the edge of the road.

To his horror, he saw Molloy start to crawl slowly towards the grass verge. Panicking at the fact that Molloy had survived the impact, Richardson shifted the automatic gearbox, putting the Range Rover into reverse. Looking over his shoulder, he drove backwards at speed, running over the prone figure of Molloy a second time.

He heard two thuds as first the rear wheel, then the front wheel passed directly over the stricken man, crushing him.

With a cruel smile on his face, Richardson calmly placed the vehicle in drive and again drove directly over Molloy. This time there was a sickening crunch as the wheels of the two-ton vehicle passed directly over the man's head.

Richardson stopped the vehicle ten yards beyond Molloy and looked back in the rear-view mirror. This time there was no movement.

As he drove away from the dead man, Richardson's thoughts turned to how he was going to cover his tracks. He knew there would be significant damage to his vehicle. Various solutions to the problem raced through his mind as he sped through the darkness.

I could abandon it, set it alight, then report it stolen.

I could remove the registration plates, then ship it abroad in a container.

I could take it to a breakers' yard for destruction, no questions asked.

I could stash it away until it's repaired at the garage.

Richardson had no thoughts for Molloy, who was dead from the catastrophic head injury he had caused when he drove the Range Rover directly over the private detective's head, crushing it like an egg.

He would decide what to do about the Range Rover in due course. For now, he was content he had dealt with the problem of Molloy and there was nothing left to connect Mason Connor to the death of Ian Drake.

51

10.00am, 20 March 1989
MCIU Offices, Mansfield, Nottinghamshire

Three days had passed since all the employee contract files had been delivered from Fossil Energy Exploration to the MCIU. Since that time, DC Jag Singh had been working flat out to find the relevant contracts from the vast mountain of files, aided by Jimmy Matheson from F.E.E.

Jag had already briefed DI Tina Cartwright on his findings, and now both detectives were updating Danny on those inquiries.

'How are things progressing?' asked Danny.

Jag said, 'It's saved so much time having Jimmy here, to work alongside me. He can interpret the paperwork so much quicker than I could. He knows exactly where to look to find the duration of contracts.'

'That's good to hear. So, what have you found?'

'We've now completed an initial trawl through every contract, and there are currently forty-two men living in Nottinghamshire who are working on six-month contracts in the oil industry. Most of those men are deployed on rigs in the North Sea, but there are a few in more exotic parts of the world. We've limited this initial search to contracts that commenced in August 1988. Of those forty-two men, only six have had previous contracts of four years overseas prior to starting this contract in August '88.'

'Have you given any leeway at all?'

'Yes. We've given a month's leeway at either end of the contract, so hopefully we won't have missed anyone for the sake of a few days.'

'What do we know about these six individuals?'

'All six men are now off the rigs and have returned home.'

'How long are they home before they have to return to the rigs?'

'That can vary, but according to Jimmy, the oil companies usually afford their employees six weeks' time off between deployments. However, in certain circumstances this can be cut short if the men are needed back on the rigs urgently.'

'How often does that happen?'

'Rarely. It's only used to cover medical emergencies, that kind of thing.'

Danny was thoughtful for a minute, then said, 'So, by that reckoning, all of these men will now be at home and not due back on the rigs until the middle of April.'

'That's correct.'

'Good work, Jag. Is Jimmy Matheson still here?'

'Yes. He's been instructed to remain here and work with

us until we've finished with the files. He's happy enough. He's living the high life, staying in the Savoy Hotel in Nottingham.'

'That's good. He'll be a godsend if we need to extend the search and go through the contacts again.'

Jag nodded. 'For sure, boss.'

Danny turned to Tina. 'I want you to start researching the six names. We need current addresses. I don't want to rely on the information in the contracts. Once that's been done and we've housed these men, you'll need to research their backgrounds. We need to know everything we can about these individuals.'

Tina replied, 'I've already started that process, boss.'

'Good. Because we're going to need to work fast. If the killer is one of these men, I think he'll be looking to strike again before he goes back to the rigs.'

52

11.00am, 20 March 1989
MCIU Offices, Mansfield, Nottinghamshire

Danny was about to start the second strategy meeting that morning and needed a few moments to turn his thoughts away from the oil industry inquiries back to the murders of Ian and Melanie Drake. Supervising all the inquiries for the two completely separate murder investigations was starting to take its toll.

There was a knock on his office door and the four detectives tasked with interviewing the five people fostered by the Drakes walked in.

Rachel Moore spoke first, 'As you know, we've now interviewed all five people who were fostered by the Drakes. When we debriefed this inquiry previously, I told you that all five had denied still being in contact with each other. Certainly, for two of them we now know that was a lie.'

'Go on.'

'We carried out financial checks on all five and have found a definite link between Kevin Briar and Dominic Finch.'

'What's the link?'

'Finch has regularly provided large sums of money to finance the outward bound centre run by Briar. Looking at the accounts submitted by the centre, without the substantial financial support from Finch, it would have been forced to close years ago. It's not a viable business.'

'These are the two who were literally as thick as thieves when they were being fostered.'

'Yes, boss. Finch and Briar were with the Drakes the longest and appear to have suffered the most significant abuse at the hands of Melanie Drake.'

'Didn't one of the other foster children witness that abuse?'

DC Lorimar said, 'That was Sandra Mellor. She's a school teacher now. She was there for a short time when Finch and Briar were there as well. She witnessed some of the abuse they suffered.'

'Did she say if she was still in touch with either man?'

'She said not, but did rather skate over it when I asked the question. I thought at the time she was a bit quick to say no. She did describe in detail how close she got to both boys back then, as they protected her from the worst of Melanie Drake's cruelty.'

'Did you ask her if she had seen either man recently?'

'I did ask the question, and she told me she hadn't seen Finch or Briar since leaving the Drakes' house.'

'Do you think there's any mileage in talking to Sarah Mellor again?'

'It wouldn't hurt. She was annoyed with us for interviewing her at her place of work, so she wasn't that forthcoming. If anything, I felt she came over as being slightly evasive.'

'Okay, do that. Go back and ask her again if she's aware of any recent contact between Briar and Finch.'

Danny looked at Rachel. 'I want you to concentrate on Finch and Briar. Dig deeper and see if we can find any other association between the two of them that isn't just financial.'

'Will do, boss.'

'Have you had a reply from Finch's lawyer yet?'

'No. I'll keep chasing him.'

The meeting over, the four detectives left the office.

No sooner had they left than the office manager, DC Fran Jefferies, walked in. 'I thought you should hear this, boss.'

'What's up, Fran?'

'The traffic department at Worksop are dealing with a non-stop fatal road accident that occurred at Kilton last night.'

Danny sighed. All he needed was yet another suspicious death investigation to add to the pressure he was already feeling. 'Is it suspicious? Does it fit the category where we need to be involved in the investigation?'

'Not at the moment, but they're still working at the scene.'

'What's the relevance, then?'

'The victim of this hit-and-run accident is Mike Molloy.'

'The private detective involved in tracing Ian Drake?'

'Yes.'

'Okay, get back onto Traffic and inform them that if they find anything that looks suspicious, we need to be told immediately. In the meantime, brief DS Wills and tell him from me to take Nigel Singleton and visit the scene of the accident. I want to know first-hand what's happened up there. I never did like coincidences.'

'Will do, boss.'

53

1.30pm, 20 March 1989
Kilton, Worksop, Nottinghamshire

DC Nigel Singleton parked the CID car next to the 'road ahead closed' sign and said, 'This is as close as we're going to get, Sarge.'

Andy Wills looked at the frost on the grass verges and muttered, 'Shit. It looks bloody freezing out there.' As he got out, he pulled the hood of his coat over his head and made his way on foot towards the traffic officers milling around on the road ahead. Nigel reluctantly got out of the warm car and followed on behind.

Sergeant Dave Woodrow approached the two detectives and raised a hand. 'That's far enough, gents. This is a crime scene.'

The two detectives took out their identification and Andy said, 'DS Wills and DC Singleton from the MCIU. You said crime scene, not accident scene. I take it from that, you don't think what happened here was an accident?'

The experienced traffic sergeant said, 'I'm supervising the scene examination and I know it wasn't an accident. Follow me and I'll show you how I know.'

Sergeant Woodrow walked towards the grass verge and pointed at a series of tyre tracks. 'The first point of impact with the pedestrian was twenty yards further down the road. The vehicle had been driven half-on and half-off the road. You can see where the nearside tyres have ploughed up the verge.'

Andy said, 'So, the driver swerved onto the verge to hit the pedestrian?'

'Exactly. Do you see the other tyre marks on the verge?'

Andy nodded.

'That's where the vehicle was then driven back over the victim. Not once, but twice. He may well have survived the first impact, but he was never going to survive the injury to his skull after he was run over the second time.'

Nigel muttered, 'Death by vehicle?'

Dave nodded. 'Exactly that. A heavy car's as lethal as any handgun or knife.

Andy said, 'Were there any witnesses?'

'To the collision itself, no. We've spoken to the landlord of the French Horn public house just down the road and he remembers seeing the victim as he left the pub.'

'Have you got a statement from the landlord?'

'Not yet. We've been concentrating our efforts here. Under the current guidelines, we knew this would end up being investigated further by the CID.'

'Fair enough. We'll go and talk to the landlord. What's his name?'

The sergeant flipped open his notebook. 'Landlord's Barry Westlake. He told my officers that he knows the victim well, as he drinks in his pub most evenings.'

Nigel asked, 'Did he remember any altercations or arguments inside the pub that could have led to this?'

'Nothing like that was mentioned. This Molloy character always followed the same routine. He would arrive at the pub, sit at the bar, drink until closing time and then walk home. The landlord did say he was the last person to leave the pub last night, because he stood chatting with him for a few minutes in the car park. He doesn't remember seeing anybody else or any vehicles, though.'

Andy said, 'Apart from these tyre tracks, what else have you got from the scene?'

'We've recovered debris at the initial point of impact. Some glass from a light cluster, paint and chrome flakes.'

'So the vehicle will have been damaged by the collision, then?'

'From the debris we found, I think it will have sustained quite a lot of damage. The car was obviously being driven at speed when the first impact occurred.'

'Any idea on a vehicle type?'

'We'll know more when the samples we've recovered have been analysed, but if I was to give you my best guess, based on the width of the tyre tracks and the colour of the paint recovered, I would go for one of the big Range Rovers.'

'Will you be preparing a full report of your findings to pass to us?'

'Yes. That's the protocol now. Any fatal RTA where we feel there are suspicious circumstances, we prepare a report and pass it either to the CID, or yourselves, for further investigation.'

'Okay. Well consider this inquiry to be ours from now. I'll contact our DCI and let him know that this should be treated as a murder enquiry. How much longer will you need to examine the scene?'

'Another hour and we'll be in a position to re-open the road.'

'Okay. Have you found any cameras in the area that might have captured the offending vehicle, either before or after the collision?'

'I've got two lads scouting for traffic cameras in either direction. To date they've found nothing that's going to help you. By the way, it's no coincidence that the point of impact was here.'

'What do you mean?'

'I believe the victim would have been deliberately targeted here. At night, this road is pitch black. Look around you. There are no street lights here, and no pavements. I think this part of the road was selected deliberately. I'm guessing whoever did this would have had the foresight to look out for any traffic cameras as well.'

Nigel said, 'Where's Molloy now?'

'His body was removed an hour ago. The on-call undertakers have taken him to Bassetlaw Hospital. We gave the control room instructions that the accident was suspicious and asked them to contact the hospital to delay any post-mortem examination. I figured you'd want a Home Office pathologist involved.'

Andy said, 'That's good. Thanks for that. It will need to be a Home Office pathologist. We'll go to Worksop nick and get everything organised. How did you get an identification so quickly if the head injury was so bad?'

'He still had his wallet in his coat pocket. His driving licence was inside.'

'How soon will your report be ready?'

'I'll draft a preliminary report in the next few hours. Then a more detailed report containing the results of the forensic samples we've recovered here will be forwarded to you later.'

'Nice one. I suppose this frost has knackered any chance of tyre casts.'

'You suppose right. The frost reacts badly to the casting agent we use and blurs everything. It's the moisture, I think. Anyway, not a prayer of getting any detail from them.'

'Fair enough.'

'The wallet he had on him had the South Yorkshire Police crest on. Is it true the victim was an ex-cop?'

'Mike Molloy was a retired Traffic cop. He served with South Yorkshire Police.'

'Bloody hell. One of our own.'

Andy nodded. 'We'll need that preliminary report as soon as you can. We'll be at Worksop nick for the duration.'

'I'll drop it in there for you gents. Good luck.'

54

3.00pm, 20 March 1989
MCIU Offices, Mansfield, Nottinghamshire

The telephone on Danny's desk rang twice before he snatched it up. 'DCI Flint, MCIU.'

Andy Wills said, 'Boss. It's me, Andy.'

'Have you been to the scene of the hit-and-run?'

'Yes, but I'm at Worksop Police Station now. It looks like Molloy's been deliberately targeted and killed. There's evidence at the scene that whoever knocked him over drove deliberately over him twice. I've just come from the mortuary at Bassetlaw Hospital. Molloy died because of the injuries he received when he was run over, not from the actual collision. His head has been virtually crushed when the vehicle was driven over him.'

'It's a murder enquiry then.'

It wasn't a question.

Danny paused for a few moments, allowing all the implications of another murder investigation to sink in before continuing, 'What have you organised so far?'

'I've spoken to the control room and a Home Office pathologist is en-route to do the post mortem at Bassetlaw Hospital. That's scheduled for five o'clock this afternoon. I've left Nigel at the French Horn public house. He's obtaining a statement from the landlord, Barry Westlake. He was the last person to see Mike Molloy alive.'

'I'll gather some staff and join you at Worksop Police Station within the hour. Are Traffic preparing a report?'

'Sergeant Woodrow was the supervisor at the scene. He's done a good job, considering the freezing weather conditions. I should have his preliminary report by the time you get here, boss.'

'Good work, Andy. This has got to relate to the death of Ian Drake somehow. What a can of worms.'

55

4.30pm, 20 March 1989
Mason Street, Arnold, Nottingham

Glen Lorimar slowed the CID car to a crawl as both detectives scanned the numbers of the houses on Mason Street in Arnold.

Helen Bailey pointed to a neat semi-detached house on the left and said, 'There it is, number twenty-four.'

Glen parked the car and both detectives made their way to the front door. Helen rang the doorbell and waited. She knew Sandra Mellor was at home. Glen had telephoned earlier to let the schoolteacher know they were coming to talk to her again.

The door opened and a thoughtful-looking Sandra Mellor said, 'I really don't know how I can help you, but you'd better come in.'

Helen said, 'Thank you. It shouldn't take long; we just need to go over a couple of things you told us before.'

Sandra showed the two detectives into a small sitting room at the front of the house. 'We can talk in here. I don't want to disturb Mum and Dad in the lounge.'

Glen spoke first, 'I don't want you to take offence at what I'm going to ask you; it's just that you seemed rather hesitant about some of the things you told us last time we spoke. In particular, when we spoke about Dominic Finch and Kev Briar. Is there anything you didn't tell us about them last time?'

There was a long silence as Sandra Mellor struggled with what she was going to disclose. Finally, she said in a whisper, 'I wasn't totally truthful when we spoke before. I'm aware that Dom and Kev are still close and have remained friends over the years.'

'Is there any reason you didn't tell us this before?'

The schoolteacher shrugged her shoulders. 'I don't know. I suppose I still look on them as my big brothers. If those two hadn't been there for me, that evil cow would have behaved much worse towards me.'

'You're referring to Melanie Drake.'

'Yes.'

Helen said gently, 'What else didn't you tell us before?'

'Only that Dom always swore he would get even with that evil bitch. He always said that we wouldn't be young kids forever, and that someday she would get what she deserved.'

'What do you think he meant by that?'

'I don't know. It was just something he always said.'

'What about Kevin Briar?'

'Patch always followed Dom's lead. He was like his

shadow. Whatever Dom did, Patch would be involved in it as well.'

'What were they involved in?'

'You name it, they did it. Back then, they were wild. They would nick cars for joyrides, breaking into places, nicking from shops. They were into everything. The police were always bringing them back to the Drakes. I never went with them when they did any of that stuff, but we all knew what they were getting up to.'

Glen said, 'Last time we spoke, you told us that you hadn't seen either Dominic or Kevin in years. Was that true?'

Sandra looked down at the floor and shook her head. There was a pause and then she said, 'I saw them both around six months ago. I was shopping in Nottingham and I saw them in the Broadmarsh Shopping Centre.'

'Did you speak to them?'

'No. They were quite a distance away and they were having quite an animated discussion.'

'Are you sure it was them?'

'It was definitely them; neither of them has changed that much.'

'Why did you tell us before that you hadn't seen them in years?'

'I don't really know. I'm sorry. I think I was so angry that you'd barged into my workplace to ask me all those questions. I didn't feel inclined to be straight with you.'

'Is there anything else you think we should know?'

'That's it. I'm sorry for messing you about. The boys aren't in any trouble, are they?'

'No, they're not. We're just trying to get background information on the Drakes, that's all. Thanks for being honest with us now, Sandra.'

'Am I in trouble for lying to you before?'

Glen shook his head, 'No, you're not, but it's never a good idea to lie to the police. These are serious crimes we're investigating, and we rely on people's cooperation. Thanks for seeing us today.'

56

1.00am, 21 March 1989
Wheatfield Crescent, Mansfield Woodhouse,
Nottinghamshire

The man made a final drive by the detached bungalow on Wheatfield Crescent. The target and all the neighbouring properties were now in darkness. It was time to act.

He turned left onto Peafield Lane and made his way to the layby half a mile from the junction with Wheatfield Crescent. The layby was unlit and there were no other vehicles parked there. It was a location regularly used by courting couples, but not tonight.

He parked his car as close to the hawthorn hedge as he dared, then got out and made his way across the field, back towards Wheatfield Crescent. He could see the outline of the bungalows in the distance. He knew exactly where his target was, and he headed straight for it.

He felt inside his pockets for the tie wraps, plastic bag and breaking tools. He felt comforted as his gloved hands felt the instruments of his terror.

It felt good, knowing that he was finally going to be able to complete his unfinished business. He knew his actions tonight would help banish the constant scolding from the voice inside his head. How long for was an unanswered question.

Ever since he'd returned from the oil rig, the volume and frequency of that lone voice had steadily increased. It became so oppressive that he'd felt compelled to leave the house and seek out his previous target.

As he got closer to the bungalow, he could see there was a low light on in what was the main bedroom. Everything looked as it should, the windows were the same, nothing had changed. The target would not get another reprieve. Tonight, he would make her pay for everything she'd ever done to him.

As he reached the low wooden fence that was the boundary between the farmer's field and the garden of the bungalow, a security light suddenly flooded the garden with bright white light.

Instinctively, the man ducked down below the fence and cursed under his breath.

He hadn't expected the security light, or the pandemonium that began to erupt all around him.

A dog in one of the nearby bungalows started barking ferociously, and he saw lights in neighbouring bungalows start to come on.

The man was left with no option.

He cursed under his breath again and began running away from the bungalow. Back across the field, towards the safety of his parked car.

He would start the search for a new target tomorrow.

As he ran, the volume of the voice inside his head increased. He knew he would need to kill again, and soon.

57

8.00am, 21 March 1989
Wheatfield Crescent, Mansfield Woodhouse,
Nottinghamshire

Danny Flint parked his car behind the scenes of crime van and the other CID car. He could see Andy Wills talking to a neighbour of Audrey Hollis.

As soon as Danny had arrived in the office that morning, Fran Jefferies had informed him there'd been another suspicious incident at the bungalow occupied by the elderly female, and that Andy Wills had already began inquiries.

It seemed like Audrey Hollis may have had another fortunate escape.

He got out of his car and approached Andy. 'How did you hear about this?' he asked when Andy was free.

'I got into the office early to give Jag a hand with his list of suspects from the oil company inquiry, and took a phone call from PC Chris Walker, who had just finished nights. He told me about a reported prowler he'd been sent to during the night. He rang the office because he remembered a previous incident at the same bungalow on Wheatfield Crescent some months ago. He informed me that there had been a burglary offence at that location that the MCIU had attended, as it bore similarities to the method of entry used on the White and King murders.

'I remember that incident. We thought it was identical to both the previous murder scenes and that the old lady who lived there had been very fortunate to have been away on holiday. It's good that PC Walker remembered the previous incident.'

'Very fortunate, but Chris is a good cop. Anyway, as soon as I realised that the prowler had been disturbed at the rear of Mrs Hollis's bungalow, I thought I'd better get out there. I left a message with Fran to inform you what had happened.'

'Any witnesses?'

'Audrey Hollis was oblivious to everything. The light didn't wake her, and she was unaware anything had happened. I've spoken to the neighbour who saw the man running away across the field. The only light was from the security light, so the description isn't great. He says the man looked to be heavy set, wearing dark clothing. He said he wasn't moving fast, and that it looked like he was running in heavy boots.'

'Is that it?'

Andy nodded. 'That's it, I'm afraid. That field's pitch black at night.'

'How soon were the police contacted?'

'The neighbour who saw the man running away towards

Peafield Lane called it in. But he waited ten minutes after he'd seen him to make the call. He put the kettle on first, apparently.'

'Bloody hell.'

'The control room sent units to search Peafield Lane, but by the time they arrived there was no sign of anybody in the area.'

'Any vehicles spotted?'

Andy shook his head. 'No, boss.'

'I see you've called out scenes of crime. Have they found anything?'

'They've taken casts of fresh boot prints found near the fence, which do corroborate what the witness said. We should be able to compare those with the boot prints we found at the previous break-in.'

'It looks like our killer may have returned to complete some unfinished business.'

'It's possible, boss. But it could just be somebody looking to break in and steal.'

'Have you got a statement from the witness yet?'

'I wanted to make sure I didn't miss anyone else who may have seen something first. I've visited all the neighbouring bungalows now and there are no other witnesses. I'll get the statement and liaise with scenes of crime about the boot print samples.'

'Good work, Andy. I don't believe in coincidences. I want you to arrange for this bungalow to be watched during the hours of darkness and ensure there are regular patrols along Peafield Lane for the next two weeks. I don't want to risk this maniac coming back for another go.'

'No problem. I'll get that sorted.'

58

11.00am, 21 March 1989
MCIU Offices, Mansfield, Nottinghamshire

Danny walked into the main briefing room and found Glen Lorimar and Helen Bailey already there. 'How did you get on with the schoolteacher last night?'

Glen replied, 'It was very interesting. Let's just say Sandra Mellor was economical with the truth when we spoke to her the first time.'

'Go on.'

'She saw Dominic Finch and Kevin Briar together in Nottingham about six months ago.'

'I thought she told you she hadn't seen either of them since she left the Drakes' house.'

'She did say that.'

'So, why the lie?'

'Two reasons. Firstly, because she was pissed off at us for going to the school to talk to her, and secondly, out of some misguided loyalty to the two lads she looked up to when they were all in foster care.'

'And Finch and Briar have both denied having any contact with each other now?'

'Yes.'

'That begs the question, why would they lie about that? I think we need to talk to Finch and Briar again.'

'I thought you might suggest that, boss, so I've already contacted Finch's office in London. He's out of the office for a week, as of now. He left early today and is having a break from the office. His secretary informed me that he's intending to spend the week at his holiday cottage in Derbyshire.'

'Whereabouts in Derbyshire?'

'Near Wirksworth.'

Danny was thoughtful for a while, then said, 'Has Dominic Finch's lawyer answered those questions yet?'

'Yes. They arrived this morning. One of the questions on that list was whether Finch was still in contact with Kevin Briar.'

'And?'

'A straight denial.'

'Yet they were seen together just six months ago, and Finch is regularly supporting Briar's business with cash injections. I think we need to use this opportunity while Finch is just over the border in Derbyshire. I want you, Rachel, Helen, and Jane to set up observations on Finch and Briar. Let's see for ourselves if the two of them are still in contact. If they are, they'll get together while Finch is up here in Derbyshire. In the meantime, I'll ask Fran to do some more digging on the finances of Finch. Let's see if she can find a connection between Finch and the bogus company that was used to lure Ian Drake back to Nottinghamshire.'

'When do you want us to set up on Finch and Briar?'

'No time like the present. Overtime's not an issue. If those two meet up, I want to know about it.'

At the thought of unlimited overtime, Glen's eyes lit up. 'I'll talk to DS Moore and DC Pope and get everything organised. We should be able to start the obs this afternoon.'

'Keep me informed.'

59

1.00pm, 21 March 1989
Nottinghamshire Police Headquarters

Danny had been summoned, via a terse telephone call, to travel immediately to headquarters and meet with Chief Superintendent Potter. There had been no pleasantries exchanged, just a sharp "get yourself to headquarters now" order from his supervisor.

He knew exactly what the meeting would be about.

He knocked once on the door and waited for the customary order to enter.

It never came.

Instead, the door opened and Potter said quietly, 'Come in, Danny.'

Now, he was really alarmed. In all the years he had worked with Potter, he had hardly ever referred to him by his

Christian name, and he couldn't remember ever seeing his boss look so worried.

Potter closed the door behind Danny and both men sat down. The chief superintendent steepled his fingers and rested his chin on them before saying quietly, 'Please tell me you've made progress on your inquiries with the oil companies.'

'We've been able to make great strides ever since we received all the documentation and employee contracts from Fossil Energy Exploration. We initially had a list of thirty-two possibles, but that's now been narrowed down to just six names. My team are working tirelessly to narrow that down even further. I'm convinced that somewhere in that list of names is our killer.'

'What do you intend to do with that information?'

'We already have the forensic evidence to trap our killer, but we need to ensure we're looking at the right man before we do anything hasty. In the meantime, while we're engaged in that research, I intend to have surveillance teams watching the six individuals who are the closest to our parameters. I need to ensure that nobody else is attacked while we're doing the necessary research. There was another incident at a bungalow in Mansfield Woodhouse last night that makes me think our killer is back in the area. This also fits in with the inquiries we're doing with the oil company.'

'How soon do you think you'll be in a position to make an arrest?'

'Sir, I know how desperate you are to get a result on this inquiry, but I need to make sure everything is done properly so we have the best chance of achieving a conviction. If we dive in too early, we could lose everything.'

'And you're convinced the killer is within these contracts?'

'It's always been our best hope.'

'I hope you're right.'

Potter paused before continuing, 'Immediately after this meeting I've got to join the chief constable and Councillor White to update them on the progress being made in the Margaret White murder inquiry. I'll tell them exactly what you've told me and pray you're right and the killer is on your list. I don't want to contemplate what will become of the MCIU if you're wrong about this.'

Danny could feel his anger and resentment bubbling just below the surface. He could understand the grief felt by Richard White, and empathise with his need for justice, but that didn't give him the right to dictate to a chief constable how a criminal inquiry should be run. He expected the chief constable to fight more to support his officers not cave in to the pressure being exerted from the councillor.

He was just about to say as much when Potter waved his index finger in the air and said, 'Don't say it, Danny. I know what you're thinking and for once I totally agree with you. I've been fighting your corner ever since this inquiry started and Richard White got involved. I'll continue to argue your case and espouse to the chief that your team offers the best chance we have of catching this maniac. I just don't know how much longer Jack Renshaw will listen when he's being put under so much pressure.'

There was more than a hint of desperation in Danny's voice when he said, 'We'll know one way or the other in a week's time. We'll either have our killer by then, or we won't.'

'And that in turn might be a case of Nottinghamshire Police will either have a Major Crime Investigation Unit, or it won't. I'll make sure you get that week, Danny. Don't let me down.'

60

3.00pm, 21 March 1989
MCIU Offices, Mansfield, Nottinghamshire

Danny had driven at speed from headquarters, his thoughts consumed by his meeting with Potter. As soon as he'd arrived back at the MCIU, he called a meeting with Tina Cartwright, Fran Jefferies, Jag Singh and Simon Paine. He needed answers on the inquiries they were doing to shorten the list of suspect names. After his meeting with Potter, he knew time was running out.

Trying to keep the desperation from his voice, he asked Tina, 'How are you getting on with our six favourites?'

'Good news. We've now managed to whittle it down to two. We now know that the four others on that list were all still out of the country when either Florence King or Margaret White were killed. It's a risk, but as we believe the same killer is responsible for both deaths, it's fairly safe to assume they had to be in the country at the time of both.'

'I normally don't like assumptions, but that's a fair one. What details do we have on the remaining two suspects?'

'The first one lives at Bingham. His name's Benjamin Pearson, he's forty-five years old, married with two kids. He works as a specialist electrician on the rigs. He earns massive money, because if anything electrical blows it's down to him to repair it, there and then.'

'And the second?'

'A man named Amos Varley. He's in his late twenties and has an address at Old Clipstone. The house was previously owned by his parents, but he now lives there alone. Both parents are now deceased.'

'What does he do on the rigs?'

'He's employed as a rigger.'

'What does that entail?'

Jag Singh replied, 'The riggers are responsible for placing and assembling the various parts of equipment that make up the rig. Basically, they're the men who prepare the rig for drilling.'

'Would that bring our man into contact with the crude oil?'

'On a daily basis. Jimmy Matheson says it's one of the shittiest, dirtiest and most dangerous jobs on the entire rig.'

Danny paused for a moment, then said, 'Tina. I want you to arrange observations on both suspects.'

'Will do, boss.'

Simon Paine said, 'There was one thing I discovered when I was researching Varley that seemed a bit of a coincidence.'

Danny said, 'Go on.'

'Amos Varley's own mother died a month before Florence King was murdered.'

'Did you research the mother's death?'

'It's still on my to-do list.'

Danny was thoughtful for a minute. 'Do you have any idea what Mrs Varley looked like?'

'No, sir. Sorry.'

'It's just a thought, and something I've been toying with. There's a definite physical similarity between Florence King, Margaret White and Audrey Hollis. I was wondering if Mrs Varley also fitted a similar description.'

'I'll look into the woman's death and find out, boss.'

'I'm conscious that we need to work fast. A prowler was disturbed at the rear of the bungalow owned by Audrey Hollis last night. If that was our killer, it means he's already active and looking to strike again. Tina, I want you and Fran to carry on the research into Benjamin Pearson and Amos Varley.'

He paused before looking at Jag Singh and Simon Paine. 'Are you two both okay to work overtime tonight?'

The two detectives looked at each other and nodded before Jag said, 'No problem, boss.'

'Good. I want you two to set up on the address at Old Clipstone and start surveillance on Amos Varley. From what you've all said, I think he's far more likely to be our man. Geographically, he's much closer to these offences than Pearson, and his role on the rigs is far more likely to bring him into regular contact with crude oil.'

He turned to Tina. 'Having said that, I still want you to arrange a two-man surveillance team to set up on the Pearson house tonight.'

Tina nodded. 'No problem.'

Danny spoke directly to Jag and Simon. 'It's obvious from last night's attempt on Audrey Hollis's bungalow at Mansfield Woodhouse that our man is already out and about at night. If Amos Varley moves from his house, I want you two right behind him, watching his every move. If he so much as steps on a crack in the pavement the wrong way, arrest him. We've got the suspect's DNA profile. All we need is an arrest.'

Tina added a note of caution. 'It's not quite that simple, sir. Under the Police and Criminal Evidence Act we would still need Varley's consent to obtain an intimate sample so we can make that comparison.'

Danny nodded and muttered under his breath, 'I know, I know. Bloody PACE.'

There was a heavy silence in the room, before Danny looked towards Jag and said, 'Get out there, and watch Amos Varley like a hawk. Don't let him out of your sight.'

'Will do, boss.'

61

1.15am, 22 March 1989
Greenshank Road, Warsop Vale, Mansfield,
Nottinghamshire

The man in the dirty overalls had been driving round the deserted streets for hours. He stopped the car when he saw the signpost for Warsop Vale. He turned off the ignition and stared at the crossroads. His thoughts turned to the old woman he'd seen earlier that evening.

He had left the house at four o'clock, unable to wait for dusk to fall, and started hunting. He had driven around several old age pensioner complexes, seeking the perfect victim.

It had been pure chance when he saw the old lady leaning on the wooden fence at the rear of her house on

Greenshank Road. She was far too busy gossiping with her neighbour to notice his car as he drove slowly past.

This was not an OAP complex. The house was an ordinary terrace, so he needed to make sure that the old lady lived alone. He'd parked up and returned on foot to watch the house. After four hours, nobody else had either come to, or left the house.

He had walked to the front door of the property and knocked loudly.

The door was answered by the same elderly woman.

He asked if either she, or her family, had noticed a little terrier dog running around the streets, as he'd lost his beloved dog after it chased a rabbit into one of the nearby fields.

His carefully phrased question had achieved the desired response. The woman had told him that she hadn't seen his dog, and there was nobody else in the house to ask, as she lived there alone.

He had thanked her and walked away, smiling broadly.

Now that he had seen her up close, he knew she was perfect.

The very sight of her had been enough for him to experience some of the feelings of relief he craved so desperately. He knew that when he revisited the house and killed the dreadful woman, it would cause the nagging voice inside his head to fall silent once again.

He turned the ignition key and started the car.

After a moment's hesitation, he drove the car into the junction, heading slowly towards Warsop Vale.

62

1.15am, 22 March 1989
Greenshank Road, Warsop Vale, Mansfield,
Nottinghamshire

Simon Paine started the CID car and said, 'Looks like we're going back to Warsop Vale.'

Jag Singh replied, 'I'm not really surprised. He's spent so much time there yesterday evening, I always thought he intended to come back tonight.'

The two detectives had been following Amos Varley ever since he left the house at Old Clipstone the previous afternoon. They had shadowed his every move, taking care not to be spotted by their target.

Varley didn't appear to be surveillance conscious. He had carried out none of the manoeuvres associated with someone who's aware they're being followed. He drove around aimlessly in his high-powered Ford Sierra Cosworth, travelling to most of the small mining communities in the area.

It was Simon who had noticed the pattern in amongst the random locations they had visited. After the fourth such location they had driven around, he had exclaimed, 'Why is he visiting OAP complexes?'

Jag had shrugged his shoulders. 'It can't be random. Don't forget the victims of the maniac we're looking for have all been elderly white females.'

Jag had kept a running log of all the locations visited and had been half-surprised when the Cosworth stopped just outside Warsop Vale. There were no such OAP complexes in this tiny village, just rows of terrace houses that used to house the miners employed at Warsop Main Colliery.

Amos Varley had got out of his car and walked slowly back towards the rows of houses. Simon had followed him, keeping a discreet distance. A long four hours had passed before Varley approached one of the houses and knocked on the door. He had a brief conversation with the elderly woman who opened the door, before returning to his car.

Since then, he had driven around the area, only stopping once, to buy fish and chips from the Blue Dolphin chip shop at Mansfield Woodhouse.

Jag glanced at his watch. 'It's just gone one o'clock in the morning. What do you think he's up to?'

'My guess is he's going back to the house he spent hours watching earlier.'

'The old lady's house?'

'Yeah.'

'Do you think we should get some backup out here?'

'The nearest station's at Warsop, not too far away. Let's just see how things develop before we call in the cavalry.'

Simon was the more experienced of the two detectives and Jag trusted his judgement. 'Okay. Don't forget you said the occupant of that house looked old and frail.'

'Don't worry, mate. If he tries anything dodgy, we'll be all over him like a rash.'

The Sierra Cosworth being driven by Varley turned into one of the back alleys that serviced the rows of terraced houses and came to a stop.

Simon switched off the lights of the CID car and parked up so he still had Varley's vehicle in view. The detectives were seventy yards away. Luckily, Varley had parked his car near one of the few street lights, so his car was clearly visible.

The driver's door opened, and Varley got out. He scrunched up the empty fish-and-chip wrappers and hurled them over a low wall, into the yard of one of the houses. He then leaned back in the car and took out a white carrier bag from inside. The detectives looked on as Varley stuffed the carrier bag and its contents inside the donkey jacket he wore over his overalls, before walking slowly away from the car.

Jag said, 'I don't like the look of this. Call for backup. I'm going to follow him.'

He turned off the interior light, slipped out of the CID car, and crept into the darkness after Amos Varley.

63

1.30am, 22 March 1989
Greenshank Road, Warsop Vale, Mansfield,
Nottinghamshire

Jag silently followed Amos Varley through the rows of terrace houses. Both men kept to the shadows and Jag took extra care where he was walking. He knew he couldn't afford to alert the suspect to his presence.

After five minutes, both men were in the alleyway immediately behind the houses on Greenshank Road. Jag could see the suspect was now motionless, standing directly outside the gate that would give him access to the elderly woman's house he'd visited earlier.

Jag could feel his heart pounding in his chest and tried to control his breathing as he crept ever closer to the suspect.

Turning off his personal radio, he crept closer still, only stopping when he was twenty yards from the suspect. He squatted down in the dark shadows, waiting to see what Varley did next. The detective had heard nothing from his partner before he silenced his radio, and he hoped Simon had managed to get backup travelling.

Suddenly, Varley removed the white carrier bag from his jacket and reached inside. He took out an eight-inch metal pry bar before stuffing the bag and its remaining contents back under his jacket.

Being this close, Jag could now see that Varley was wearing work gloves.

He reached inside his own jacket and grabbed the radio. He needed to find out what was happening and whether backup was on its way. Before he had the chance to switch on the radio, he saw Varley open the gate and step inside the yard.

He quickly turned on the radio and whispered, 'DC Singh to DC Paine. I need backup immediately, at the rear of the address on Greenshank Road.'

Without waiting for a reply, he stepped forward to the rear gate and slowly pushed it open. He could just make out the dark figure of Varley standing by the rear window of the house. He was no longer wearing the donkey jacket; it had been dropped at his feet.

Jag could see that Varley now had the pry bar in his hands and was attempting to force the transom window.

Suddenly, blue lights splashed across the brickwork and Varley turned. Jag saw the look of surprise on Varley's face as he realised that somebody else was in the yard with him.

Jag could now hear the diesel engine of the police patrol car as it screeched to a halt in the alley, directly behind him. He saw Varley react instantly to the blue lights and leap over the adjoining wall into the neighbouring yard. Reacting to the suspect, Jag immediately gave chase.

He continued to pursue Varley as he clambered over several walls, trying to escape. Both men eventually came to a yard where the far wall was too high for Varley to clamber over at the first attempt.

Jag yelled, 'Police officer. Stand still!' before grabbing the suspect and pulling him down from the wall. As both men landed in a heap, Jag got up and was confronted by Varley, who swung the pry bar he still held towards him. Jag managed to dodge the pry bar, but the ducking motion threw him off balance and he was unable to prevent the suspect from landing a heavy punch, just above his right eye. The force of the blow knocked him down.

Jag recovered quickly, leaping to his feet just in time to see the suspect disappearing through the gate of the yard. He flung the gate open and saw the suspect running along the rear alley heading in the direction of his parked car. He could see the police patrol car in the distance and shouted, 'Down here! We're down here!' before chasing after Varley.

Not knowing the area, Varley ran into an alley that was a dead end, and Jag knew he had him. He quickly caught up with him, cornering him at the end of the alley. As Varley turned to face him, Jag could see he was still holding the pry bar in his right hand. He could hear the police car approaching rapidly and headlights now illuminated the end of the alley. He could see Varley clearly now. His suspect was dressed in dirty, stained overalls and wore heavy work boots.

Jag shouted, 'I'm a police officer! Put the weapon down!'

He heard car doors open and close again behind him, and he knew the uniform officers were now standing directly behind him. He took a step towards Varley and shouted, 'I said, drop the weapon!'

Reluctantly, Varley dropped the pry bar at his feet and held his hands up. The two uniform officers stepped forward and used handcuffs to restrain him.

Jag touched his fingers to the bleeding gash above his right eyebrow and said, 'I'm arresting you on suspicion of attempted burglary, going equipped to steal, and police assault.'

He turned to one of the officers and said, 'Will you be taking him to Mansfield?'

'Yeah.'

'Before you go, bring him back to the yard where I found him. He's left a coat in there.'

As they all walked back towards the yard, a breathless Simon Paine appeared. 'Bloody hell, Jag, are you okay? Your eye looks a mess.'

'Good job you got the troops here. He wouldn't have come without a scrap otherwise. Where were you?'

'The cops weren't sure which way you'd gone out of the yard. I chose the wrong way. Sorry, mate.'

'Don't worry about it; we've got him now. That's all that matters.'

One of the officers lit up the rear yard with his torch and the detectives saw the donkey jacket below the window. Jag said, 'That coat's his. There's a white carrier bag inside it.'

Simon Paine slipped on a pair of plastic gloves and retrieved the bag.

Jag said, 'What's inside?'

Varley shouted, 'That's not mine. I've never seen it before in my life.'

Simon opened the carrier bag and took out a pair of snips, a clear plastic bag, and cable ties.

From the donkey jacket pocket Simon retrieved a bunch of keys. He held up the Ford key, looked directly at Varley and said, 'And I don't suppose this Ford key fits the Cosworth you parked a couple of streets away either.'

Jag turned to the two officers and said, 'Get him out of here.'

64

2.15am, 22 March 1989
Mansfield, Nottinghamshire

Danny was instantly awake as the telephone next to his bed started to ring. Snatching up the receiver, he said quietly, 'Hello. Danny Flint.'

The control room inspector said, 'Sorry to call you at this hour, sir, but two of your detectives have made an arrest and have asked that you be contacted immediately.'

Wiping the sleep from his eyes, Danny sat up in bed. 'Who's made the arrest and what for?'

There was a brief pause before the inspector said, 'DC Jag Singh and DC Simon Paine have arrested a man by the name of Amos Varley at Warsop Vale. He's been detained for attempted burglary, going equipped to steal and police assault.'

Hearing the name Amos Varley, an excited Danny was

now wide awake, but his thoughts turned to a previous late-night phone call he had received, when DC Fran Jefferies had been badly assaulted following the arrest of Joanna Preston for murder twelve months ago.

He said, 'Arrested for police assault? Who's been assaulted and how bad is it?'

'DC Singh was punched during the arrest and has a cut over his eye. I don't know any other details. Sorry, sir.'

'I take it Amos Varley's been taken to Mansfield?'

'The officers are booking the suspect in now, sir.'

'Right. I'm on my way. I'll be there in thirty minutes.'

'I'll let the custody suite know you're travelling.'

Danny put the phone down and got out of bed. A sleepy Sue stirred behind him and mumbled, 'What's happening? Is Hayley alright?'

Danny knelt next to her and whispered, 'It was work, sweetheart. I need to go in and sort something out. Go back to sleep.'

'What time is it?'

He glanced at the bedside clock. 'It's quarter past two. Hayley will sleep through for another few hours if I don't wake her. Go back to sleep. I'll call you later, when I know what's what.'

Sue turned over and mumbled, 'Be careful. Love you.'

Danny kissed her on the back of her head and started to get dressed. Tiptoeing into the bathroom, he splashed water on his face, brushed his teeth and quickly combed his hair.

Without bothering to knot his tie, he crept downstairs and slipped on his shoes before grabbing his jacket, coat, wallet and car keys.

He closed the front door of the house as quietly as he could so he didn't wake his child, and got in his car.

Questions now flooded his brain. *What was Amos Varley doing that caused Jag to arrest him? Is this the breakthrough I prayed for? Have we finally caught a cold-blooded and dangerous killer?*

As he drove his powerful car through the dark, empty streets, he hoped the answers to those questions, and many more, would come soon enough.

65

2.45am, 22 March 1989
MCIU Offices, Mansfield, Nottinghamshire

Danny walked into the main briefing room of the MCIU and saw Tina Cartwright talking to a smiling Jag Singh, and Simon Paine.

He said to Jag Singh, 'For someone who's been punched in the face, you're looking very happy.'

The smile instantly disappeared from Jag's face, and in a professional voice he said, 'It's looking good, boss. We've been following Varley all afternoon and evening. He spent hours earlier watching a house on Greenshank Road, at Warsop Vale, before finally approaching the house and speaking to the old lady who lived there.'

'Is this the same house where you arrested him?'

'Yes. After speaking to the old lady, he left Warsop Vale and drove around aimlessly for hours. He finally returned to the same area about an hour ago. We watched him park his car a couple of streets away and walk to the house he'd visited earlier. I followed him on foot to the rear of the old woman's house and caught him trying to force entry to a transom window in the rear yard.'

'How was he trying to break in?'

'He had an eight-inch pry bar he was forcing the window with.'

Danny pointed at the gash above Jag's right eye and said, 'Tell me how you got that.'

'Simon had radioed for backup and the uniform lads arrived with the blue lights on. When Varley saw the lights and heard the car engine he bolted and started hopping over the neighbours' walls. I chased him and after four or five yards I caught up with him. I managed to pull him off the wall before he could climb over it. I identified myself as a police officer and he swung the pry bar at me but missed. Because I'd ducked to avoid the pry bar, I couldn't get out of the way when he threw a punch at me. The punch knocked me on my arse, and he ran out of the gate. I got up, chased after him again and finally caught him in one of the alleys that's a dead end. I thought at first he was going to have another go at me with the pry bar, but then the uniform lads arrived and he thought better of it. He dropped the pry bar and gave himself up.'

'That's great work, Jag. How's the eye feeling now?'

'It's smarting and I've got a bit of a headache.'

Tina said, 'I've told him it needs a few stitches. He's going to the hospital as soon as we've finished briefing you.'

'Let's make it quick then. Did Varley say anything when he was arrested?'

Jag said, 'Not initially, but when I took him back to the

yard of the old woman's house to retrieve the coat he'd dropped, he did say something.'

'What?'

Simon said, 'When I recovered the black donkey jacket, I found a carrier bag inside it that contained a pair of snips, a clear plastic bag and cable ties. Varley protested, saying that he'd never seen the coat before, and that it wasn't his.'

Danny said, 'Was anything else in the coat?'

Simon grinned. 'Varley's car keys were in one of the other pockets. It's his coat all right, boss.'

Danny could feel his excitement building. This was indeed looking good.

'What else was he wearing?'

Jag said, 'Dirty overalls, gloves and work boots.'

'Have you seized his clothes?'

Tina said, 'All his clothing's been seized. He's in the cell wearing one of our paper suits now. The pry bar was recovered from the scene of his arrest and his Ford Sierra Cosworth is being recovered by the vehicle examiners to the forensic bay at headquarters.'

'Excellent. Who seized his clothing?'

Simon said, 'I did, boss. There are oil stains all over the overalls and the boots feel oily to the touch. There's a strip of cloth missing from the right sleeve of the overalls that could match the strip of cloth we found at the Margaret White murder scene.'

Danny said, 'Tina, have you contacted Tim Donnelly yet? I want him called out to get a grip of these forensic opportunities.'

'Will do, boss.'

'Have you organised a search of Varley's home address?'

'The duty inspector's aware of the arrest and is coming in to the station to sign the Section 18 authority for the search.'

'Good work. I'll contact the control room now and arrange for a section of the Special Operations Unit to be called out to carry out the search of his home address.'

Danny paused to think, then said, 'Is there anything else I need to know from the actual arrest?'

Jag shook his head, but Simon said, 'There was one other thing, boss. When I searched the donkey jacket and found the snips and cable ties, I looked at Varley and he was smiling. When he saw I was looking at him, his expression changed, and he denied the coat was his. He was smiling about something, though.'

Danny nodded. 'That's interesting. He sounds a strange character.'

He turned to Tina. 'When can we interview Varley?'

'I've spoken to the custody sergeant and there can be no interviews until eight o'clock this morning. PACE regulations mean Varley's entitled to a rest period now.'

'Bloody hell.'

After initially cursing, Danny paused to think before saying, 'Well, let's use this time to our advantage. I want Tim Donnelly to get cracking with the forensic opportunities, and I want a full search of Varley's home address. Jag, I want you to go straight to the hospital and get that eye seen to. Are you okay to remain on duty?'

Jag smiled. 'I'm not going anywhere, boss. I'll get this patched up and be straight back. It's nothing a couple of paracetamol can't sort out.'

'Good man.'

Danny turned to Simon. 'I want you to go back to Greenshank Road and speak to the woman whose house Varley was trying to break into. I want a full statement from her. I want to know exactly what Amos Varley said when he visited earlier in the day. I want to know what she looks like as well. Get an up-to-date photo if you can. My guess is that physically, she'll closely resemble Florence King and Margaret White. I think this is all about the victims. Tina, as staff start arriving, I want them researching everything we can about Amos Varley. I want to know about his family background, what he was doing before he went on the rigs, who his friends and associates are, the works. Let's get cracking and we'll reconvene at eight o'clock to start preparing for interviews.'

66

5.15am, 22 March 1989
Archway Road, Old Clipstone, Nottinghamshire

Sergeant Graham Turner and his team from the Special Operations Unit had almost completed the search of Amos Varley's home address.

The suspect's property was a neglected four-bedroom detached house tucked away in a remote location between Clipstone and Edwinstowe. Archway Road was little more than a country lane that led to nowhere. Varley's house was a hundred yards further along Archway Road than the previous dwelling, and was also the last house on the road. From there, the lane petered out, eventually becoming a footpath that led across the fields to the main Edwinstowe Road.

The décor of the house obviously hadn't changed in years. For the sergeant and his team, it had been like stepping into a time machine that transported them back to the late sixties, early seventies.

Evidentially, the only items the team had found were a bag of cable ties purchased from a local DIY store. The ties had been found in a cupboard under the sink, in the kitchen. Sergeant Turner had made the decision to seize them, as they looked like ties he'd seen in photographs taken at the scene of Margaret White's murder.

PC Matt Jarvis suddenly shouted, 'In here, Sarge.'

Turner walked into the lounge that was being searched by Matt and his colleague Tom Naylor. 'What's up?'

'In the briefing it was mentioned that we should look for photographs of Varley's parents. Do you think this could be his mother?'

Matt Jarvis handed over a framed photograph of an elderly woman standing in the garden of the house. She was standing with her arms folded across her chest and looked very displeased to be having her photograph taken.

'I don't know. We'll seize it anyway. She looks a fierce woman.'

Matt nodded. 'The maternal instinct doesn't look very strong, does it? I bet she was a tough old bird.'

The sergeant ignored the comment. 'Where did you find the photograph?'

'It was in the drawer of that writing bureau.'

'That's odd. It's a framed photograph; you'd think it would be on display, not shoved in a drawer.'

'It was right at the bottom of the drawer, buried beneath a ton of documents.'

'Very odd. Have you found anything else in here?'

Tom Naylor said, 'We've recovered some documentation about the rigs and bank account paperwork, but that's about it. I've also seized a file of papers from a solicitor about the will and the estate left for Amos Varley following his mother's death.'

'Have you got much more to go through?'

'About another hour should see us finished in here, Sarge.'

'Okay. There's no rush. The rest of the lads are about done but take your time. I don't want you to miss anything.'

'Will do, Sarge.'

67

7.30am, 22 March 1989
MCIU Offices, Mansfield, Nottinghamshire

Danny was in his office with Tina Cartwright and Sergeant Turner, discussing the result of the search at Varley's home address and the statement obtained from the potential burglary victim at Warsop Vale.

He said, 'What did the search yield?'

Sergeant Turner handed Danny a full list of the items seized by his search team. 'There wasn't that much there, boss. The main thing was the bag of cable ties we found in the kitchen. Hopefully, forensics can match them to those that were recovered at the murder scenes. There's also a lot of documentation that will need to be properly read through, to see if there's anything relevant to your inquiries.

I've erred on the side of caution and brought anything I thought may be relevant.'

'Good. I'd much rather you did that than leave something that could be important.'

'It's mainly employment documents and bank account statements, but there's also a file that deals with the death of his mother. Copies of the death certificate, the last will and testament, and documentation from a solicitor dealing with his mother's estate.'

'Do you have the death certificate of his mother to hand?'

'The lads are just filling out the exhibit labels and booking everything in the property store. Give me a minute.'

Turner left the office, returning a few minutes later clutching the death certificate of Joan Varley, which he handed to Danny.

Danny quickly read the document, before passing it to Tina and saying, 'Her death was recorded by Dr Partridge. I want you to find out if he or she was Joan Varley's own GP. As you know, if her own GP certified the death, there would be no need for a post mortem. It states on this document that the cause of death was heart failure. I need you to speak to Dr Partridge and establish exactly what that means.'

Sergeant Turner handed Danny the framed photograph recovered at the house and said, 'I brought this for you to look at. Do you think this is Varley's mother?'

Danny's eyes widened when he saw the photograph. He placed the frame on his desk and took out the photographs of Florence King and Margaret White. The three women looked identical in appearance. The expressions on the faces of the two murder victims were much softer than the hard, embittered expression on the face of Joan Varley.

He said, 'Look at this, Tina. The physical likeness is uncanny.'

'Don't forget Audrey Hollis. She's very similar in appearance as well.'

'Now I'm even more convinced that the key to these murders lies with Amos Varley's mother. I need chapter and verse on the circumstances surrounding her death and anything else you can find out about her. I want detectives going door to door on Archway Road. Let's see if anyone's still living there who can remember what Joan Varley was like.'

'I'll see who's available and get them travelling straight away. I'll team up with Fran and see what we can find out about her death.'

'Is the first interview with Varley all arranged?'

'I've spoken to the custody sergeant, and everything's in place for Varley to be interviewed at eight o'clock.'

'Who's doing the interview?'

'Jag's back from the hospital now. I've told him and Simon to carry out the first interview. I thought it prudent to allow the arresting officers to do at least the first interview. That way, Varley won't think we suspect him of anything other than a burglary.'

'Good thinking, but at some stage we're going to have to question him about the murders and he'll need arresting for those offences before then. But for this first interview, let's question him about the attempted burglary and the assault on Jag.'

'Is his solicitor here?'

'Varley's declined legal advice for the time being.'

A shocked Danny said, 'What?'

He was thoughtful for a moment before continuing,

'Okay. Let's see if that changes as things develop. One last thing. What did Varley speak to the woman at Warsop Vale about?'

'I've got the statement from Tilly Bowers here. Basically, he was asking her if she had seen his terrier dog, as he'd lost it when it chased a rabbit in one of the nearby fields.'

'A bullshit story, then?'

'Sounds like it. He asked if Mrs Bowers, or any of her family in the house, had seen the dog.'

'And she told him that she was the only person who lived there now?'

'Exactly. He knew she would be in the house alone last night, and that's why he returned.'

'I want to know the minute Jag and Simon have completed the first interview, and I want you or Fran to keep me abreast of anything you find out about Joan Varley. As a priority, I need you to find and speak to Dr Partridge.'

Tina and Graham left the office, leaving Danny alone with his thoughts.

His eyes were locked on the photographs of the three women on his desk. He was confident Amos Varley was a killer. He also felt he was getting closer to understanding why Varley had chosen to kill two defenceless old ladies.

68

8.15am, 22 March 1989
Mansfield Police Station, Nottinghamshire

Jag Singh and Simon Paine had gone through the introductions preceding the interview, before Jag said, 'At the moment, you've declined the right to free and independent legal advice. Are you happy for this interview to continue without a solicitor being present?'

Amos Varley looked up, shrugged his shoulders, and said quietly, 'I don't need a solicitor. This is all something and nothing. It's no big deal.'

There was a brief pause before Varley continued, 'Before we start, I want to apologise to you for that.'

He pointed at the bruising above and around the detective's right eye, before saying, 'I honestly didn't realise you were a cop. You didn't look like one in the dark. I thought you were going to beat me up.'

Jag said, 'I identified myself to you.'

'Yeah, but anybody could say that. I thought you knew the person who lived there and you were waiting to give me a good hiding.'

'Let's talk about that, then. What were you doing in that yard in the middle of the night? You obviously thought it was something you might get a good hiding for, so why were you there?'

'I was mooching around, looking for stuff to have away.'

'Such as?'

'Whatever I could find. Tools, bicycles, anything really.'

'Don't forget I was standing behind you. I saw you trying to force the window. That's a bit more than mooching around.'

'I wasn't trying to force the window. I was just seeing if any were open.'

'Why?'

He shrugged his shoulders and said, 'If I'd found one already open, I probably would have gone in to see what I could get.'

'Probably?'

'Okay. If one of the windows had been open, I would have gone in.'

'I saw you using a small pry bar to try and force the window. We've recovered that pry bar from where you dropped it when you were detained.'

'That's not my pry bar. I found it in the yard.'

'The householder's made a statement saying she doesn't own any such tool. Why had you taken it with you? Was it your intention to break into houses?'

There was a long pause, then Varley said quietly, 'Okay. It's mine. I went out looking to do a burglary. I need money urgently and was looking for something to steal that I could maybe sell on.'

'Why do you need money?'

Varley grinned and said, 'We all need a bit of extra cash when we can get it, don't we?'

'What were the plastic bag and the tie wraps for?'

'I use them at work. I just forgot to take them out of my pocket.'

'Have you been to that area before?'

'No. It was a spur-of-the-moment thing. I thought it looked like a good place to find something to nick.'

'I've no other questions for you at the moment, but we may need to talk to you again.'

'What about? I've admitted what I was doing there. Can't you crack on and charge me? I don't want to be stuck in here any longer than I need to be.'

'There's a few more things we need to check, but I can't see you being here much longer.'

Jag ended the interview and returned Varley to his cell.

As he and Simon completed the custody record, Simon asked, 'What do you think?'

'I can see right through his little game. He thinks if he admits the burglary and the assault, he'll be out of here before we can talk to him about anything else. I don't think so, mate.'

69

9.00am, 22 March 1989
MCIU Offices, Mansfield, Nottinghamshire

Still juggling the two separate murder investigations, Danny walked into the main briefing room, seeking out Rob Buxton. Seeing him talking to Tina Cartwright, he walked over. 'Rob, I'm aware the surveillance we planned on Kevin Briar and Dominic Finch is scheduled to start this morning. Have you got enough staff to carry out an effective surveillance?'

'The staffing level isn't ideal, but I've got enough to mount an effective follow. Whether I'd call it a full-blown surveillance is a different matter. Hopefully, Finch and Briar won't be surveillance conscious and we get away with it.'

'How many have you got?'

'Andy and Helen are watching Briar, Rachel and Jane are on Finch.'

'Have they set up on them yet?'

'They were out and on plot at seven thirty this morning. There's been no movement from either of them yet.'

'Okay. Keep me informed of any developments.'

He turned to Tina. 'Any progress finding Dr Partridge?'

'I've just come off the phone to the Mansfield Woodhouse Health Centre. I managed to speak to Dr Jill Partridge. Joan Varley had been her patient for years and suffered from congenital heart disease. Dr Partridge had treated her for two very mild heart attacks in the six months leading up to her death. She attended the house on Archway Road the morning Joan Varley died and was happy to write the death certificate, as all the signs indicated she'd suffered another heart attack.'

'So she saw nothing suspicious about the woman's death?'

'Apparently not, but I got the impression she may not have been looking at the scene how we would. On that note, I've also managed to talk to the uniform officer who attended the scene. PC Bob Kilder said he saw nothing suspicious and examined the body with Dr Partridge. There were no marks of violence anywhere.'

'It's all academic, as it's too late to do anything about it now. Who called the sudden death in?'

'The death was reported to the police by Joan Varley's son, Amos.'

'Was anybody else in the house?'

'No. The husband died several years before. It was just Amos and his mum.'

'Have you had anything back from the detectives doing the door-to-door enquiries on Archway Road?'

'Not yet. I can contact them on the radio and see if anyone's got any updates.'

'Give it another hour. If you still haven't heard anything by then, chase them up.'

Danny returned to his office. There was a knock on his door and Jag and Simon walked in.

Danny said, 'How did the first interview go?'

Jag replied, 'Varley coughed being there to burgle the house. He was looking to get inside and steal whatever he could sell on, as he needed some extra cash.'

'That seems a bit easy. What are your thoughts?'

'I don't buy it, boss. I got the impression he's taking the line of least resistance. Admit the burglary and the assault on me, maybe get a few months inside, and dodge being questioned about the real reason he was there. He's also lied to us, saying that it was a spur-of-the-moment thing to try that house, but we know he spoke to the elderly occupant earlier. Crucially, I think he knows if he's charged now, we won't be able to prevent him getting bail.'

'Did you ask him about the items he had with him?'

'He skated over that, saying he used the bag and tie wraps at work.'

Danny was thoughtful, then he said, 'How did you end the interview?'

'I told him there were a few more things we needed to check, but that we wouldn't be much longer.'

There was a long silence before Danny continued, 'This is what I want you to do. Research any other burglary offences that have occurred in the Warsop Vale area. Once you've done that, inform Varley you're now investigating a series of burglaries that have occurred in the surrounding area. I want you to arrest him on suspicion of those other burglaries, then ask for his consent to provide a blood sample. I'll ask the superintendent to authorise the taking of the intimate sample. Don't make the request until the police surgeon's arrived at the cell block. If he does consent to the intimate sample being taken, I don't want to give him the chance to change his mind while we wait for the surgeon to arrive. If he doesn't consent, then it's tough shit anyway.'

'Do you think he'll go for it, boss?'

Danny shrugged his shoulders. 'I don't know, but I think it's worth a try. Research any other burglaries you can find, then come and see me before you go back into the interview room. I want to ensure we have the superintendent's authority signed, and that the police surgeon's ready and waiting at the cell block.'

70

9.30am, 22 March 1989
Mansfield Police Station, Nottinghamshire

Jag Singh and Simon Paine entered the interview room with Amos Varley. As he sat down, Varley grinned and said, 'Are we about done, lads?'

Jag shook his head. 'Not quite. We're investigating a series of dwelling house burglaries that have all occurred in and around the area where you were arrested. We need to question you about those offences, so I'm now arresting you on suspicion of committing further burglary offences.'

While Jag said the caution, Varley laughed and said, 'You've got to be joking. I haven't done any other burglaries.'

Jag said, 'In relation to other offences, I am now requesting you to provide an intimate sample. If you consent to this request, a sample of your blood will be obtained by a police surgeon. That sample will then be checked against those other offences.'

Varley stopped laughing and was thoughtful for a moment before saying, 'Why not. I haven't done any other burglaries.'

Jag handed the consent form to Varley, who immediately signed it.

Varley was then escorted back to the custody sergeant who said, 'Mr Varley, you've signed a consent form allowing the police to obtain an intimate sample. The request for this intimate sample has been authorised by a superintendent. These officers will now escort you to the police surgeon, who will obtain a blood sample from you. Any questions?'

Varley shook his head and followed Jag into the doctor's room. The two detectives stood in the doorway while the doctor obtained the blood sample.

As soon as it had been obtained, and while Jag returned Varley to his cell, an excited Simon phoned Danny. 'He went for it, boss. He signed the consent, and the police surgeon has taken the sample.'

Danny said, 'How was Varley when you made the request?'

'When Jag informed him that a doctor would take a blood sample, I could see the cogs in his brain turning. He was desperately trying to remember if he'd left blood anywhere. He obviously doesn't understand DNA, or the connection between blood and semen.'

'Excellent work. Get that blood sample up to my office as soon as you can.'

71

9.45am, 22 March 1989
MCIU Offices, Mansfield, Nottinghamshire

Danny picked up the phone and dialled the number for the Forensic Science Service in Birmingham. As he waited for his call to be answered, he stared at the blood sample just obtained from Amos Varley.

After several rings the phone was eventually answered. 'Dr Weaver. Can I help you?'

Danny took a deep breath and said, 'Good morning, Dr Weaver. It's Detective Chief Inspector Flint at Notts MCIU. I've got a question for you.'

The scientist replied, 'This sounds intriguing, Detective. Go on.'

'If I have a blood sample hand-delivered to you this morning, how soon could you obtain a DNA profile from it?'

With a note of indignation in her voice, Fay Weaver said, 'As well you know, Chief Inspector, the system doesn't work like that. I can't short-cut our procedures just to please you.'

Danny had expected her response and said quietly, 'The blood sample I'm talking about has just been obtained from the man I strongly suspect is responsible for the brutal rape and murder of two elderly women. Unless I can gather enough evidence to prevent it, I will be forced to release this man by tomorrow afternoon. I could charge him with burglary and police assault, but there's no way I'll be able to remand him in custody. This means he would be released on bail, free to potentially rape and kill again. As you know, we already have this killer's DNA profile, so all I need is for this sample to be profiled and see if it's a match. I was hoping you could make this one exception to your rules.'

There was a long silence.

Danny held his breath.

Finally, Dr Weaver said, 'How soon can you get the blood sample here?'

Stifling a small cheer, Danny said, 'A Traffic car will be despatched forthwith. It will be at your laboratories by eleven thirty this morning.'

'It will speed things up considerably if you could send somebody with the sample, to walk it through the booking-in procedure.'

'Tim Donnelly will bring the sample and remain with it throughout your procedures.'

'Understand this, Chief Inspector. This in no way sets a precedent and is strictly a one-time-only offer. I will not entertain other requests such as this, so don't ask. Get the sample here as soon as you can, and we'll get it done.'

Wearing a grin that stretched from ear to ear, Danny

said, 'I understand. Thank you so much, Dr Weaver. You may have just saved someone's life.'

72

9.45am, 22 March 1989
Mansfield Police Station, Nottinghamshire

Amos Varley cradled the plastic beaker that contained the piping hot coffee the cell officer had just bought him in both hands.

He'd tried to engage the officer in conversation but had been largely ignored. The only reply he got to his questions had been a surly, 'Two sugars. Be careful; it's very hot.'

The cell door had then been slammed shut. The sound of the heavy metal door being closed in such dramatic style had made him shudder.

He tried to sip the coffee, but the water was scalding hot. He placed the beaker on the floor of the cell to cool and stared at the walls that now seemed to be closing in around him.

He was worried.

He knew he hadn't left any blood anywhere, so he hadn't been particularly bothered about giving a sample. He hoped if anything, it would speed up his release.

But something the Asian detective had said and done when he escorted him back to his cell after being seen by the police surgeon was now deeply troubling him.

The detective had touched two fingers to the deep gash above his eye. The swelling was more pronounced now and Varley could clearly see where the wound had been recently stitched.

Ignoring any obvious discomfort caused by Varley's punch, the detective had grinned and said, 'Thanks for this, mate. It was worth every stitch.'

It was such a strange thing to say and do.

The more he thought about it, the more convinced he became that he was missing something.

73

**11.20am, 22 March 1989
Forensic Science Service, Marston Green, Birmingham**

Tim Donnelly felt nauseous.
He enjoyed driving fast, but to sit in the back of a Traffic patrol car with its blue lights and sirens on as it was driven at high speed from Nottingham to Birmingham had been a total nightmare.

It was like being on the world's longest rollercoaster ride.

The Traffic car had been accompanied on the high-speed journey by four police motorcycle outriders. The presence of the motorcycles had meant there was never any let-up in the speed.

Every red traffic light and roundabout had been negotiated at top speed, after any opposing traffic had been halted by the skilled outriders.

As the powerful car came to a skidding halt outside the

main reception of the Forensic Science Service offices, Tim could see Dr Fay Weaver waiting just inside the door.

Clutching the all-important blood sample, he exited the vehicle and walked on jelly legs towards the reception area.

Fay Weaver met him just inside the building. 'Are you okay, Tim? You look as white as a ghost.'

Tim swallowed hard and said, 'I'm fine,' before handing Amos Varley's blood sample to the scientist. The exhibit label was immediately signed by the scientist.

She said, 'Tim, I want you to walk through the entire process with me to ensure there's no break in the evidential chain. We don't want to mess this opportunity up.'

Tim said, 'Before we go, how long do you think this will take?'

'If all goes well, we should have a profile of this sample by six o'clock this evening. Then it will just be a case of comparing the profile with the ones we already have from the crime scenes. I'm hopeful you'll have a definitive answer by eight o'clock tonight.'

Tim quickly stepped back outside and said to the driver of the traffic car, 'Contact the Force Control Room and get a message to DCI Flint. We should have an answer, one way or the other, by eight o'clock tonight.'

'Will do.'

Tim walked back inside and said, 'Okay, Fay. Let's get this done.'

74

12.30pm, 22 March 1989
Matlock, Derbyshire

Andy Wills and Helen Bailey were pleased to be on the move. They had remained stationary in their car for over four hours, watching the High Peak Outward Bound Centre in the village of Youlgreave.

Andy had slipped their nondescript vehicle in behind the Land Rover driven by Kevin Briar as it emerged from the centre.

He maintained a good distance as the two vehicles were driven along the country lanes near the centre. It was all he could do. The lack of staff meant there was no possibility of being able to change positions with other officers. He needed to follow the Land Rover without causing Briar to become suspicious.

As the Land Rover was driven onto the busy A6 road that

led into Matlock, the other vehicles using the road made his task much easier.

Helen said, 'He's definitely heading into Matlock.'

Andy remained tight lipped. He was aware his colleagues, Rachel Moore and Jane Pope, had already tailed Dominic Finch into Matlock town centre.

After parking his BMW in the car park adjacent to Hall Leys Park, Finch had remained in the vehicle.

Andy managed to keep one other vehicle between himself and Briar's Land Rover as they entered the town of Matlock.

Helen spoke into the radio, 'DC Bailey to DS Moore. Over.'

The reply was almost instant, 'From DS Moore, go ahead. Over.'

'We're entering Matlock, heading in the direction of Hall Leys Park. Is your target still at that location? Over.'

'Affirmative. I've a clear view of the car park and the target is still in his vehicle. DC Pope's in the café on the park, in case he decides he wants refreshments. Over.'

'We're at your location now. Target vehicle is a dark green Land Rover, registration number Delta Two One Mike Bravo Tango. I've a nearside indication. Stand by. Over.'

From her position in the car park, Rachel saw the Land Rover drive in and park two bays along from where Finch had parked his BMW.

Andy drove his vehicle into the car park and parked at the far end, away from the two target vehicles. There were other vehicles parked between his car and the two target vehicles, but he still had a good view of Finch and Briar.

Almost as soon as Briar arrived, Finch got out of his car and walked towards the Land Rover. As Briar got out of the

Land Rover the two men shook hands. It was a formal greeting, lacking any real warmth. Having greeted each other, they immediately began to walk towards the path that led alongside the river.

Andy said, 'DS Wills to DS Moore. Helen and I will follow the targets on foot. Remain here and stay with the vehicles. Over.'

Rachel replied, 'Will do. Over.'

Andy and Helen got out of the car and walked towards the path. Andy could see the two men walking slowly in front of them. They were less than twenty yards away. He whispered to Helen, 'I'm going to put my arm around you; we need to be a couple.'

Helen instantly snuggled in beside Andy and the two dawdled slowly along, pretending to stare at the picturesque river as it flowed through the park.

Andy could see that Briar and Finch were having quite a heated conversation. The discussion between the two men became more and more intense, until Briar reached over and grabbed the lapels of Finch's overcoat before roughly pushing him away again.

Andy could see that Finch was not in the least bit intimidated by Briar's threatening actions. He watched as the smaller man stepped forward and prodded Briar's broad chest with his index finger, shouting, 'No more! That's it, we're done!'

Briar turned away and began walking back along the path towards Andy and Helen. Andy pulled his colleague in close and hugged her, keeping one eye on the approaching Briar. He could see that the outward bound centre owner had a face like thunder. Whatever had been discussed by the two men, it was obvious that Briar wasn't happy about the outcome.

As Briar stormed by the two detectives, Andy glanced back towards Finch. The contrast in the mood of the two men could not have been more pronounced. Finch was beaming a wide smile and chuckling to himself as he walked slowly back towards the car park.

The two detectives made their way back to the car park and arrived just in time to see Briar starting the Land Rover. Knowing that traffic in Matlock town centre would be quite heavy, Andy didn't run for his car. He knew he would be able to locate the Land Rover in quick time.

Four minutes later he was three vehicles behind the Land Rover as it was driven out of town, back towards Youlgreave.

He snatched up the radio and said, 'DS Wills to DS Moore. We have eyeball on Briar again. Have you got Finch?'

Jane Pope answered, 'Affirmative. We have eyeball on Finch. He's driving towards South Wingfield. Looks like he's returning to his holiday cottage. Over.'

There was a brief silence before Rachel spoke on the radio, 'DS Moore to DS Wills. Over.'

'Go ahead. Over.'

'What happened on the path?'

'There was a very heated discussion between the two of them. For two friends, who according to both of them haven't seen each other in years , it all got very heated, very quickly.'

'Were you in a position to hear anything that was said?'

'Not really. I did hear how it ended, though, because Finch ended up shouting at Briar. Let's get them both housed, then we can debrief properly with the DCI. It was all a bit bizarre. Over.'

'That sounds like a plan. What time are our reliefs due to arrive? Over.'

'The arrangement was for them to be here at three o'clock. Hopefully, that hasn't changed. Over.'

75

4.00pm, 22 March 1989
MCIU Offices, Mansfield, Nottinghamshire

Danny, Rob, Andy, and Rachel were debriefing the surveillance operation on Dominic Finch and Kevin Briar. Andy had gone through the conduct of the two men during their meeting at Matlock earlier that day. He finished by saying, 'If nothing else, it confirms what Sandra Mellor told us. Finch and Briar are still very much in contact.'

Danny said, 'It makes no sense. Why would they lie about something so trivial? We were aware they were close friends back in the day, so why try and pretend they no longer kept in touch?'

Rob said, 'It's not just Sandra Mellor's word. Don't forget the regular transfers of cash from Finch's personal bank account into Briar's outward bound centre. We already know these cash transfers have been propping up Briar's business for years.'

Andy said, 'That could be what the shouting match was all about. When Finch shouted, "No more! That's it, we're done!" maybe he meant cash. Perhaps he was telling Briar there would be no more cash payments, and that he wasn't prepared to subsidise his business anymore. That would certainly explain the look of anger on Briar's face when he stormed off.'

Danny said, 'It's possible.'

He paused before looking at Rob. 'Have we gleaned anything else from the financial records of Finch?'

'There was one other interesting point the Met Fraud Squad found. There is a financial link between Dominic Finch and Douglas Richardson.'

'Go on.'

'Finch has enabled finance on several deals brokered by Richardson for property developments overseas. The Met have flagged up these transactions between Finch and Richardson as part of an ongoing investigation into a man named Mason Connor. Connor's a top-level target for the Met's organised crime team. They're carrying out an ongoing surveillance operation on him.'

'Have you spoken to anyone at the Met on that operation?'

'I've been in regular contact with DI Barnes, from their organised crime team. He believes Finch is using money from Mason Connor's criminal enterprises to facilitate the finance in Richardson's overseas property development schemes. When the profits from those developments come in, the original amount of cash, plus a healthy interest, is returned to Connor.'

'A simple money-laundering scheme?'

'The Met are so convinced, they've placed a watch order on Finch and Richardson whenever they are in London.'

'Why not a full-blown surveillance?'

'The Met feel that would be too labour intensive and cost prohibitive, so they've limited their surveillance to the Metropolitan Police area.'

'Anything interesting from their surveillance on Finch and Richardson that could help us?'

'There are several recorded meetings between Connor and Finch, and Connor and Richardson.'

'Have Finch and Richardson ever met?'

'There are no such meetings shown on the surveillance record. What their records do show is that Richardson and Finch have both recently spent time at the British Library in London, but not at the same time.'

Danny was silent, deep in thought.

He looked at Rob and said, 'I want you to work with Andy and Rachel and prepare an operational order for the arrest of Dominic Finch and Kevin Briar tomorrow morning. I want them detained on suspicion of the murders of Ian Drake and Melanie Drake. They've both been caught out in a lie, and both have revenge as a motive. Maintain regular updates from the teams watching them tonight. We need to ensure they remain at their respective properties in Derbyshire. It's important we detain both men at the same time.'

'No problem. We'll get straight on it. Any word from the Forensic Science Service yet?'

Danny moved his head from side to side, trying to alleviate the pain in his neck and shoulders as his muscles tensed up again. 'Nothing yet. The last update I had was this morning. They're hoping to have an answer, one way or the other, by eight o'clock tonight.'

As Rob and the others left the office, Danny leaned back in his chair and closed his eyes, not daring to entertain the possibility that the scientists would say the DNA profiles didn't match. He knew if that unthinkable scenario happened, it could spell the end for the MCIU.

76

7.00pm, 22 March 1989
Mansfield Police Station, Nottinghamshire

Amos Varley continued to bang his clenched fists on the cell door.

After ten minutes of continuous pounding, his hands were starting to hurt. Ignoring the pain, he continued to hammer on the metal door.

Suddenly, he heard the key in the lock and the heavy door was flung open. The bulky figure of the custody sergeant filled the door, and Varley could see two other uniform cops standing behind him. Feeling the anger emanating from the big sergeant, Varley took a step back.

'What's your fucking problem?' demanded the sergeant.

Not intimidated by him or the uniforms behind him, Varley snarled, 'How much longer are you going to keep me locked up in here? I've cooperated in every way I can and

I'm starting to get the feeling you lot are just pissing me about.'

The big sergeant took a step inside the cell and said quietly, 'Nobody's pissing you about. These things take time. If you stop banging on the door, I'll go and talk to the detectives dealing with you. That way I can find out how much longer they intend to be. Is that okay with you, Varley?'

Although delivered in a soft voice, the implied threat behind the sergeant's final sentence was obvious.

'Do I have a choice?'

'Not really. And if you continue to batter the cell door with your fists, I'll have no choice either. I'll restrain you for your own good. The last thing I need is you causing yourself an injury.'

The sergeant took the hard edge off his voice and continued, 'To be perfectly honest, that's paperwork I can do without. Do we understand each other?'

Varley nodded and sat down on the hard bench.

As the sergeant stepped back outside the cell door, he said, 'All things considered, I really don't see you being here much longer. Now, can I get you a hot drink?'

'Yeah.'

'I'll sort you out a brew, then talk to the detectives. I'll find out what the holdup is. In the meantime, calm yourself down. Okay?'

'Okay. I'm just getting a bit pissed off, that's all.'

As the heavy cell door closed, Varley turned and lay down on the bench.

Something was wrong; he knew he should have been charged and released by now. He cursed himself for giving that blood sample. His head was spinning with unanswered questions.

What is the delay? What do the cops know that I don't? What haven't they told me? What am I missing? Why did I agree to provide a blood sample? How much longer am I going to be in here? Should I have a solicitor now?

77

7.45pm, 22 March 1989
MCIU Offices, Mansfield, Nottinghamshire

The tension in Danny's office was unbearable. He was leaning forward with his elbows resting on the desk, staring at the telephone, willing it to ring.

On the other side of the desk sat a very tense-looking Tina Cartwright. Jag Singh and Simon Paine were standing in the office, also waiting. Nobody was saying a word. The only sound was the quiet action of the wall clock. Jag's eyes kept flicking towards that clock. As he stared at it, the second hand seemed to be crawling around the clock face.

Suddenly, the telephone started to ring. After the oppressive silence, the noise seemed deafening. Danny snatched up the receiver. 'DCI Flint.'

Tim Donnelly said quietly, 'Boss, it's Tim Donnelly.'

There was a second's pause before he continued, 'It's

positive. Varley's DNA profile from the blood sample is an exact match for the profiles we have from the Margaret White and Florence King murder scenes. You've got him.'

'You're absolutely positive?'

'There's no doubt. Amos Varley raped and killed both those old women.'

'That's brilliant work. Get the scientists' report back here as soon as you can.'

'Will do, boss. Can they drive a bit slower coming back? I don't think my heart will take another journey like that.'

'Stick to the speed limits, but I want that report on my desk as soon as you can. Well done, Tim.'

Danny put the phone down and looked at the three detectives opposite, all staring wide-eyed at him. He said, 'It's a match. Varley's our man.'

Jag clenched his fist and said, 'Yes.'

Danny acknowledged his detective's delight and then said, 'We've still got work to do. You need to arrest him for the two murders now. I expect he'll want legal advice, so there may be a delay before we can interview him again.'

Tina gave a note of caution, 'We'll still need to prove that he was in the area when the two offences were committed.'

Jag nodded. 'I think he'll still want to talk. Solicitor or not, if he thinks there's no way out of it, he'll want to talk. I think he'll want to try and explain why he's done something so abhorrent.'

Danny picked up the photographs of Varley's mother, Florence King and Margaret White and said, 'I wouldn't bank on that, Jag. Take these into the interview room with you. The more I look at them, the more I'm convinced the reason behind him committing these crimes has something to do with his own mother.'

As the gathered detectives all left his office, a wave of relief washed over Danny. It felt like a ton weight had been lifted from his shoulders. He quickly dismissed the feeling, knowing there was still a lot of work to be done. For the first time in months, he briefly allowed himself to entertain the possibility of a positive outcome.

78

8.00pm, 22 March 1989
Mansfield Police Station, Nottinghamshire

Amos Varley followed Jag along the corridor from his cell to the custody sergeant's desk.

Varley folded his arms across his chest and said, 'What's going on?'

Making sure the custody sergeant was listening, Jag replied, 'There's been a development. The blood sample you provided has now been forensically examined. The DNA profile taken from it has been found to match the DNA profile recovered at the scene of other serious crimes.'

Jag paused to gauge Varley's reaction. There was none. The prisoner stared straight ahead, failing to make eye contact with the detective.

Jag continued, 'As a result, I'm now arresting you on

suspicion of the murders of Margaret White and Florence King.'

There wasn't a flicker of emotion from Varley, and after Jag had cautioned him, he simply said, 'I think I need a solicitor.'

The custody sergeant took over and once again outlined Varley's rights before making a note of the request for legal advice. When Varley couldn't provide details of a solicitor, the custody sergeant explained to him that he would be provided with one from the duty list.

With the legal requirements completed, Jag was instructed by the sergeant to take Varley back to his cell.

When they reached the cell door, Varley stepped inside and said, 'I just want some advice from the solicitor. I want to know what he or she says about this DNA thing. Once I know where I stand with that, I'll be able to explain things to you better.'

Jag said, 'It's better not to say anything until we interview you. You're still under caution.'

'Okay. One thing I will say is this, I'm glad you caught me outside that old woman's house. I needed to be stopped.'

'Save it for the interview, Amos. I'll be back soon.'

79

9.15pm, 22 March 1989
Mansfield Police Station, Nottinghamshire

An hour had passed since Jag and Simon had finished giving disclosure to the duty solicitor who would be representing Amos Varley.

Tony Crane had been a solicitor for over twenty years and had represented every type of criminal in that time. He was well known to both police officers and the criminal fraternity in the Mansfield area. He knew all the tricks and was a wily operator who knew how to play the system. Like other experienced detectives, Jag was always on his guard when dealing with Tony Crane.

The world-weary solicitor had raised a suspicious eyebrow when Jag had disclosed to him how the incriminating intimate sample had been obtained.

He had voiced those concerns saying, 'My client, in

effect, thought he was providing a sample to check against other burglary offences.'

Jag had replied confidently, 'It was made quite clear to your client that the sample would be checked against other offences, not just outstanding burglaries.'

The solicitor had frowned but hadn't pushed it. Instead, he had asked for details of the two murders his client had subsequently been arrested for. Without giving exact details of the forensic evidence available, Jag had outlined the details of the two murders.

Having made copious notes, the solicitor had then gone into Varley's cell for a private consultation.

That had been an hour ago, and Jag was starting to wonder what Varley and his solicitor were still talking about during that consultation. He wondered if Varley had changed his mind about wanting to talk to him.

There was a loud banging on the door of Varley's cell. The custody sergeant unlocked the heavy metal door and said, 'Everything okay in here?'

The solicitor nodded. 'We're ready now. Is DC Singh here?'

'Yes. Why?'

'My client has expressed a desire to speak only to him. Can you also let the detective know that this could take a while, as against my best advice Mr Varley wants to answer all questions.'

Ten minutes later and Jag sat across the table from Amos Varley and Tony Crane. DC Paine was also in the room, sitting in the background making notes.

After the introductions had been made, Varley's solicitor spoke first, 'My client has decided to answer questions in relation to the matters for which he's been arrested. If you start to question him about other matters, or if your questioning becomes oppressive or inappropriate, I will interject.'

Jag took a second to compose himself. 'Thank you, Mr Crane.'

He then looked directly at Amos Varley and said, 'Amos Varley, you are currently under arrest for the murders of Margaret White and Florence King. Are you responsible for the deaths of those women?'

Varley looked up for the first time and made eye contact with the detective. There was a slight nod of his head, and in a voice barely more than a whisper he said, 'I am.'

Trying to suppress his own excitement, the detective said, 'I want you to take your time and tell me what you know about the first of those deaths, Florence King.'

Maintaining a cold stare, Varley whispered, 'Neither of the two women you have named were my first. The first woman I killed was my mother.'

Jag shot a look at the solicitor, who nodded for him to continue.

Jag took a deep breath. 'Amos Varley, I'm now arresting you on suspicion of the murder of your mother, Joan Varley.'

He repeated the caution, and when there was no reply from Varley, he continued, 'Okay. Tell me about that. What happened between you and your mother?'

'It's a long story, Detective.'

'We've got plenty of time and I'm keen to hear what you have to say. Go on.'

The level of Varley's voice raised a little as he said, 'My father died when I was ten years old. That's when everything in my life changed. From that moment, I was subjected to a living hell by that woman. I need you to understand that I have endured years of physical and sexual abuse at her hands. Can you imagine spending most of your childhood and adolescent years living in constant fear? Feeling permanently dirty and ashamed of your own existence?'

There was a long pause.

Jag used the silence. He never uttered a word, knowing Varley still had much more to say.

After what seemed an age, Varley spoke again, 'I was twenty-five years old when I finally snapped. I suffocated my mother with a pillow while she slept. The doctor who came to the house the next morning was already treating her for an ongoing heart condition. She asked me what had happened, and I just said I'd found her like that when I woke up. She examined my mother's body quickly and told me that her heart had finally given out. She wrote out Mother's death certificate in the lounge while I made her a cup of tea in the kitchen. I registered her death using that certificate and arranged her funeral and everything else later. Nobody ever asked me any questions.'

'And did killing your mother make your life better?'

'At first it did. I no longer had to endure her constant criticism running down everything I did. She wasn't there to control everything I did anymore.'

Varley paused again, as though wondering what to say next. Once again, Jag allowed him the time to compose his thoughts.

He could see Tony Crane starting to fidget, and for a second Jag thought he was going to interrupt.

Before the solicitor could voice concerns over the silence becoming oppressive, Varley spoke again, 'Gradually, I began to hear Mother's voice again. Only now it was inside my head, and it was constant. I could hear her scolding me repeatedly. It didn't matter where I went inside that house, it was the same endless noise. Even the walls of the house seemed to ooze painful memories. I felt trapped in a living nightmare.'

There was another long pause before Varley said quietly, 'I began to realise that the only time I hadn't heard my mother's voice was immediately after I'd suffocated her. Taking her last breath meant she could no longer ridicule or belittle me. I decided that if I could somehow recreate that act, it might stop her screaming inside my head all the time.'

'Having come to that realisation, what did you do?'

'This is going to sound ridiculous.'

Another long pause.

This time Jag did break the silence. 'This is your interview, Amos. It's for you to say whatever you want to. Nobody's going to think anything you say in here is ridiculous. What did you decide to do?'

'I decided to kill my mother all over again.'

'I've seen photographs of Florence King and your mother. It's fair to say that Florence King bore some physical resemblance to your mother. Is that why you chose her?'

Varley shrugged. 'I suppose so, but it was a subconscious decision. I didn't go out searching for someone who looked exactly like mother, but when I saw her, I knew she would be the one. I thought killing her might stop Mother's voice in my head.'

'Where did you first see Florence King?'

'I'd been fishing at Spion Kop ponds and was walking to the bus stop in Warsop when I first saw her. She was pegging washing out on the line. I just stopped and stared at her. She startled me because I thought she was Mother. That's when I knew what I had to do.'

'And what was that?'

'I had to kill her.'

'How did you kill her?'

'I went back to the house that night. I cut the telephone line, broke into her house and suffocated her, the same as I had my mother.'

'Did you use a pillow?'

'No. I'd taken a plastic bag with me. I tied her to the bed and put the bag over her head. The funny thing was that as soon as she stopped breathing and her eyes went funny, the voice of my mother fell silent. It was all so weird.'

'What did you do after killing her?'

'That silence didn't last long, and I realised I had to get away from my parents' house. I saw an advert in the paper, asking for young engineers who wanted to train as a rigger in the oil industry. I applied on the off chance and was surprised when I was offered a four-year contract working in Saudi Arabia.'

'Why surprised?'

'I had no experience in the oil industry, but they took me on and trained me on the job. The desert conditions were tough, with all that heat and dust, but the money was good. More importantly, it got me away from that bloody house and all those painful memories.'

'Could you still hear your mother's voice while you were working away?'

There was silence and then Varley whispered, 'I could still hear it, but it sounded distant. You know when you think you can hear somebody calling your name who's miles away? It was like that. I could bear it like that.'

'So, what changed?'

'I came home, that's what changed. I thought after four years away I'd be over everything, but as soon as I stepped back inside that house it was worse than it had been before I left. Mother's voice sounded like a howling banshee, so shrill and demanding. I should have just sold the house and moved back to Saudi permanently, but I couldn't think straight. She'd taken over my mind by then.'

Varley rested his head in his hands and a tormented expression came over his face.

Jag said, 'Are you okay?'

Varley nodded. 'I'm okay. I can still hear her now. She's still criticising me, laughing at me.'

Trying to regain control of the interview, Jag said, 'Let's talk about Margaret White, the woman who lived at Clipstone.'

The expression on Varley's face changed again. He stared directly at Jag and said flatly, 'I stood it for as long as I could, but when her wailing and screaming got too bad, I went out hunting again. By this time, I knew what I had to do to silence it. Hunting is the best word to describe what I did. I spent hours walking around, just looking at women, trying to find one that I knew would silence that bitch inside my head once and for all.'

'How did you find Margaret White?'

'I saw an old woman who looked a bit like my mother standing in the queue at the Forest Town post office. I waited outside in the rain and followed her home. I watched her little bungalow for a few days, then I killed her.'

'How did you do that?'

'I did her the same as I'd done the Warsop one. It had worked back then, so I used an identical method. I cut the phone line, broke in through a back window. Wedged all the doors open, in case I had to leg it, then suffocated her with a plastic bag. It was the same as I'd done before.'

'What happened after you killed her?'

'The silence lasted less than a week. I was distraught, wondering what I had to do to silence the din forever. Eventually, I was forced to go and try and find another. I managed to find one, but when I went to kill her, she wasn't there. I was leaving the next day so couldn't do anything about it. I had signed up to a six-month contract on a rig in the North Sea.'

'Where did you find this old lady?'

'The woman I had chosen lived in a bungalow near Peafield Lane, at Mansfield Woodhouse. I broke in the same way as I had the others, after cutting the telephone line. I realised once I was inside that nobody was there.'

'If that woman had been there, what would you have done?'

'The same as before. I would have killed her.'

'When did you get back from your contract in the North Sea?'

'I arrived back here on the twentieth.'

'Have you done anything else since you arrived back in the area?'

Tony Crane coughed and said, 'I won't have questions like that, Detective.'

Ignoring his solicitor, Varley answered, 'The first thing I did was try the bungalow at Mansfield Woodhouse again, but a security light came on and a dog started barking, so I had to run away. I ran back across the fields to where I'd parked my car.'

There was a pause and then Varley said, 'You know earlier today when you were putting me back in the cell, and I said I'm glad you caught me?'

'Yes.'

'I meant it. I would have killed that woman last night if you hadn't stopped me.'

'Is that why we found the plastic bag and cable ties in your coat pocket?'

Varley nodded. 'Exactly that. I would have suffocated her like the others.'

Jag took a moment to carefully phrase his next question. Even with the rapport he had developed with Varley, the detective knew there was a good chance he would refuse to answer questions about this element of the murders.

After careful consideration, Jag said, 'You've given me your explanation as to why you've killed these women. That it was all done to try and somehow silence the voice of your mother inside your head. Now I need to understand why you raped these old ladies before you killed them.'

Varley stared unblinking across the desk, and the detective could see the fire and pain behind his watering eyes. 'Because, Detective, that's what my mother made me do to her. On the night of my twelfth birthday, my mother took me in her bed and instructed me how to have sex. I was just a child who did everything his mother told him to do. It was only as I got older that I realised what she was making me do was wrong. My mother made me have sex with her every other night from my twelfth birthday onwards. I was so browbeaten into submission by her that I was almost twenty before I refused to do it anymore. She still controlled every aspect of my life, though. I was never allowed to see girls. For me to have a girlfriend was totally out of the question. I was totally dominated by her. I did everything I was told to do, without thinking or questioning. I'd been conditioned to do that since I was ten years old. Even when I was a grown man, I didn't dare speak back to her.'

Jag could see the tears streaming down Varley's face. It was obvious the suspect was suffering mental torment, but he allowed him to continue his narrative.

Varley's voice became angrier and louder as he continued, 'When I raped those two women, in my mind I was being forced to have sex with my mother. I could hear her voice screaming at me, "Don't do it like that, it's got to be like this, go faster, push harder, touch me there, not there, you idiot".'

Rubbing his eyes, he looked down at the desk and continued, 'The only time her nagging stopped was when I tightened the plastic bag around their heads and ejaculated. Only then was there the complete silence I craved.'

Varley slumped forward until his head was resting on the desk. He muttered, 'That was all I ever wanted, silence.'

'Is there anything else you want to tell me?'

The reply was mumbled, 'I'm sorry for what I did to those two women, but it was the only way I could stop my mother's screaming.'

80

10.30pm, 22 March 1989
MCIU Offices, Mansfield, Nottinghamshire

Danny had taken a moment before seeking out Rob. After spending hours supervising the Amos Varley interviews, he now had to reset and refocus on what needed to be done in relation to the planned arrests of Dominic Finch and Kevin Briar. He was just about to leave his office when there was a loud knock on the office door.

The door opened and an excited-looking Jag Singh and Simon Paine walked in. Danny had been half-expecting the two detectives to report a 'no comment' interview, but seeing the excitement showing clearly in the experienced men's faces, he asked, 'Did Varley talk?'

Jag said, 'And some. He's admitted everything. The murders of Florence King and Margaret White. The murder of his own mother and his intention to kill both Audrey Hollis at Mansfield Woodhouse and Tilly Bowers at Warsop Vale.'

Before Danny could respond, a joyous Simon Paine added, 'Jag snapped him like a dry twig, boss.'

Danny shot him a stern look and said, 'Calm down. This isn't a celebration. Never forget you're talking about the deaths of people's loved ones here, not some burglary you've cracked. Now take your time, and let's have a proper debrief.'

A chastened Simon replied, 'Sorry, boss.'

Danny knew only too well how both men were feeling. Their sense of euphoria after weeks of hard work was fully understandable but had to be checked.

He said, 'Look, I know how you're both feeling. Getting Varley to talk is great work. Has he given sufficient detail in the interview for us to charge him with all those offences?'

Jag replied, 'I've just been speaking to the custody sergeant, and he agrees there's more than enough evidence to support charges. I explained the forensic evidence we already have against Varley, including the DNA matches, and have outlined the detail in all his confessions. He's preparing charges now.'

'That's great. Did Varley give a reason for committing the murders? I always want to try and understand why.'

'It's as you suspected, boss. It's all connected to his own mother. The abuse Varley suffered after his father died, at the hands of his own mother, was truly horrendous. From the age of twelve he's been forced into an incestuous relationship with his mother. He described her total control over his very existence. After years of abuse, he finally snapped and suffocated her as she slept, but following her death he claims he could still hear her voice inside his head. He killed the other women in the hope it would stop him continually hearing his mother's voice.'

'Sounds to me like he's putting on a show for an insanity plea.'

Jag replied, 'I thought that at first, but he was genuine in what he was saying. The emotion he displayed was way too raw to be faked.'

'And just maybe he is insane. Raping and murdering old women in their own homes is hardly the act of a rational mind. That's one the psychiatrists can argue about. It really is great work, gents. Did you have any problems with his solicitor during the interviews?'

'None at all. I don't think Tony Crane could quite believe what he was hearing. He didn't try to interrupt, and only once tried to prevent his client from answering my questions.'

'What time are you going to charge him?'

'We didn't know if you wanted to charge him, boss.'

'Varley's your arrest. You've done all the interviews. I want you to charge him, Jag. I'm coming down to see him charged, though. I don't even know what Amos Varley looks like, and it would be nice to put a face to the shadow I've been chasing all these months.'

'I would think the charges will be on by now.'

'Right, let's go.'

81

11.00pm, 22 March 1989
Mansfield Police Station, Nottinghamshire

Danny stood in the background, staring at Amos Varley as Jag Singh charged him. The short, stocky killer showed no sign of emotion as he was charged with what were truly horrendous crimes. There was a haunted look behind his expressionless eyes as he stared straight ahead.

This pathetic-looking individual was the man who had caused Danny countless sleepless nights and could have brought about the downfall of the MCIU.

Danny felt a flush of anger as he thought about the pressure that had been applied to him by Potter and the chief constable during the running of the inquiry. He totally understood why the councillor, Richard White, had used his political clout to question the investigation into his mother's brutal murder. What he couldn't comprehend was the fact that Jack Renshaw hadn't tried to protect the investigation team. It was something he knew he would have to deal with later. Right now, he was just pleased this dangerous killer was under lock and key.

At the end of the charges, Jag stated the caution and invited a reply from Varley. In a flat, monotone voice Varley said, 'I can't hear Mother anymore.'

As Varley was led back to his cell, Danny couldn't help but glare after the shuffling figure in the white forensic suit. He thought of all the pain and suffering that one individual had caused to the families of his victims. There was no room in his thoughts for the suffering this deranged individual had endured at the hands of his own warped mother.

Feeling he could finally close the book on Amos Varley, Danny turned to Rob Buxton and said, 'Is everything in place for the arrests of Finch and Briar tomorrow morning?'

'The arrest and interview teams have been briefed and will be coming on duty at six o'clock. I'll be here to carry out a final briefing with them and a section of the Special Operations Unit. The SOU lads will carry out the physical arrests and then undertake the searches of the premises where Finch and Briar are located. The outward bound centre could take a while, but the holiday cottage where Finch is shouldn't take long at all.'

'Good work, Rob. You'd better get yourself off home. You've an early start tomorrow. I'll be going to headquarters first thing, to update Potter on Amos Varley. I want to be kept informed as soon as Finch and Briar are detained. I don't anticipate being at headquarters very long, but there are some things I need to get off my chest that won't wait.'

Rob knew that look on his friend's face. 'You're not planning on doing anything stupid, are you, Danny?'

'I need to say my piece, that's all. I've felt harassed throughout this inquiry by the very people who should have been supporting me. I've tried to shield you and everyone else from it, but I know that feeling of pressure seeps through. My fear has always been that my detectives start to feel it and begin cutting corners to get a result. It's counterproductive and very harmful to the integrity of any investigation.'

'It's also the way of the world, Danny. I've known you long enough to consider you a friend first and foremost, so I feel comfortable saying this to you. Please don't say or do anything you might regret later. I can see how you feel about this, and of course everyone's noticed the pressure being exerted on you from above. But I can assure you, your fears are unfounded.'

Rob paused before continuing, 'Not one of the detectives on this unit has ever cut any corners to achieve a result. They've been professional throughout, and the result of that unswerving professionalism is that pathetic individual in the cell downstairs has just been charged. All I ask is that you think about what you're going to say to Potter and Renshaw. Any criticism of them could destroy the MCIU just as easily as if we'd failed to find and charge Amos Varley.'

Danny smiled at his old friend, placed a hand on his shoulder and said, 'Thanks, Rob. I needed that. I know nobody's cut any corners and how professional everyone's been. Don't worry, I'll rein in what I'm going to say, but I will let them know what I think.'

'I know you will, boss.'

'I'll get back here as soon as I can, to oversee the interviews of Finch and Briar.'

'No problem. I'm sure we'll have everything in hand.'

82

8.00am, 23 March 1989
MCIU Offices, Mansfield, Nottinghamshire

Danny walked into the main briefing room, which was already a hive of activity. He saw Rob Buxton in deep conversation with Sergeant Graham Turner from the Special Operations Unit and made his way over.

'Do we have our targets in custody?' he asked.

Rob said, 'Everything went as planned. Kevin Briar was arrested at the outward bound centre. Unfortunately, he didn't want to come quietly and has sustained an injury to his face that the police surgeon is examining now.'

Exasperated, Danny sighed. 'What happened?'

Sergeant Turner answered, 'He went ballistic when my men broke the door down. They had been knocking for three minutes, so I gave the order for them to push the door in. Briar came at them with an ice axe. Obviously, my men defended themselves, brought him down and arrested him. In the scuffle, he sustained some bruising to his face. I've seen him, and it's nothing serious. Compared to what he could have done with that bloody ice axe, it's nothing. He'll be fit for interview, I'm sure of it.'

'Are all your staff okay?'

'No injuries to report, boss.'

'Thank God for that. Has the ice axe been recovered?'

Rob said, 'That was my first question. I remembered Seamus Carter talking about an ice axe as a possibility for the murder weapon used on Ian Drake.'

Graham replied, 'That axe has been recovered, along with another five we've found so far.'

'What about Finch?'

Rob said, 'Dominic Finch was arrested with no problems whatsoever. There's an interesting development with Finch. I was expecting him to be really arsey when arrested, but apparently he's been the complete opposite. Rachel and Glen conveyed him back to Mansfield and they both reckon he's shitting himself, now he's under arrest on suspicion of murder.'

'That is interesting. When Rachel went to see him in London, she emphasised to me how cool and matter of fact he'd been.'

'Well, not anymore. He's flapping big style.'

'I suppose he's got used to his millionaire lifestyle. There's a lot of truth in the old saying, "the more you have, the more you've got to lose". Is it something we could use to our advantage in the interviews?'

Rob shrugged. 'Both men have asked for solicitors. His

demeanour could change by the time his brief has finished prepping him.'

'I've got to be at headquarters for nine o'clock. When do you anticipate a first interview with either of them?'

'Depending on the outcome of the police surgeon's examination of Briar, I don't think we'll be speaking to either of them much before midday.'

'Okay. Hopefully I'll be back way before then. Keep me informed.'

Danny walked towards his office but was stopped by Fran Jefferies, who said, 'I've just had the result of the inquiry you asked me to do in respect of the vehicles owned by Douglas Richardson.'

Danny was thrown for a second but then said, 'Yes, yes. Richardson. What does he own?'

'Registered in his own name are three vehicles. He has a Ford Sierra Cosworth, an Aston Martin and a Range Rover. His wife Beth has a Triumph TR4 sports car registered in her name.'

'What colour's the Range Rover?'

'It's grey. I followed up the vehicle inquiry with a check on the paint samples recovered from the body of Mike Molloy. It's the same paint. Obviously, we would need to recover the vehicle and take paint samples to prove an exact match.'

'That's great work, Fran. Thanks.'

Danny was thoughtful for a second, then turned and walked back to Rob.

'Who's not involved in the arrests of Finch and Briar today?'

Rob said, 'Obviously Jag Singh and Simon Paine are busy with paperwork from last night, and Tina is in meetings with the Force lawyers about the unused material question in respect of all the files from Global Fossil Energy Exploration. I've kept Andy Wills, Jane Pope and Sam Blake as cover, in case anything else broke this morning.'

'Has anything else come in?'

'No.'

'Good. Thanks.'

Danny searched the sea of faces in the office until he saw Andy Wills. He walked over and said, 'Andy, I want you to find Jane Pope and Sam Blake, then come and see me in my office.'

'Will do, boss.'

As he walked to his office, he took the paperwork for the vehicle inquiry from Fran Jefferies.

After a few minutes, Andy Wills walked into Danny's office followed by Jane Pope and Sam Blake. 'You wanted to see us, boss?'

Danny said, 'I've had my suspicions about Douglas Richardson being involved in the murder of Mike Molloy. I've just been informed that he owns a grey Range Rover that's a colour match for the paint samples found on Molloy's body. I want you to arrest Richardson on suspicion of Molloy's murder and seize the Range Rover he owns for forensic testing. I've been assured by Tim Donnelly that if we find the offending vehicle, we'll be able to achieve an exact match to the samples we already have from Molloy's body.'

'The grounds for arrest sound a bit thin, boss. Even if we find the vehicle and it's proved to be an exact match, it doesn't prove Richardson was the driver.'

'I know, and you're right, it's very thin. My worry is that if we don't act and Richardson gets rid of the vehicle, our one chance of a conviction will have disappeared with it. No, we need to move. I'll take any flak that comes our way.'

'Don't you think we should at least get a search warrant? That way, if we do find the vehicle and it has accident damage, it will give us better grounds to arrest. And if we don't find the vehicle, we haven't put ourselves open to a wrongful arrest claim. The courts will have sanctioned the search.'

Danny was thoughtful; there was a lot of merit in what his detective sergeant was advocating.

'Okay. Go with that. I just hope you get the warrant, or we'll be scuppered.'

Andy smiled. 'Don't worry, I'll get the search warrant. I'll also get in touch with the vehicle examiners and arrange for them to meet us at Richardson's house when we execute the warrant. If the Range Rover's still there, we'll need a full lift to the forensic bay at headquarters.'

Danny said, 'I'll talk to Tim Donnelly when I get to headquarters and make sure he has staff that can work on the vehicle today. Ask Sergeant Turner if he's any staff free to assist in searching Richardson's house. By all accounts, it's a bit of a mansion and would take the three of you an age to search properly.'

'Will do, boss.'

83

9.00am, 23 March 1989
Nottinghamshire Police Headquarters

When Danny arrived at Chief Superintendent Potter's office, his secretary was waiting for him.

'Good morning, Chief Inspector. Chief Superintendent Potter is waiting for you in the chief constable's office.'

Danny carried on walking to the end of the corridor, towards the chief's office. As he passed Potter's secretary, she whispered, 'Councillor Richard White's in there as well, Danny.'

He turned and smiled at the secretary. 'Thanks for the heads-up.'

He knocked once on the chief's office door and waited. The door was opened by Adrian Potter, who ushered Danny inside.

Danny could see Councillor Richard White sitting beside Jack Renshaw. Potter sat down the other side of the chief.

Danny remained standing in front of the chief constable's desk, until Jack Renshaw said, 'Sit down, Chief Inspector. I understand you have an update of interest to all of us?'

Danny made eye contact with the chief and said, 'A man was charged late last night with three murders.'

He paused and looked directly at Richard White, before continuing, 'He was charged with the murders of Florence King, Joan Varley, and your mother, Margaret White. He's also been charged with other offences, in relation to burglary.'

Jack Renshaw said, 'Do you have the evidence to support these charges?'

'Yes. There's strong forensic evidence linking him to the murders, as well as confessions to all his crimes.'

Richard White stared hard at Danny before saying, 'You're certain you've got the right man, Chief Inspector?'

'He wouldn't have been charged if he wasn't. He's the man responsible for your mother's death.'

'Who is he? Why did he kill my mother?'

Danny glanced towards Jack Renshaw, who nodded almost imperceptibly for him to continue.

'His name's Amos Varley. The first person he murdered was his own mother. After suffering years of physical and sexual abuse at her hands, he killed her. The other murders, including that of your own mother, were as a direct result of that first murder. I don't think it's appropriate to go into any more detail at this time. There will be a trial and all this information is sub judice.'

White grimaced and said, 'I'm not trying to put you on

the spot. I'm just trying to make some sense of all this, Chief Inspector.'

'All I can tell you is that I'm certain Amos Varley is the man responsible for your mother's untimely death.'

'Well, thank you for that, at least, Chief Inspector.'

Renshaw whispered something to Potter, who stood and said, 'Richard, would you come with me, please? I need to talk to you about other, rather pressing, matters in my office.'

White stood. 'Of course.'

He followed Potter but paused next to Danny. He waited for Danny to stand then offered his hand. As the two men shook hands, the councillor said, 'Please pass on my heartfelt thanks to everyone who helped bring that evil monster to justice.'

'I will, sir. Thank you.'

Danny remained standing until Potter and White had left the office.

Jack Renshaw said, 'Sit down, Danny.'

He waited for Danny to be seated and continued, 'Thank Christ for that. I genuinely thought you were never going to catch that bastard.'

Danny was about to answer, when he recalled Rob Buxton's words of caution. When he did speak, he chose his words carefully. 'I'm pleased we were able to bring Councillor White and all the other bereaved families some resolution. It's been a very difficult investigation, and only the hard work and professionalism of everybody involved has brought about that resolution.'

Jack Renshaw stared across the desk at Danny, making eye contact before he spoke. 'I think I owe you an apology, Danny. In the cold light of day, I can see that some of the pressure I applied to you and the MCIU was uncalled for. For that, I'm genuinely sorry. I hope you can understand the situation I was in. I'm still relatively new in post, and I've had conversations with Richard White on an almost daily basis. Most of those discussions centred on what he perceived as the poor performance of the unit tasked with investigating his own mother's brutal murder. Remember, this is the man who ultimately controls the budget this police force must work to.'

'I understand all that, sir. But the lack of perceived support could have been very damaging for the investigation. All it would have taken was for a single detective to engineer evidence, or to see a suspect where there wasn't one, and it would have all failed. The wrong person gets convicted and we still have a killer on the loose. I refused to allow that to happen, whatever pressure was being brought to bear by you and Chief Superintendent Potter. Why didn't you trust me to talk to Richard White?'

He paused, trying to gauge Renshaw's reaction before continuing, 'If you had allowed me to speak directly to him, I could have explained the difficulties we faced. I could have explained the length of time some of our work takes. You should have trusted me.'

There was a long silence, then Jack Renshaw began to nod slowly. 'You're right, Danny. I think that would have been the better way to deal with things, but hindsight's always twenty-twenty vision. Moving forward, I need to know if you're happy to continue in your role as head of the MCIU, or if you're ambitious and ready for a change?'

The response and question from Jack Renshaw weren't what Danny had been expecting. Trying to regain his composure, he finally asked, 'What change?'

'What I'm about to tell you doesn't leave this room, understood?'

Danny nodded and waited. 'Adrian Potter will be promoted in the very near future. He's applied for an Assistant Chief Constable post with the Surrey Constabulary. I'm almost certain he'll be offered the job. Which will leave me looking for a new head of CID. If you take on the role, it will mean promotion immediately, better working hours, no more 'on call' telephone conversations in the middle of the night, far greater renumeration, and a better pension.'

Danny was thoughtful. He still had eight years' service to complete, and while everything Jack Renshaw had just said was positive, he didn't know if he could sit behind a desk for that long.

'How long have I got before I need to make a decision?'

'I don't foresee Adrian leaving for at least another three months, but obviously I'd like your decision sooner rather than later. If you don't take the offer, the opportunity may pass you by, as I'll have to appoint somebody ready to replace Adrian. I sincerely hope you'll take the job, Danny.'

'I need to discuss things with my wife before I make any decisions.'

'Of course. I understand. Please add my thanks to those of Councillor White, to everybody at the MCIU. When I've received all the details of the investigation, I'll be considering commendations for you and your staff.'

'I will, and thank you, sir.'

As Danny walked away from the office, his head was spinning. It was the last thing he'd been expecting to hear at the end of this meeting.

Questions raced around inside his head. *Am I ready to*

leave the MCIU? Can I perform the role of head of CID? Who will take over the MCIU? What will Sue think? Will I be happy sitting behind a desk?

He walked briskly towards the scenes of crime department and tried to clear his head. He still had an ongoing investigation to supervise. All his focus must be on that for the time being. There would be plenty of time to mull over his future.

Right now, he needed to talk to Tim Donnelly. He needed to ensure the forensic bay was available to receive any incoming vehicles seized from Douglas Richardson.

Then he needed to get back to the MCIU.

That single thought caused a smile to form on his lips.

84

**10.30am, 23 March 1989
Laburnum House, Milton Street, Ravenshead,
Nottinghamshire**

The two CID cars pulled in behind the plain white Transit van that was parked in the layby at the entrance to Newstead Abbey. Also waiting in the same location was the vehicle examiners' recovery truck.

Andy Wills got out of the first CID car and spoke to Sergeant Turner, who was sitting in the passenger seat of the van.

'How many men have you got?'

'You've got me and three; should be plenty.'

'Should be. I don't foresee any problems with Richardson, but apparently it's a big property to search. If you wait here, we'll go in first and execute the search warrant. Once he's got over the shock, I'll call you in for the search.'

'Whatever way you want to play it, Andy. Why don't we wait on Milton Street, then if you do start having a problem we're right there?'

Andy nodded. He didn't really know what the reaction of Douglas Richardson would be and there was always safety in numbers.

He walked over to the vehicle recovery truck and spoke to the driver, 'Just follow the van and wait on Milton Street. I'll call you in if we find a vehicle to recover.'

The driver nodded.

Andy walked back to his car. 'Okay, Jane. Let's get going.'

A few minutes later and the two CID vehicles drove through the open gates and onto the driveway of Laburnum House.

Andy glanced towards Jane Pope and said, 'Bloody hell, Jane. You weren't kidding when you said this place was massive. Those three garages are as big as my house.'

Jane didn't reply but brought the car to a stop outside the double oak doors at the front of the palatial house. Already parked on the drive were a Ford Sierra Cosworth and a Triumph TR4 sports car. There was no sign of the Aston Martin or Range Rover that were also registered to Douglas Richardson.

Andy, Jane and Sam Blake got out of their cars and walked to the front of the house.

Andy knocked loudly and after a couple of minutes the door was opened by a woman.

Jane stepped forward and said, 'Hello, Mrs Richardson. I don't know if you remember me, DC Pope from the Major Crime Investigation Unit. This is DS Wills and DC Blake. Is your husband home today?'

Beth Richardson was more than a little shocked and she

spluttered, 'Yes, he's home. Well, he's home, but he's out now. He's just nipped to the shop in town for cigarettes. He shouldn't be long.'

Regaining her composure, she continued, 'Is there anything I can help you with?'

Andy Wills said, 'I'm DS Wills. We're investigating a hit-and-run accident where a man sadly died. We're in possession of a warrant to search your property for evidence in relation to that accident. I can see two cars on the drive. Do you own any other vehicles?'

'What hit-and-run? Where? I don't know anything about an accident.'

Andy persisted, 'Do you own any other cars, Mrs Richardson?'

'Dougie's out in the Aston, and the Range Rover's in one of the garages.'

'Are the garages locked?'

'What sort of an idiotic question is that? Of course they are.'

Andy took the search warrant from his pocket and said, 'This is the search warrant. You'll need to find the keys for the garages so we can have a look inside.'

Beth Richardson tutted. 'Wait here.'

She disappeared back inside the house. Andy made sure the front door remained open. He spoke into his radio, 'DS Wills to Sergeant Turner. You can join us on the driveway now. We're about to gain access to the garages at the property. Over.'

There was no reply, but Andy could hear the diesel engine of the Transit van as it drove onto the driveway of the property.

Sam Blake grinned. 'That doesn't sound like an Aston Martin to me.'

Beth Richardson appeared in the doorway. 'Here are the keys. I would prefer if you waited for my husband to return before you started rummaging around in the garages.'

Andy said, 'How long do you think he'll be?'

'He only nipped out for cigarettes. He'll be back any moment.'

'If you could come with us to unlock the garages, I don't mind delaying the search a little, until your husband returns.'

'Very well. Follow me.'

Beth Richardson unlocked each of the garage doors. Sam Blake followed on behind her, raising each of the doors in turn as soon as they were unlocked.

In the last garage was what appeared to be a large vehicle covered by a dust sheet.

Andy said, 'Is this your Range Rover?'

Beth Richardson shrugged. 'I don't know. I never drive the bloody thing. It's too big for me.'

Andy removed the dust sheet and immediately saw accident damage to the front of the Range Rover.

Graham Turner walked into the garage. 'Andy. You've got company.'

Andy stepped outside and saw the silver-coloured Aston Martin being driven slowly up the driveway. The vehicle accelerated as the police vehicles came into the view of the driver, eventually skidding to a halt outside the garages.

A red-faced Douglas Richardson got out of his vehicle and stormed towards the open garages. 'What the hell's going on?' he blustered.

Andy Wills again produced the search warrant and said,

'Douglas Richardson, my name's DS Wills. I'm from the Major Crime Investigation Unit. I have a warrant to search your property for evidence in relation to a fatal non-stop road traffic accident. I notice your Range Rover has accident damage to the front. How did that damage occur?'

'I hit a deer a few nights ago. The garage is collecting it later today. It needs a full lift to go for repair.'

'Where did this collision with the deer take place?'

'Not far from Clumber Park.'

'Did you stop?'

'No, I didn't stop. I knew it was a deer. I saw it in my headlights just before I hit it. Bloody thing leapt straight out in front of me. Made a right bang; frightened me to death. My car was just about driveable, so I limped home and arranged for the repairs to be done. I haven't driven it since.'

'Was anybody with you at the time?'

'No.'

'Where had you been?'

'I can't remember... Worksop, I think. This is ridiculous.'

'Can you remember exactly when this was?'

'Yes. Three or four days ago. The garage should have recovered it the day after, when I called them.'

'Which garage did you call?'

'The Land Rover dealers at Chesterfield. They always do my repairs and servicing. They'll have a record of when I called them. The bloody car should be with them by now. They've been dragging their feet. I'm not happy.'

Andy was aware that the fatal collision had occurred on the nineteenth of March, just four days ago. He had heard enough.

He cautioned Richardson, 'Douglas Richardson, I'm

arresting you on suspicion of the murder of Mike Molloy. You'll be taken to Mansfield Police Station for questioning while officers remain here to complete the search of your property.'

Richardson shouted, 'Murder? You said you were investigating a fatal road accident. This is outrageous! I've told you, I hit a fucking deer! I'll have your fucking job for this. I don't think you realise who you're dealing with.'

Sam Blake stepped forward, handcuffed Richardson and said, 'Calm down. Everything will get sorted at the station. Don't make matters any worse.'

Richardson snarled, 'Fuck off!'

Andy looked at Sam and Jane. 'You two transport Mr Richardson to Mansfield. I'll stay here and organise the vehicle examiners to remove the Range Rover to headquarters for forensic examination.'

As Douglas Richardson was driven away by the two detectives, his shocked wife cautiously approached Andy and said, 'Can you tell me what's happening, please? Why has my husband been arrested? Does he need a solicitor?'

'He needs to answer a few questions in respect of the fatal road accident I mentioned to you earlier. He'll be asked if he wants legal representation when he gets to the police station. In the meantime, I still have to execute this search warrant. As well as searching the garages, I'll need to look in the house for any paperwork in respect of repairs carried out on the Range Rover already. I don't want to disrupt your house any more than I need to. Where do you think any paperwork like that will be?'

Beth Richardson thought for a while, then said, 'I can only imagine that anything like that will be in my husband's study. You'd better come in and have a look. I really can't see

Dougie being involved in anything like this. He's an extremely competent driver.'

Andy turned to Graham. 'Graham, while I sort out the vehicle examiners to lift the Range Rover, can you and your men go with Mrs Richardson to search the study? I'm interested in any paperwork that mentions Mike Molloy, Sentinel Investigations Agency, Ian Drake, Diamond Foster Investments or Dominic Finch.'

'Will do, Andy.'

After Andy had contacted the vehicle examiners on the radio, the vehicle recovery truck was driven onto the driveway. The two examiners got out of the truck and the driver spoke to Andy, 'PC Davenport, Sarge. I take it you've found the vehicle you want recovering?'

'It's the Range Rover in the garage.'

'We'll need the keys. There's an immobiliser and a steering lock fitted on this model.'

'Give me a minute.'

Andy walked to the house to find Beth Richardson. He returned shortly after, having been given the Range Rover keys.

In his absence, the two examiners had been having a look around the Range Rover. As Andy approached, PC Davenport said, 'Did this bloke say what he'd hit?'

Andy replied, 'He reckoned it was a deer, somewhere near Clumber Park. Why?'

PC Davenport shook his head. 'Nah. Not a chance. Whatever he hit was around six feet tall. Let me show you.'

Andy followed the burly PC into the garage.

PC Davenport said, 'Can you see those dents in the bumper and grille at the front of the vehicle?'

'I see them.'

'Well, if you look at the bonnet, in line with those dents at the front, you'll see more dents, with another larger dent near the windscreen.'

Andy nodded. 'I can see them. What does that all mean?'

'It means, in my experience, those marks and dents at the front of the vehicle have been caused by the initial impact, probably thighs or hips. The other dents on the bonnet were then caused after the body doubled over from the impact. That larger dent near the windscreen was probably caused by your victim's head. Did your fatality have massive head injuries?'

'Yes, but the post mortem revealed he'd been run over several times. His head was virtually crushed.'

Without saying a word, PC Davenport crawled on his back under the front wheels. Shining his torch into the wheel arches, he said, 'You're in luck, Sarge. It must have been dry on the night of the collision. There's a lot of stuff under here. I think forensics are going to have a field day with this.'

85

11.30am, 23 March 1989
MCIU Offices, Mansfield, Nottinghamshire

Danny and Rob were discussing the imminent interviews to be held with Dominic Finch and Kevin Briar. Also present in his office were Rachel Moore, who would interview Finch with Danny, and Glen Lorimar, who would interview Briar with Rob.

Danny said, 'So, we all know the information we have in respect of the financial dealings between the two men. If either man decides to answer our questions, I want to know if they've had any financial dealings with Douglas Richardson in the past. I think this will probably relate more to Finch than Briar, but you never know.'

The gathered detectives all acknowledged Danny, and Glen said, 'Are there any specific tactics you want to employ for this initial interview?'

'We're going to have to wait and see if they want to talk to us first. They've both been spoken to already about their time in foster care with the Drakes, so we have some idea of what line they're going to take. It will be interesting to see if either man has had a change of heart, now they're under arrest on suspicion of murder.'

Rob said, 'A lot will depend on the advice given by their solicitors. I'll be surprised if both men don't say "no comment" to everything.'

'We'll soon find out, Rob. The solicitors have been with their respective clients for almost forty minutes. I can't see them being much longer.'

There was a knock on the door and Danny shouted, 'Come in.'

Jane Pope walked in and said, 'Sorry to interrupt, boss. I've got an update for you in respect of Douglas Richardson.'

'Go on.'

'Richardson's in custody downstairs. DS Wills has arrested him on suspicion of the murder of Mike Molloy. His Range Rover has been seized and is en-route to headquarters for a full forensic examination. DS Wills is just finishing off the search of the property with the Special Operations Unit, then he'll be back here for the interviews with Richardson.'

'That's great. Who else is doing the interview?'

'I'll be interviewing alongside DS Wills.'

'Do you know if the search of the house has yielded anything?'

'I've had no update on the search of the house. The last report I had was that the vehicle examiners believe the seized vehicle is a forensic gold mine.'

'Okay. Keep me informed of all updates and tell DS Wills

to contact me on his return. I want to run all three of these interviews alongside one another. That way we'll be able to exploit any discrepancies and should be able to play one suspect off against another.'

'Will do, sir.'

The telephone began to ring, and Danny snatched it up. 'DCI Flint.'

'It's the custody sergeant, sir. Just letting you know that the solicitors for Finch and Briar have finished their consultations. Both men are now ready for interview.'

'We'll be right down.'

86

11.30am, 23 March 1989
Laburnum House, Milton Street, Ravenshead,
Nottinghamshire

Andy Wills and one of the SOU officers had made a cursory search of all the rooms in Douglas Richardson's home address. They had been accompanied by an extremely anxious Beth Richardson, who constantly tutted every time either officer opened a cupboard door or a drawer. Nothing of any significance had been found.

That had left Sergeant Turner and the other two SOU officers to carry out a far more thorough search of Douglas Richardson's study.

The officer tasked with searching the drawers of Richardson's desk said, 'Sarge, you'd better have a look at this letter. I've put it back in the envelope, but you need to read the contents. I found it stuffed under other papers in the bottom drawer.'

Graham Turner took the brown envelope. Douglas Richardson's name and address had been handwritten and it had been posted using a second class stamp.

The envelope had been opened with a letter opener, so it was easy to slip the contents out.

The letter inside consisted of a short handwritten note from someone demanding a meeting. There was a veiled threat that stated it would be in everyone's best interest to meet. It stipulated a telephone number to be used to arrange the meeting.

The letter had been signed M. Molloy.

Graham Turner let out a low whistle and left the study to find DS Wills.

Andy and the other SOU officer were just making their way down the stairs, followed by Beth Richardson.

Graham said, 'This is interesting, Andy.'

Andy took the letter and read it.

He turned to face Beth Richardson and showed her the handwritten brown envelope. 'Can you remember when this letter arrived?'

She knew exactly when the letter had arrived.

It had arrived on the same day her Dougie had returned home from London. The same day he'd beaten her ribs until it was painful for her to even draw breath for yet another unknown, minimal indiscretion on her part.

She could still feel the soreness in her ribs, even now, after a week, and in that instant she decided she would no longer do or say anything to protect her abusive pig of a husband. She was sick of his domineering, uncaring attitude and all the unnecessary beatings.

She barely glanced at the envelope. 'That letter arrived exactly one week ago, on the sixteenth. I remember it because I put that one and a couple of other letters on the desk in the study, ready for Dougie to deal with when he got back from London that evening. Have you finished searching the house now, Detective?'

Andy glanced at Graham Turner, who nodded and said, 'We're all done, Sarge.'

He looked back at Beth Richardson and repeated, 'We're all done. Thanks for your cooperation. Before I go, I'd like to get a quick statement from you about the date this letter arrived.'

'I'll be more than happy to provide you with a statement —if it doesn't take forever. It's my bridge club this evening, and I still have a ton of stuff to do.'

'Twenty minutes max.'

Beth Richardson let out an exaggerated sigh and said, 'Very well.'

87

11.45am, 23 March 1989
Mansfield Police Station, Nottinghamshire

After the introductions in the interview room had been made, it was Dominic Finch's solicitor who spoke first. He was red faced and sweating, as though he had been engaged in strenuous exercise. When he did speak, Danny understood instantly why the solicitor looked like a man under pressure.

He blustered, 'I've advised my client not to answer any of your questions and there is no prepared statement at this time.'

The lack of a prepared statement spoke volumes to Danny. The anxiety on the face of the solicitor betrayed the struggle he was having to get his client to agree to his strategy of a 'no comment' interview.

Danny looked hard into the troubled eyes of the expensive solicitor and said, 'Thank you. I do intend to question your client on these matters. How he chooses to respond to those questions is, as we both know, ultimately his decision. After all, this is your client's interview and his only chance to get on record what he wants to say about the matters for which he's under arrest.'

Without waiting for a response from the solicitor, Danny looked at Finch and said, 'Are you responsible for the death of Ian Drake?'

Finch had been looking down at the desk but slowly looked up when he heard the question.

Danny could see the fear in the man's eyes. He was now a very different person to the tearaway youth he'd been in the past. The thought of losing his luxurious millionaire lifestyle loomed large and forced him to fight to defend himself.

He muttered a single word, 'No.'

The solicitor immediately interjected, 'Dominic. You really don't need to say a thing. Please listen to my advice.'

Finch rounded on the solicitor, snapping, 'I didn't kill Drake. I'm not going to spend the rest of my life in prison for something he's done.'

The solicitor muttered, 'You're making a huge mistake,' then sat back in his chair.

Danny said, 'Who's he, Dominic?'

'I think you already know who he is. Patch killed Drake. All I did was set up the meeting between him and Drake. After what happened when we were kids in foster care, he was obsessed with the guy. All he ever talked about was getting even with Drake. I don't think he's ever got over the abuse he suffered when we were at the Drakes' house. He did have it worse than me.'

'When you say Patch, who do you mean?'

'Kevin Briar. Patch was always his nickname when we were kids. I still call him that at times.'

'Okay, thanks. How did you set up this meeting between the two men?'

'I managed to track Ian Drake down and arranged for him to travel from Scotland to Nottingham for a bogus job interview.'

'How did you manage that?'

'Through a third party.'

'Who?'

'I'm not prepared to say. All I can tell you is that a mutual acquaintance of myself and the third party hired a private detective to track down Ian Drake and then set up the bogus company for the non-existent job interview.'

'Are you prepared to tell me who the mutual acquaintance was who actually hired the private detective?'

Finch thought for a moment and then said, 'He's somebody that has business dealings with both of us. That's all I can say, really.'

'It would help me believe what you're saying if you could give me at least one name that might corroborate your story.'

Again, there was a long pause.

The solicitor leaned over and whispered something to Finch, who responded by hissing, 'No.'

Finch then made eye contact with Danny and said, 'The private detective was hired by a business acquaintance of mine. His name's Douglas Richardson. He arranged for and paid the private detective to trace Drake and then set up a bogus company in Nottingham.'

'What sort of business acquaintance is Richardson?'

'I've provided the finance on a couple of overseas developments his company has carried out.'

'How did you know when the private detective had set it all up and that everything was in place?'

'I was contacted by the private detective.'

'How was that contact made?'

'I wanted to remain anonymous, for obvious reasons, so the private detective was told to call a telephone number at a certain time to pass on the information he had. The number he was given by Richardson was a payphone at the British Library in London. I waited at the specified time and took his call. He never knew who he was talking to.'

'Did Richardson know that it would be you the private detective was contacting?'

'No, he didn't.'

'Once you had everything in place and Ian Drake had travelled from Scotland for the bogus job interview, what happened?'

'A meeting was arranged through the private detective for Ian Drake to meet the two directors of the company at a restaurant just outside Mansfield. It was sold to Drake that he already had the job, and this would just be the formality of signing the lucrative contract and then celebrating over a meal.'

'Did you go to that meeting?'

'Yes.'

'Why did you go?'

'I went as moral support for Patch. To be honest, we were both quite nervous. We didn't know how Drake was going to react. As kids, we all knew that his wife had mysteriously disappeared, and there were rumours that it was Drake who'd bumped her off. I told Patch I'd drive him to the meeting but that I didn't want to speak to Drake.'

'Can you remember the name of the restaurant?'

'Yeah. The Young Vanish at Glapwell.'

'The pub?'

'It's a pub, but there's a fancy restaurant at the back.'

'What happened when Drake arrived?'

'It had been a mistake arranging the meeting to be there. It was packed that night; there was some sort of party on. There was no chance for Patch to talk to Drake there, so he suggested to Drake they go somewhere else where he could air his grievances.'

'Did Drake agree?'

Finch shook his head and said, 'No way. He was raging. He realised the job offer had all been a load of bollocks. He just wanted to leave, but he couldn't because the taxi that dropped him off had already left.'

There was a pause, then Finch continued, 'Anyway, Drake started to walk off. That's when Patch grabbed him.'

'Then what?'

'The two of them started brawling in the car park. Patch was much stronger and battered him. He told me to get the car, which I did. He bundled Drake onto the back seat and got in the back with him. He told me to drive to Cresswell Crags.'

'Why there?'

Finch shrugged his shoulders. 'I don't know. It was somewhere we used to go when we were kids and had nicked a car. We'd park up there to smoke fags and have a drink.'

'Was Drake conscious at that time?'

'Yeah. I could hear him muttering something to Patch.'

'What happened at Cresswell Crags?'

'I stayed in the car.'

'Does that mean Briar and Drake got out?'

'Yes. Patch marched Drake off towards the lake, while I stayed in the car.'

'So, Drake walked alongside Briar?'

'Kind of. He was obviously a bit groggy, but he could still walk.'

'Do you know what happened?'

'No, I don't. Look, I keep telling you, I didn't do anything to Drake. That's why I'm so pissed off at being dragged in here. All I did was set up the meeting and then do a bit of driving.'

'How long were they gone?'

'Ten or fifteen minutes.'

'What happened when they came back to the car?'

'Only Patch came back.'

'Did you ask where Drake was?'

'Yeah. Patch said the prick wouldn't accept that what he'd done all those years ago was wrong, so he'd given him a good hiding.'

'Did you go and check on Drake?'

'Did I, fuck! I didn't do anything to him, but that doesn't mean I had any time for the prick.'

'So, what did you do?'

'Patch said, "Fuck him, he can walk back to Mansfield". So, we left. I just drove off. When Patch said that, I genuinely thought he'd just beaten him up and that Drake would be okay. Like I keep telling you, I did nothing wrong that night. I didn't know that Patch intended to beat the crap out of him. If I'm being honest, I thought he was going to try and get some money out of him, that's all.'

'We have Kevin Briar in custody as well. Is he going to say the same as you?'

'Patch won't say anything to you lot. He hates coppers with a vengeance.'

Danny looked towards Rachel. 'Anything you want to ask?'

Rachel said, 'When we spoke in London about your time in foster care, you refused to answer any questions and everything had to be done through your lawyer. As requested, we sent your lawyer a list of questions. One of those questions was whether you had remained in touch with any of the people who'd been fostered by the Drakes at the same time as you. Why did you deny you were still in regular contact with Kevin Briar?'

'By the time you came to see me I was aware that Drake had died that night. It was stupid of me to deny our contact over the years, but I wanted to try and distance myself from Kevin Briar. I didn't want to get dragged into something he was responsible for.'

'Do you regret setting that meeting up now?'

'Of course I do. Patch has always been a bit on the edge, but I had no idea he intended to do this. I genuinely thought he just wanted to talk to Drake.'

Danny looked at Rachel, who shook her head, indicating she had nothing else to ask, so he said, 'Once we've checked some of the things you've told us we'll need to talk again.'

88

11.45am, 23 March 1989
Mansfield Police Station, Nottinghamshire

Glen Lorimar was an experienced interviewer. As he entered the interview room, he saw the confidence displayed in the body language of Kevin Briar.

Glen and Rob took their seats opposite Briar and his solicitor. In that instant, Glen decided to ignore the interview plan he'd discussed with Rob Buxton and change the tone of the interview. He believed if he aimed his questions in a more general sense, rather than being direct, there would be more chance of getting a response from Briar.

He knew if he challenged the confident businessman too early, he would clam up and not answer any questions.

He knew Rob was experienced enough to go along with

the interview, without interrupting, whichever direction it went in. The most important thing was to get Briar to respond to questions.

After the introductions had been completed, Glen smiled amiably and said, 'Thanks for your patience this morning, Kevin. I only have a few questions for you right now. Can you tell me about your relationship with Dominic Finch?'

A very relaxed Briar smiled back and said, 'I've already spoken about this to your officers when they came to see me at work. We were best friends when we were kids.'

'When you were both being fostered by the Drakes?'

'That's right.'

'Are you still close?'

'Not like we once were, but yeah, I'd say we're still close.'

'Would you help him out if he was in trouble?'

Briar smiled again. 'Of course I would. That's what friends do, isn't it?'

'And I take it that feeling would be mutual. If you were ever in any trouble, you'd expect Dominic to help you?'

'I'm sure he would.'

'He's been helping you for years already, hasn't he?'

The smile disappeared from Briar's face, and he said sharply, 'I didn't ask him to. He offered.'

'We've checked the financial accounts of your business, High Peak Outward Bound Centre. Over several years, there have been regular injections of large amounts of cash into your business, from a company called Small Bird Finance. That's the finance company owned by Dominic Finch, isn't it?'

'Yes, it's Dominic's company. Like I said before, we became very close when we went through all that shit being fostered. We were like brothers back then. When he found out my business was failing, he offered to help me, and he has done ever since. He's doing well, so he doesn't mind.'

Now that Briar was answering his questions, Glen changed tack and became more direct. 'You've already told us about the abuse you suffered at the hands of Melanie and Ian Drake. Is that the reason you were so desperate to meet Ian Drake again?'

A puzzled expression came over Briars face. 'I don't understand that question. I haven't seen Ian Drake since I left his foster care, and more to the point, I have no desire to meet that horrible bastard again.'

'Okay. When was the last time you met Dominic Finch?'

'I haven't physically met Dom for years. We've spoken on the phone now and then, but that's it.'

'Are you aware that Dominic has a holiday home in Derbyshire? It's not that far from your outward bound centre. Have you ever met him in Derbyshire?'

'No. I've just told you, I haven't seen him in years. I didn't know he had a place up here. Where is it?'

Glen ignored Briar's question. He had now caught him out in two lies, and decided to close the first interview. He looked at Rob to see if he wanted to ask anything. The slightest shake of Rob's head let Glen know there was nothing the DI wanted to ask Briar.

Glen looked at Briar and said flatly, 'Are you responsible for the death of Ian Drake?'

The smile returned to Briar's face. 'Of course I'm not. I haven't seen the man since he stopped fostering me.'

'I've no further questions at this time, but we do have other enquiries to complete, and we will need to talk again. Would you like to speak with your solicitor?'

Briar looked towards his solicitor, who said, 'I'll need a few minutes with my client. How long do you think these other enquiries will take?'

'They shouldn't take long. We don't want to keep you, or your client, any longer than we need to.'

89

12.30pm, 23 March 1989
MCIU Offices, Mansfield, Nottinghamshire

Danny and Rachel walked into the main briefing room.

He said, 'Let's grab a quick coffee and debrief that first interview. Then as soon as Rob and Glen are finished, we can compare notes. What did you make of Finch?'

'He's desperate to blame Briar for everything. He's done a pretty good job of distancing himself from the worst that happened.'

'My thoughts exactly. I don't buy it though. You wouldn't go to all the trouble to trace Ian Drake to then take a back seat. It will be interesting to see what Briar's said, if he's said anything at all. Finch seemed confident that he wouldn't talk to us.'

Danny glanced at his watch before continuing, 'Would you mind getting the coffees? I need to call Sue before she goes back to work. She's working a split shift today and will still be at home now. I need to let her know I'm going to have a late finish.'

'No problem, boss.'

Danny walked into his office and picked up the phone. His call was answered by a breathless Sue on the third ring.

Danny said, 'Are you okay? You sound out of breath.'

'You just caught me. I was just leaving to get back to work when I heard the phone ringing, so I dashed back in the house. Is everything okay?'

'Everything's fine, but I won't be home on time tonight. Is the babysitting covered?'

'No problem. I'll finish on time, at five, so I can pick Hayley up from the childminder on my way home. Are you sure you're okay?'

'I'm fine, but there's something we need to have a chat about, when I do get home. Do you think you'll still be up?'

'I'll make sure I am. Do I need to be worried?'

'Definitely not. It's good news... if I want it. If *we* want it.'

'Now I'm really intrigued. I've got to go, or I'll be late. We'll talk later. Be careful, sweetheart.'

Danny said, 'Love you,' and put the phone down.

There was a single knock on his door before Rob and Glen walked in, followed by Rachel clutching two coffees.

Danny asked, 'No comment?'

Glen replied, 'Not at all. He was happy to talk to us. He's still lying, but he was answering the questions. Why did you think he'd go no comment?'

'Finch told us that Briar would never talk to you, as he

detests the police. I think he's hoping he doesn't, anyway. He's trying to shift all the blame onto Briar.'

'In what way?'

'Finch admitted setting everything up to lure Ian Drake back to the area, but he's saying it was Briar who attacked Drake on his own. Finch has told us he had nothing to do with Drake's death, and that it was all down to Briar.'

'Has he admitted the meeting at the Young Vanish pub?'

'Yeah. He said he thought Briar was going there to talk to Drake and demand cash as some half-arsed compensation for the abuse he'd suffered.'

'Blackmail?'

'He didn't use that word but that's what he's inferring.'

'Did he say how Drake ended up at Cresswell Crags?'

'The meeting in the car park at the Young Vanish pub ended in a fight. Briar bundled Drake into their car and told Finch to drive to Cresswell Crags. It was somewhere they used to go when they were teenagers.'

'What happened at the Crags?'

'According to Finch, Briar walked off with Drake towards the lake, while he stayed in the car. After fifteen minutes, only Briar came back. He apparently then told Finch he'd given Drake a good hiding, but that he'd be okay and that he could find his own way back to Mansfield.'

Rob said, 'Bloody hell. No wonder he's hoping Briar doesn't talk. He's hung him out to dry, good and proper. I think we need to re-interview Briar and let him know exactly what his so-called best friend has had to say.'

'Grab a quick coffee, then get straight back into another interview and see what he has to say this time. Drop out that he was seen with Finch at Matlock. That might focus his mind and let him know you're not lying to him about what Finch is saying to us.'

Danny paused and then continued, 'Rachel has all the notes from our first interview with Finch. Sit down with her in the briefing room before you re-interview. That way you can sort out exactly what you need to put to Briar.'

As Rob, Glen and Rachel left the office, Andy Wills walked in and said, 'Have you got a minute, boss? There's been a couple of interesting developments in respect of Douglas Richardson.'

'There's been a development from this side as well. Dominic Finch has just named Richardson as being the person who arranged the private detective to trace Ian Drake on his behalf. Apparently, Richardson was given the job by a mutual acquaintance, whom he refused to name.'

'Are you thinking that mutual acquaintance could be one of the organised crime figures the Met are interested in?'

'Could be. He didn't mind coughing up Richardson's name, but there was no way he was going to say who the mutual acquaintance is.'

'How does Finch know Richardson?'

'Business dealings. Finch has provided finance for overseas developments built by Richardson's company.'

'Did Finch name the private detective Richardson used?'

'He doesn't know the name. He was only contacted on two occasions by the private detective. Both times were by phone at the British Library in London, at pre-arranged times.'

'Fair to assume it was Molloy, then. The contact number he had for his anonymous client was that library.'

'It's looking that way. What are the developments you mentioned?'

'The SOU found a letter signed by Mike Molloy at Richardson's house, requesting a meeting with Douglas Richardson. In it he stated it would be in everyone's best interests if he attended.'

'Sounds like Molloy may have been after another pay day.'

'That's how I interpreted it as well, so you can bet your life Richardson saw it the same way. I've also got a statement from Richardson's wife stating that letter arrived on the sixteenth of this month.'

'Three days before Molloy was run over and killed.'

Andy nodded. 'Exactly. I don't think he wanted to make any more payments to Molloy. Before I came in here, I phoned Tim at scenes of crime for an update on the Range Rover. They've recovered samples from the front wheel arch they believe to be human tissue. They're submitting them immediately to the lab for a full forensic analysis. Tim's confident the samples are human tissue and that there's enough to obtain a full profile for a DNA comparison. If that's the case, it will prove Richardson's vehicle was the one used to run over and kill Mike Molloy.'

'It won't prove who was driving, though. When are you going into interview with Richardson?'

'We've given disclosure to his solicitor, and she's in consultation with her client now.'

'What did you give his solicitor in disclosure?'

'I told her we've recovered the letter. I haven't told her about the statement made by his wife, pinpointing the date it was received. I've also told her that we're currently undertaking a full forensic examination of the seized Range Rover, and that it will be some time before we have any results.'

'Good. So, there's every chance Richardson will talk to you?'

Andy shrugged. 'It doesn't really matter if he goes "no comment". I think we're going to have more than enough evidence to convict him of the Molloy murder. I would like to get him to repeat what he said at the house, though—that he was driving the vehicle on the night of the murder, and that the accident damage to his vehicle was caused when he hit a deer.'

Danny nodded. 'You're right, it's important you get that repeated if you can. It'll be interesting to see what he's got to say about Finch giving him up as the go-between. Let me know how you get on. Rob and Glen are about to reinterview Briar. I'll wait until they've interviewed him and you've interviewed Richardson before I speak to Finch again.'

90

1.00pm, 23 March 1989
Mansfield Police Station, Nottinghamshire

Andy Wills rested his elbows on the table in the interview room and waited for Douglas Richardson to finish whispering something to his solicitor.

When Richardson stopped muttering, Andy said, 'Douglas Richardson, you've been arrested on suspicion of the murder of Mike Molloy. Are you responsible for his death?'

Richardson was barely able to keep his fiery temperature in check as he snarled, 'I told you at the house, I've never heard of Mike Molloy. This whole business is an outrage. I'll be instructing my solicitor to sue this force for every penny it's got once this farce has played out.'

'You also told me at the house that the substantial accident damage I saw on your Range Rover was caused by a collision you'd been involved in a few days before our visit. What was the nature of that accident?'

Richardson let out a huge sigh. 'This is so bloody tiresome. Why do I have to keep repeating myself to you people? I hit a deer near Clumber Park.'

'And when was this?'

'On the night of the nineteenth. I was on my way back from Worksop.'

'What had you been doing in Worksop?'

'I don't see that's any of your business, Detective.'

'If what you're telling me is the truth, the more you can tell me to verify that story, the more it will help you.'

Richardson's solicitor said, 'Really, Sergeant? It's not my client's job to disprove your allegations. Either you have evidence to justify his arrest, or you don't.'

Oh, I have the evidence, thought Andy.

Andy continued, 'I'm just trying to build up a picture of your client's movements that night. All he's told me so far is that he was driving his Range Rover and that he'd been to Worksop. What time did your vehicle collide with the deer?'

'I can't remember. It was late.'

'Did you stop?'

'Very briefly. I got out and had a look around to see if the animal was still in the road, but when I couldn't see it, I checked the damage to the car, got back in and managed to drive slowly home.'

'Was anybody else in your vehicle that night?'

'No.'

'I've seen your vehicle at the house. The damage to the front of it was extensive. Has anybody driven it since?'

'I don't think that would have been a good idea. That's

why it was in the garage at home, waiting to be towed away by the Land Rover dealers for repair.'

'Hitting a deer must have been a hell of a shock.'

'It was. The noise it made frightened me to death.'

'Did you have any chance to brake at all?'

'I think I did hit the brakes hard, yes.'

'As I understand it, the temperature that night was below zero and there was a hard ground frost. Did your vehicle go into a skid when you braked?'

'I can't remember. Is that relevant?'

'If your vehicle skidded, it's possible it left skid marks on the road. If we can find those, it could help us pinpoint exactly where this accident happened, that's all. Unless you can remember exactly where it happened.'

Richardson allowed a greasy smile to form on his lips and said, 'I can't remember. You'll just have to go out and find the bloody skid marks.'

'And there was no sign of the dead, or badly injured, animal?'

'I didn't see it. It might not have been that badly injured.'

'I've seen the damage to your car. I think it's fair to say it would have been badly injured.'

'Whatever.'

Rachel handed Andy the letter that had been recovered from Richardson's house. It was inside a clear plastic pocket.

Andy held onto the letter but turned it around so Richardson could read it. As he did so, he said, 'This is police exhibit number AW 1. It's a letter recovered from the study at your home address. Have you seen it before?'

As Richardson read the letter the colour drained from his face. He shot a panicked look towards his solicitor, who said, 'You know my advice, Douglas.'

Richardson looked back at Andy and said, 'No comment.'

Andy said, 'The letter is inviting you to a meeting that the writer describes as being in everyone's best interests. Do you know what was meant by that statement?'

'No comment.'

'I asked you at the beginning of this interview if you were responsible for the death of Mike Molloy and you told me then that you had never heard of a person of that name. This letter was signed M Molloy, so you obviously did know him.'

'No comment.'

'What was your relationship with Molloy?'

'No comment.'

'Mike Molloy was a private investigator who owned Sentinel Investigations Limited. Have you ever had any reason to hire the services of that private investigation company?'

Andy could see the beads of sweat forming on the company director's head as Richardson muttered, 'No comment.'

'Do you know a man named Dominic Finch?'

Again, Richardson glanced towards his solicitor.

She looked at Andy and said, 'I haven't received any disclosure about the involvement of Dominic Finch. What's the relevance of your question?'

'Dominic Finch is also in custody here. He's currently being investigated for other matters. When Finch was questioned about those other matters, he's informed officers that your client hired Mike Molloy to carry out a trace on a man named Ian Drake, his own brother-in-law.'

Andy looked directly at Richardson and said, 'Is that

what happened? Did Dominic Finch ask you to trace your brother-in-law, Ian Drake?'

Richardson looked at his solicitor, who shook her head.

Richardson immediately said, 'No comment.'

'How do you know Dominic Finch?'

'No comment.'

'Has Finch provided your company with finance to complete overseas developments?'

'No comment.'

'Finch has told officers that you were tasked to find Drake by a third party who's a mutual business acquaintance. Is that correct?'

What remaining colour Richardson had, now completely drained from his face, as his brain tried to process the implications of what the detective was saying. *Surely Finch hadn't named Mason Connor in this mess.*

He spluttered, 'No comment.'

'Finch was quite happy to name you as being the person who hired, and paid, Mike Molloy to trace Ian Drake. He also told us that you had instructed Molloy to set up a bogus company in Nottingham to lure Drake here on the pretext of a job offer. Do you have any comment on that?'

'No comment.'

'Do you think this letter from Molloy was the pretext to obtaining another payment from you for the information he'd already been paid for?'

'No comment.'

'Did you believe Molloy was going to attempt to extort money from you because of what had subsequently happened to Ian Drake?'

'No comment.'

'Molloy had been aware that Ian Drake, the man he'd

traced on your behalf, had been found murdered shortly after he was lured back to this area. Drake was your brother-in-law, so you were also fully aware that he was dead, and that his death was being investigated as a murder. You were complicit in that murder because you hired the private investigator who traced him.'

'No comment.'

'I believe you feared Mike Molloy was going to blackmail you for further payments and to prevent this you murdered him by driving your Range Rover into him on the nineteenth of this month, at Worksop.'

A look of desperation spread across Richardson's face, and he spluttered, 'Prove it.'

'I've no further questions for you at this time.'

91

1.15pm, 23 March 1989
Mansfield Police Station, Nottinghamshire

Kevin Briar still looked very relaxed as he sat down next to his solicitor in the interview room.

Glen reminded him he was still under caution and said, 'At the same time as you were detained this morning, we also arrested Dominic Finch. He's also been interviewed and has given a very different account in respect of Ian Drake to the one you gave us earlier.'

From being sat in a relaxed position, Briar suddenly sat upright and leaned forward, his elbows resting on the table in front of him. 'I don't believe you.'

'Finch has told us that you were desperate to meet Ian Drake again, and that you wanted to extort money from him for all the suffering he caused you as a youngster.'

'That's bollocks. Dom wouldn't say anything like that.'

'He's told us a lot more than that. He told us that the two of you met Drake at a pub called the Young Vanish at Glapwell. That you beat him up and dragged him into the back of Finch's car.'

Briar shook his head. 'This is such bullshit. You're making this shit up.'

'Finch told us he drove the car to Cresswell Crags, and that you dragged Drake towards the lake while he stayed in the car. And that you returned alone, fifteen minutes later.'

There was silence.

Glen continued, 'Can't you see what's happening here, Kevin? He's trying to put everything on you, because he expects you not to talk to us.'

There was a long pause before Briar said, 'How can I trust you? This could all be bollocks, and a trick to get me talking.'

'This isn't a trick. I'm telling you exactly what Finch told my colleagues. If you've a different version of events, I suggest you tell it to me now. Because, right now, the only person suspected of killing Ian Drake is you. Finch has put you at the scene where the body of Ian Drake was found, and he's told us that you'd already beaten him up once. And that you were the last person to be seen with him alive. What you do now is your choice. Do you want to talk to your solicitor again?'

Glen had gambled that Briar would be too angry to bother with his solicitor.

It was a gamble that paid off.

Briar growled under his breath, 'The snide, grassing bastard.'

Glen pushed, 'Do you want to tell us what really happened?'

There was a brief pause before Briar said, 'For a start, this was all Dom's fucking idea. I could quite happily have lived the rest of my life without clapping eyes on Ian Drake again.'

'What was Finch's idea?'

'To get Drake back down to Nottingham.'

'Why did he want to do that?'

'I thought he just wanted to batter him, to get some revenge for how he treated us as kids. But I found out the real reason yesterday.'

'What did you find out?'

'Dom told me he wasn't going to subsidise my business anymore.'

'Was that when the two of you met in Matlock yesterday?'

'Has he told you about that as well?'

Glen remained silent, ignoring the question.

Eventually, Briar said, 'Yes, it was in Matlock. Were you lot watching or something?'

Rob said, 'Officers were there, and they witnessed the meeting. They saw how angry you got. Why were you so angry?'

'Because I knew I'd been tricked.'

Glen said, 'Tricked, how?'

'Finch set me up to kill Ian Drake to make us even.'

'Tell me how you killed Ian Drake.'

'Like I said, all of this was Finch's idea from the outset. He arranged for a private detective to find Ian Drake. Somehow this detective found him and lured him back here. I don't know all the details of how that happened.'

'After Drake had been lured back to Nottinghamshire, what happened?'

'Finch arranged a meeting with him at the Young Vanish pub.'

'What happened at the Young Vanish?'

'Finch called me on the phone and said a meeting with Drake had been set up, and that it was at the Young Vanish. I genuinely thought the idea was just to meet Drake and beat the shit out of him as payback for what he used to do to us. I drove to Finch's holiday home and picked him up.'

'You were driving?'

'Yes. We went together in my Land Rover.'

There was a long pause in which Glen remained silent. He knew Briar had a lot more to say.

'The pub was packed when we got there, so we had to think again. By the time Drake arrived in a taxi we'd already decided to take him to Cresswell Crags. We knew it would be quiet there. I still thought we were just going to give him a good hiding. We waited until Drake got out of his taxi and watched it drive off before we approached him.'

'What happened?'

'Drake was raging when he realised the job offer was bogus and that it was us two. He was swearing at us and began walking out of the car park. So, we jumped him.'

'Both of you?'

'Yeah. We both battered him and chucked him in the back of the Land Rover. I drove to Cresswell Crags, not Dom.'

'Was Drake still conscious?'

'Yeah. He was conscious but groggy. When we got there, Dom opened the back door and Drake came flying out, swinging punches.'

'Did he hit either of you?'

'No, he missed us. He was still a bit unsteady on his feet

from the battering we'd given him at the pub. He swung at us but overbalanced and ended up on the floor. He went down hard.'

'What did you do?'

'He was going nuts, shouting and bawling at the top of his voice, so I punched him again to shut him up then grabbed some rope from the back of the Land Rover and tied his hands behind his back.'

'What sort of rope?'

'It was a length of old nylon climbing rope. When the rope gets old and isn't safe for climbing anymore, I cut it into lengths to use for other jobs. It's still good rope.'

'How did you secure Drake?'

'I can't remember for sure, but I would have used some sort of climbing knot. Probably a bowline; I can do them in my sleep.'

'Once Drake was secure, what did you do?'

'I made sure the place was deserted, then we walked him towards the caves, near the lake.'

'Both of you?'

'Yeah. We dragged him up some steps, towards one of the caves. That's when he started crying.'

'Crying?'

'Yeah. He kept blubbering that he was sorry, and that it was his wife who'd made him behave the way he did back then.'

'What happened next?'

'Him blubbering on like that made us even angrier. He was so pathetic. We started beating him again.'

'Both of you?'

'Yeah. Both of us. I must admit, it felt good kicking the shit out of the snivelling bastard. Anyway, Drake ends up in this weird sitting position. He's just sat there rocking, half out of it, and that's when Dom showed me the ice axe. I hadn't even seen him take it from the back of the Land Rover.'

'Go on.'

'So, Finch hands me the axe and tells me to finish him.'

'What do you think he meant by that expression?'

'He wanted me to kill him.'

'What happened next?'

'I knew he was serious, and I asked why. He said, "Just do it. It will make us even".'

Glen remained silent, waiting for Briar to speak.

After a long pause, Briar said quietly, 'I only hit him once. Right on top of his head. The axe went in up to the handle, and I had a hell of a job getting it out again. Drake fell forward onto his face, and we legged it.'

'Did you think he was dead?'

'I knew he was dead.'

'Where's that ice axe now?'

'At the bottom of the fucking lake. I threw it in as we ran back to the Land Rover.'

There was silence in the interview room as the enormity of what Briar had just said registered with everyone present.

It was Rob who broke that silence, 'You said earlier that Finch said it would make you even. What did he mean?'

'It made us even for the other thing we did. I can guarantee he won't have said a word about that, the grassing bastard.'

'I don't understand. What other thing?'

'When he killed Drake's wife.'

'Melanie Drake?'

'Yeah.'

'What do you know about the death of Melanie Drake?'
'I was there when she died.'
'Go on.'
'We were just kids back then. We were pissed off at how that evil bitch had treated us when we were being fostered, so we decided to get our revenge. That was all Dom's idea too.'
'What did you do?'
'I nicked a car from Woodhouse and we waited in Mansfield for the cow to finish her night class. We snatched her up and drove her to this deserted cottage out near Pleasley.'
'What was the plan?'
'We didn't really have one. We just wanted her to experience some of the terror she made us feel when she was having her evil fun. When we got her to the cottage, I tied her up and we marched her inside.'
'How did you tie her?'
'I was mad into climbing back then and I used to practice my knots all the time. It would have been a bowline.'
'What did you tie her up with?'
'I always had a length of nylon cord in my pocket to practice knots. I used that.'
'What happened at the cottage?'
'Dom lit a fag, then started stubbing the end out on her face. I was laughing, because it was what she used to do to us.'
'Apart from laughing, what else did you do?'
'I had to hold her up. She was kneeling on the floor, but she kept flopping forward, so I held her while Dom stubbed the cigarette out on her face. I could feel her shaking every time Dom lit the cigarette. She was terrified, but it served her right.'

'You said he killed her. What happened?'

'Back then, Dom used to lose his temper dead easy. I can't remember exactly what it was, but he got mad about something she said or did. He picked up this piece of old floorboard and before I could say anything, he smashed her on the head with it.'

'How many times did he hit her?'

'He only hit her once, because the wood got stuck to her head.'

'What do you mean, stuck to her head?'

'There was a great big fuck-off nail in the wood that had gone straight into her head.'

'What did you do?'

'I was panicking and saying we needed to get her to a hospital, but Dom said it was too late for that. We hid her body under the floorboards and got out of there. We dumped the car and burnt it out near Shirebrook.'

'Is that why Finch has been paying you money all these years?'

'Yeah. He offered at first, but then I thought, life was so much easier when his money was coming in that I wanted it to be a regular thing. I knew he was a millionaire and could afford it. I gave him a gentle reminder that I knew something about him that could cause his luxurious lifestyle to disappear.'

'So, what was the conversation you had at Matlock that became so heated?'

'That was when he told me that now I'd killed Ian Drake, there would be no more money paid into my business account. He laughed and told me that he knew something about me as well now.'

Briar shook his head and continued, 'There was no need

for him to be like that. He never paid me that much. It was a drop in the ocean for the greedy bastard. And then to top that off, he's tried to stitch me up today. He shouldn't have done that. If he hadn't grassed me up about Cresswell Crags, I would've taken his secret to the grave with me.'

92

2.30pm, 23 March 1989
MCIU Offices, Mansfield, Nottinghamshire

Danny and Rachel, Rob and Glen, Andy and Jane were in the main briefing room discussing how the interviews with Douglas Richardson and Kevin Briar had gone.

Rob said, 'Briar's now fully implicated Finch in the murders of Ian and Melanie Drake. He'll either listen to his solicitor now and go "no comment" or strive even harder to put everything on Briar.'

Danny said, 'From what you've told me, I don't see how he can distance himself from the murder of Melanie Drake.'

Glen said, 'He can distance himself from the intent. If his intention was only to cause her injury, then we're going to have a hell of a job to get a murder conviction. We would need to prove that he knew the nail was in the wood and that his action of striking her on the head would result in her death. Even Briar's account doesn't help us with that, because even he's saying it was a surprise when the wood ended up stuck fast into her head.'

'I agree with what you're saying, but we have to try.'

'The problem is, boss, even if he goes "no comment" it will be a stretch to prove an inference of guilt because it's all so long ago.'

'As soon as you give disclosure of Melanie Drake's murder to his solicitor, he's going to be all over Finch. Don't be surprised to get a prepared statement and "no comment" response to everything this time.'

Danny nodded. 'I hear you.'

He looked at Andy and said, 'What did Richardson have to say about Finch?'

'Nothing. As soon as we started questioning him about his involvement with Finch, he answered, "No comment".'

'Did he say anything about the mutual acquaintance who brought the two of them together?'

'No, he didn't. And from the look on his face when that was mentioned, I don't think he ever will.'

'Do you have enough evidence to convict Richardson for the murder of Molloy?'

'Provided the forensic evidence found under the wheel arches of the Range Rover can be matched to Molloy's DNA, we'll get a conviction. Richardson has admitted being out on his own, driving the Range Rover on the night of the murder. From the scene examination and the injuries identified at the post mortem, we can also prove that Molloy was not only struck by the vehicle, but also that the vehicle was then driven over him on two further occasions. I've got officers out making enquiries at the Dukeries estate to ascertain if any of the staff there have found a dead or badly injured deer. All the roads on the estate are being checked for fresh skid marks and accident debris. The bottom line is we've got enough to charge, but the forensic evidence will be pivotal for a conviction.'

Danny could feel a sense of pride at the professionalism and dedication being shown by his team. He had relished being involved in the interviews and realised just what a wrench it would be to leave the MCIU and his colleagues.

He was slowly realising how he saw his immediate future, but he wanted to get a sense of Sue's thoughts before he made a final decision.

Before he could talk to Sue, he still had work to do. He needed to give disclosure to Dominic Finch's solicitor and then sit down with Rachel to prepare a final interview.

93

3.00pm, 23 March 1989
Mansfield Police Station, Nottinghamshire

The first hurdle had been negotiated. The introductions of everyone present in the interview room had been done and there was no offer of a prepared statement from the solicitor, who cut a very sullen and frustrated figure beside his client, Dominic Finch.

Danny said, 'Dominic Finch, my colleague arrested you earlier on suspicion of the murder of Melanie Drake. You've now had the opportunity to speak with your solicitor about the details of that allegation. What can you tell me about the death of Melanie Drake?'

'The first thing I want to say is that no part of what happened that night was my idea. It was Kevin Briar who stole the car, and it was his idea to snatch her up and scare the shit out of her. I just went along for the ride.'

'Tell me what happened when you abducted her.'

'Patch knew that she was going to this night class in Mansfield, so he parked the car not far from the bus stop she would use. He jumped out of the car, grabbed her, tied her wrists, put a gag on her, and told me to get in the back of the car with her.'

'Surely, she would have recognised you?'

'We wore ski masks so she couldn't see our faces.'

'Did you help Briar grab her?'

'No, I stayed in the car.'

'Then what happened?'

'He drove us to some place out near Pleasley. It was a rundown cottage in the middle of woods. I'd never been there before. It was at the end of a farm track, and we had to walk the last hundred yards or so to get to the cottage.'

'What was Melanie Drake saying at this time?'

'She was trying to say something, but Patch had gagged her.'

'What did you do when you got to the cottage?'

'I was only a kid. I wasn't thinking straight. I was angry at her because of everything she'd done to me, so I did something stupid.'

'Go on.'

'That evil bitch used to delight in smoking a cigarette and stubbing it out on our skin. She used to refer to us as her two favourite ashtrays. She always thought it was a huge joke, so I decided to do the same to her, to see how she liked it.'

'What was Briar doing while you did this?'

'He was cracking up laughing. Every time I stubbed the fag out, she almost fainted. He kept holding her up and telling me to give the evil cow some more. I kept relighting the fag and stubbing it out on her face. I could see she was terrified, but back then, I didn't care.'

'Briar's described how you picked up a piece of wood and struck her on the head with it. Why did you do that?'

'It's so long ago it's hard for me to remember now. I think the gag slipped a little and she said something to me, but I can't remember what. All I remember is getting angry, snatching up this piece of old floorboard and giving her a crack with it. I wanted to shut her mouth, that was all.'

'Then what happened?'

'After I hit her, the floorboard stayed stuck to her head. I yanked at it, and when it came away, I saw the nail for the first time. It was a big six-inch nail, and it was covered in blood where it had gone into the top of her head. There was blood pumping out of the hole in her head, and her eyes had gone white. I knew she was dead.'

'Did you check her pulse?'

'No.'

'So, how do you know she was dead?'

'She looked dead. I don't know. I was only a kid. I just panicked and ran.'

'Did you run straight away?'

'What?'

'When you saw what you'd done to her, did you and Briar run off straight away?'

'No. We shoved her under the floorboards and covered her up.'

'Even though she may still have been alive.'

'She was dead.'

'You weren't panicking that much if you still had the presence of mind to hide her body.'

'It was an accident. I never meant to kill her.'

'Then what did you do?'

'Patch drove the car to a layby near Shirebrook. We set light to it and ran off.'

'Have you and Briar ever spoken about this since?'

Finch shook his head. 'We never talk about it.'

'And now you've made a success of your life you must have been worried this could all come out one day. Did you know that Melanie Drake's body had been found?'

Finch nodded and said quietly, 'I read about it in one of the local newspapers. Patch sent me a copy.'

'Did you panic when you read the article?'

'Not really. It was that long ago I didn't think there would be anything left to connect me and Patch to the body.'

Finch was silent for a few moments, then continued, 'I've made a good life for myself. I've tried hard to forget about that night and the terrible accident that happened.'

'Why don't you tell me about that good life? How did that all come about?'

'I'd always been good at maths as a kid. Even though I was bit of a tearaway, I was bright and did well at school. I've always had a way with finance. I understand how it works. How having money can make you a lot more. It's all about how it's invested. I can take a large sum of money and know I can double or even treble it. When I was eighteen, I got a job at an investment company in London. Instead of getting pissed on champagne and eating two-hundred-quid lunches like everyone else, I saved hard and started making money for myself, not the company.'

Danny didn't interrupt. He remained silent, letting Finch continue his story.

'Eventually, I'd saved enough to set up my own finance company. I now use that company to help wealthy people invest their money into various schemes and enterprises. Those schemes then make huge profits for them and me. The work I do has made me an extremely wealthy man.'

Danny said, 'You're obviously very astute with money. Didn't it bother you, paying all those large sums of money into Briar's business account?'

'Yes, it did. It was blackmail, pure and simple. He knew that at any time he could bring this wonderful life I'd worked so hard to achieve crashing down around me. I had no choice but to keep paying him whatever he wanted. I got sick of him always coming to me with the begging bowl.'

'What did you do about it?'

'I didn't do anything. I couldn't.'

'Why did you set up the meeting with Briar and Ian Drake?'

'That was his idea. He was always fantasising about seeing him again, giving him a beating and getting money off him. I just thought he'd got a taste for blackmail, so I set it all up in the hope he'd start blackmailing Drake instead of me.'

'You told us earlier that it was Douglas Richardson who hired the private detective who eventually traced Drake on your behalf. At that time, you refused to say who it was who'd brokered Richardson to get involved.'

'I haven't changed my mind on that. I won't be giving you any other names. All you need to know is that it was Richardson who hired and paid the private detective.'

'Were you aware that Douglas Richardson was Ian Drake's brother-in-law?'

'Really? I had no idea. It's a small world.'

'Was Douglas Richardson aware of the reason you wanted to trace Drake when he hired the private detective?'

'No. He didn't know anything. I never spoke about the reason I wanted Drake back down here.'

'Let's talk about that reason. What happened when you met Kevin Briar at Matlock yesterday?'

For the first time in the interview, Finch looked shocked. He glanced at his solicitor, who leaned forward and whispered something in his ear.

Finch immediately said, 'No comment.'

'Detectives observed the entire meeting between you and Briar. It didn't take long for it to become very heated. Why was that?'

'No comment.'

'What was it you said that upset Briar so much?'

'No comment.'

'Was that the moment you told him how you'd set him up to kill Ian Drake?'

'No comment.'

'When you told him there would be no more cash payouts into his failing outward bound centre?'

'No comment.'

'And the reason there would be no more money was because you had urged him to kill Ian Drake and now you were both even?'

'No comment.'

'Briar has given us a full account of what happened that night at Cresswell Crags. It's your right to make no comment when I inform you what Briar has told us, but you must bear in mind that a court may make an inference if you say something you could have said now at any subsequent court hearing. Do you understand?'

Briar again looked at his solicitor, who shook his head.

Danny said, 'Briar has told us that he drove you to the meeting with Drake at the Young Vanish. Is that correct?'

'No comment.'

'It was both of you who attacked and assaulted Drake outside the pub that night. Is that correct?'

'No comment.'

'That he then drove to Cresswell Crags and that both of you dragged Ian Drake towards the caves, where he was further assaulted by you both. Is that correct?'

'No comment.'

'That it was you who took the ice axe from the Land Rover and gave it to Briar, urging him to finish Drake once and for all. Is that correct?'

'No comment.'

'Kevin Briar has no reason to lie about any of this. He's admitted striking Drake with the ice axe, killing him.'

'No comment.'

'Far from this being Briar's idea, the whole plan was thought up by you, so you didn't have to make any more cash payments to Kevin Briar. The sole reason for luring Ian Drake back here was so you could manipulate Briar into killing him. It was always your intention that Drake would be murdered by Briar.'

'No comment.'

'I've no further questions.'

94

9.00pm, 23 March 1989
MCIU Offices, Mansfield, Nottinghamshire

Danny was alone in his office, going over the documentation for the charges for Finch, Briar and Richardson. The three men had all been charged earlier and Danny was reading the accompanying paperwork one last time before he went home.

It had been a long, tiring day, but one he had thoroughly enjoyed.

Throughout the day, he'd come to realise that he was happiest being hands-on with cases, and he wondered how he would cope with a purely management role. He enjoyed being involved in the day-to-day running of investigations, following the leads until they identified the offender, and bringing them to justice. The thought of that being replaced with sitting behind a desk worrying about the cost of everything filled him with an icy dread.

The very thought of that scenario made him shudder involuntarily.

He heard a noise in the main office.

He had thought he was alone, but then he heard footsteps approaching his office door.

There was a single knock before the door opened.

Detective Chief Superintendent Adrian Potter walked in. 'I was passing the station and I thought you might still be here. How did everything go today? I never got the chance to speak to you before you left headquarters this morning.'

'Everything went as well as it could, sir. We've charged two men, Dominic Finch and Kevin Briar, with the murders of Melanie and Ian Drake. And we've charged a third man with the murder of Mike Molloy.'

Potter sat down opposite Danny. 'Will you get them convicted?'

'We've enough evidence to charge, but it's still going to be a lot of hard work before I'm feeling confident enough to say the three of them will be convicted at crown court. You know how it is. The hard work continues even after charge.'

As soon as he said the last comment, Danny regretted it. He knew that Potter had very little experience in actually running a murder investigation.

The diminutive senior officer never registered the comment. He seemed distant, as though his mind was focussed on other matters.

Danny said, 'Is everything alright, sir?'

Potter looked directly at Danny. 'Did he offer you my job?'

'Excuse me?'

'Did Jack Renshaw offer you the job as head of the CID?'

Danny was taken aback at the comment, but recovered quickly. 'He asked me if I would be interested, should you ever decide to move on.'

Potter smiled and said, 'No need to be coy, Danny. He knows I've applied for a promotion in another force. I don't blame him for asking you. You are an extremely talented detective who gets results. And you're someone who now has the full backing of Councillor White on the Police Committee at the council.'

The unspoken 'but' was deafening in the silence.

Danny said it for him, 'I sense a "but" coming, sir.'

'That job is not a good fit for you, Danny. Trust me on this. Not only would you hate it, but you would also be terrible at it too.'

There was a heavy silence in the room, before Potter continued, 'I'm not saying this to insult you, or to try and put you off going for the job. I genuinely believe you would be happier staying here and running the MCIU.'

Danny was thoughtful for a long time and neither man spoke.

Eventually, Danny said, 'I'll be honest with you, I've been thinking much the same thing all day. It's such a massive decision, though. I have to consider the promotions it would entail, and the pension benefits of those promotions. I need to discuss everything, all the pros and cons, with my wife before I make any decision.'

Potter stood up and said, 'I'll let you into a secret, Danny. This afternoon I've been offered the job I applied for, so I'll be leaving the force in three months' time. I haven't told the chief yet. In fact, you're the first person I've told. I just wanted to have this chat with you.'

He paused, choosing his words carefully as he continued, 'Everything I've said tonight has been meant as a compliment. I know the chief will be pushing you hard for an answer as soon as I tell him my news. My last word of advice to you is something my father always said to me, "You're a long time at work, so make sure you're happy doing your job".'

Potter extended his hand and said, 'I know we've had our ups and downs since I arrived, but I've the utmost respect for you. I wanted to wish you all the very best, whatever you decide to do. Good luck, Danny.'

Danny shook hands and said, 'Good luck, Adrian.'

95

10.30pm, 23 March 1989
Mansfield, Nottinghamshire

Danny closed the front door quietly so he didn't wake his young daughter. When he turned round, Sue was standing in the hallway behind him.

'I heard the car on the drive. You look shattered. I'll put the kettle on.'

'Don't bother about the kettle. Come and sit down. We need to talk.'

A worried-looking Sue followed him into the lounge and sat next to him on the sofa. 'What's going on, Danny?'

'Don't look so worried; it's good news. But it's also a massive dilemma. Let me tell you what's happened today. I'm still a little shocked by it all myself, to be honest.'

Sue let out a deep sigh. She hadn't realised she'd been

holding her breath. She stayed silent, waiting for her husband to speak.

He leaned back on the sofa and said, 'I had a meeting with the chief constable this morning. I was expecting it to be a rough one, as I'd made my mind up to tell him exactly what I thought about his lack of support during the recent murder investigations. You know how I've been feeling.'

Sue nodded. She did indeed know the pressure her husband had been feeling during the recent investigations. 'And how did that go down?'

'This is the surprising part. After I'd said my piece, the chief asked me if I was happy where I was, or if I was ready to face a different challenge. Before I could defend myself against what I thought was going to be an attempt to move me sideways, he asked me if I wanted Potter's job.'

'What? Bloody hell, where did that come from?'

'Adrian Potter has applied for a promotion with another force, so the chief is looking for his replacement. He wants me to be the new Head of CID.'

Sue was thoughtful, then she said, 'And how do you feel about that?'

'If I'm being honest, I'm not enamoured about the prospect of being stuck in an office, doing a managerial role. I've been hands on, doing interviews all day, and it's really brought it home to me where I'm happiest. I think I'd be stuck in that office at headquarters and be bored rigid in no time.'

He paused before continuing, 'But it will mean at least two promotions, better working hours, a bigger salary and huge improvements to my pension when I eventually retire.'

'But would you be happy doing that job, or be like a bear

with a sore head, weighed down with frustration by the time you got home every evening?'

'Something else weird happened tonight. Before I left work, Adrian Potter dropped into the MCIU to talk to me. He told me that he's been offered the job he applied for, so he'll definitely be leaving in the next three months.'

'It's happening, then?'

'Yes, it's happening. Somehow, he'd got wind that the chief had asked me if I wanted his job. He asked me straight out if I'd been offered it.'

'What did you say?'

'I told him that the chief had asked me to consider it.'

'I bet that went down well.'

'Here's another surprise: he was very complimentary about me and my work on the MCIU. He advised me against taking the job, saying it wasn't a role I'd be suited to and that I'd be better off staying where I was.'

'Hmm, sounds like he doesn't want you to get the job.'

'It wasn't like that, Sue. He seemed genuinely concerned for me. He was talking about the role itself. He even quoted something his father used to say to him, "You're a long time at work, so make sure you're happy doing your job". He obviously thinks the job would make me miserable.'

'What do you think?'

'I think there's some merit in what he was saying. You know what I'm like when I've been stuck in my office at the MCIU for a few days. I hate it, so what would I be like if that was all I had to look forward to every day for the rest of my working life?'

'How long have you got before you need to make a decision?'

'I don't know. I think the chief will be pressing me for an answer, especially now Potter's leaving.'

'You need to think everything through, sweetheart. This is your future; it isn't a decision you can rush.'

'I know that. What I need are your opinions, your thoughts. This decision will have an impact on all of us. It's about our future, not just my future.'

'If you want my initial thoughts, I'll give them to you. But like you, I'm going to need time to process everything.'

'I understand that. I'd still like to hear your thoughts, though.'

Sue was thoughtful for a while, choosing her words carefully. 'First of all, forget about the extra salary. We both earn good money and lead a comfortable life, so the money's not important. That said, the pension ramifications need to be examined closer, to see exactly what difference the expected promotions would make to your final pension. The better hours would be a huge plus for me when it comes to collecting Hayley from the childminder. It would take some of the pressure off me always having to leave the hospital on time.'

She paused and then said, 'The most important thing for me, and for our daughter, is your happiness. You already have a stressful job with the MCIU, but it's a role you're happy and comfortable with. You work every day with great people, who are more like family than colleagues. You can't put a price on that. There's a lot of truth in what Potter's old man used to say; you need to be happy at work, or you won't be happy anywhere else. What's the point of you being able to collect Hayley from the childminder every day if you're grumpy and miserable when you do?'

There was an even longer pause, then she said, 'My

initial thoughts are that you should turn Jack Renshaw down and stay where you're happy.'

'I'll contact the chief tomorrow and tell him I want a month to weigh everything up properly before I give him an answer. If he wants an answer before then, it will be a resounding no.'

Sue cuddled into her husband on the sofa and said, 'I think it's bed time, don't you?'

96

10.00am, 24 April 1989
Nottinghamshire Police Headquarters

The day had finally arrived when Danny had to give his decision to the chief constable. After many talks with his wife, weighing up all the pros and cons of the promotion he was being offered, he had finally reached a decision.

The most important thing for Danny was that it had been a decision reached mutually with his wife.

He knocked on the chief's office door and waited.

An unmistakeable Cornish accent bellowed, 'Come in!'

A smiling Jack Renshaw greeted Danny. 'Take a seat, Danny.'

Danny sat down and waited for the chief to speak first.

Renshaw said, 'Have you reached a decision?'

'I've thought very hard about the promotion you offered

me, sir. And I've had many discussions with my wife, Sue. I've decided to turn the promotion down and remain in post on the MCIU. That's where I think I can be of most use for the force. I'm just not suited to an administration role. I'm sorry, sir.'

Jack Renshaw sat back in his chair, the smile gone from his face.

After a few moments, he said, 'Well, I wasn't expecting that. I admire your honesty, and of course I'm happy for you to remain in post on the MCIU. I've got to admit, that was another headache troubling me—wondering whom to replace you with on the MCIU.'

'This wasn't an easy decision for me, and I'm flattered to have been offered the role.'

'I just hope it's a decision you don't come to regret later in your service.'

'That's part of it, sir. I think it's come a little too early for me. I still have at least another eight years' service to do. In all honesty, I still enjoy being hands on, dealing with investigations on an everyday basis.'

'Part of me wondered if you would take on the job. Certainly, Adrian didn't think you would. He describes you as a round peg in a round hole. I know you two have clashed in the past, but he really respects you.'

Renshaw paused before continuing, 'I do have a few options in mind for the role that I've already sounded out. Adrian still has a couple of months before he transfers, so it's not a massive problem. Any updates on Finch, Briar and Richardson?'

Danny was relieved by how the chief had taken his decision. In typical Jack Renshaw fashion, he was straight back to business.

Danny said, 'All three are currently on remand. After receiving the results of the forensic samples recovered from his Range Rover, DS Wills and DC Pope went to see Douglas Richardson at HMP Wakefield. Those results proved the human tissue found in the wheel arches of the vehicle matched the DNA of Mike Molloy.'

'Did Richardson talk to the detectives?'

'He was further interviewed at the prison in the presence of his solicitor and admitted the offence. He also suggested he had significant information that would be of use to the Metropolitan Police. We've informed the Met of this development and they're planning to interview both Richardson and Dominic Finch soon.'

'Any idea what that's about?'

'Our investigation revealed some very close links between Finch and Richardson and a man named Mason Connor. Connor's someone the Met believe is heavily involved in serious and organised crime.'

'It will be interesting to see how that develops.'

'There's one other matter that needs your attention, sir. Our lawyers have suggested that a commendation letter be sent to Robert McCloud, the chief executive of Global Fossil Energy Exploration. Something along the lines that without his massive co-operation we may never have solved the murders committed by Amos Varley. The lawyers will then be able to use that letter when the question of disclosing the unused material—namely all their confidential personnel files—comes before the judge.'

'No problem. Let me know the details and I'll draft the letter today.'

'Will do, sir.'

Jack Renshaw stood and walked around his desk. He

walked with Danny to the door, placing a hand on his shoulder. 'Rest assured, there'll be no hard feelings from me because you turned down the job. I fully understand your reasons and admire the fact you didn't just take it for the sake of it. Stay at the MCIU and keep up your high standards.'

97

6.00pm, 25 April 1989
HMP Wakefield, West Yorkshire

Association was the usual noisy mixture of petty squabbles, raucous laughter and shouted opinions. It wasn't only the prison officers who were watchful. The inmates all knew that this hour was a potentially difficult and dangerous time. There were only two officers watching over the area that housed the single television. The television area was the main draw that evening, as it was showing a European Cup match involving an Italian club and an English team from the North West.

Douglas Richardson had been on remand at the grim Yorkshire prison for just over one month, and he was struggling. He had always lived a life of plenty and privilege and had no idea of the rules and hierarchy that every prison contains. He'd already been badly assaulted on two occasions, just for saying the wrong thing at the wrong time to the wrong person.

He was the proverbial fish out of water.

When the cell doors had opened for association, he had remained on his bed. The prison officer doing the rounds had forced him out of the cell and downstairs to the TV room. The rules stated he wasn't allowed to remain in his cell, so he had to join his fellow inmates.

Richardson had slid in unnoticed and sat on one of the hard chairs towards the back of the viewing area.

Unnoticed, except for one pair of eyes that held an evil intent.

Leigh Francis had been looking for Richardson. The London night-club bouncer had been given instructions to deal with the new inmate that evening.

The Jamaican with a hard face and shaven head was a short, powerful man with a muscular physique. He spent hours maintaining his size and strength in the prison gym. The other inmates all knew the lifer was a man to be avoided, as he had a propensity for extreme violence.

Even the prison officers were wary and afforded the giant plenty of space.

When Francis had entered the TV viewing area, it was only Douglas Richardson that hadn't noted the arrival of the dangerous muscle man. He'd been too intent on staring straight ahead, trying not to make eye contact with anybody.

As soon as Francis had manoeuvred himself immediately behind Richardson, a pushing and shoving match started on the other side of the room. Two inmates began shouting obscenities at each other. Within seconds, violence erupted in the room as both men swapped insults and then blows. In no time at all, other fights began breaking out in the packed, confined space.

The two prison officers did their best to calm things down but were soon forced to retreat for their own safety.

A panicking Richardson remained rooted to the spot in terror. He stayed seated on the hard wooden chair, his hands by his side, gripping the base of the chair. In his terrorised state, he never felt the presence of Francis standing directly behind him.

Francis waited until the prison officers had retreated out of view, then he snaked a powerful arm around Richardson's neck, clamping his throat in a vice-like grip.

The muscular Francis held Richardson in a classic head lock, cutting off all air and crushing his larynx. Richardson began to thrash his legs and grab at the Jamaican's massive arm with both hands, in a futile attempt to break the formidable grip that was killing him.

With his brain starved of blood and oxygen, Richardson quickly passed out.

Francis continued to apply the same massive pressure until he knew the man was dead, then with a twist of his powerful arms he snapped Richardson's neck, smiling as he heard the bones crack.

Finally, he released his grip and moved away from the dead man, leaving Richardson slumped forward on the chair.

Other prison officers, alerted by their overwhelmed colleagues, were now flooding into the TV-viewing area, forcing the scuffling inmates back to their cells. Leigh Francis walked slowly through the mob and made his way back to the landing, where a prison officer pushed him back into his cell.

At any other time, the muscular Jamaican would have protested at being shoved, but now he just smiled and lay down on his bed.

A young prison officer entered the TV room to make the last man leave. He grabbed Richardson by the shoulder and said, 'Come on. Back to your cell.'

Richardson's head lolled to one side alarmingly, and he toppled forwards from the chair. Realising the man was seriously injured, the prison officer shouted for help and began first aid on the stricken inmate.

He felt for a pulse in the man's neck but couldn't find one. He could see his lips were already turning blue, so he tried to tip his head back and start mouth to mouth. The youngster couldn't understand why the inmate's head kept falling to one side. There had been no mention that might happen when he had undergone his first aid training.

Manually holding the man's head in the correct position, he placed the plastic cover over the injured inmate's mouth and began resuscitation.

He tried to blow air into the man's lungs but struggled. Every time he tried to inflate the lungs, all he could hear was a loud wheezing sound coming from the inmate's crushed airway.

He persevered but knew there wasn't enough air getting through the damaged windpipe to the lungs.

Another, more experienced, prison officer arrived in the TV room. He took one look at Richardson and said, 'Leave it, kid. He's gone.'

The youngster moved away from the body and muttered, 'I tried my best but there's something wrong with his neck.'

'Looks like it's been broken. Did you see anybody near him?'

'No. By the time I got in here, the others were already being put back in their cells. I came in to get him back to his cell because he hadn't moved.'

'Better get the gaffer down here. He hasn't died by accident.'

'For Christ's sake. Who is he?'

'I think his name was Richardson. He's in for murder.'

'What's going to happen now?'

The older man ignored the youngster's question, reached for his radio and said, 'PO Jackson to SPO Reid. We've a one oblique one in the TV room. Doesn't look like natural causes to me. I think his neck's been snapped.'

The voice on the radio said, 'Do you know who it is?'

'It's that new bloke, Richardson. He's on remand for murder.'

'Okay. Seal the area and try not to touch the body. You know the drill. I'm on my way to you.'

'Bit late for no touching, boss. PO Foster has attempted mouth-to-mouth resuscitation.'

'For fuck's sake. I'm on my way.'

98

5.00pm, 25 April 1989
HMP Wormwood Scrubs, London

Dominic Finch had been pleased to be transferred from HMP Lincoln back to a London prison. At least here he could get regular visitors. He knew his legal team were working hard to help him evade the murder charges he faced. He was confident the charge would be reduced to manslaughter for Melanie Drake, and dropped altogether for Ian Drake.

He could afford the best legal brains in the capital and had willingly paid their exorbitant fees. He didn't want to spend one day longer in prison than he had to.

At his lawyer's suggestion, he'd continued to provide further information to the detectives investigating the murders. This information further implicated Kevin Briar as being the only person culpable for Ian Drake's murder.

Finch didn't see it as grassing on an old mate. He saw it as self-preservation by the better man.

Others in the prison system had a less charitable view.

Most of the other inmates at Wormwood Scrubs knew that Dominic Finch was someone with powerful connections on the outside. For that reason, he had been left alone while he served time on remand.

The cell door opened. An overweight prison officer stood in the doorway. 'Off the landing, Finch. Downstairs for association.'

Finch answered, 'I'll get my boots on.'

Unusually, the prison officer didn't wait to see him out of his cell.

Instead, he said, 'Don't take all day about it,' before leaving.

Finch was in a cell of his own. His previous cell mate had been released the day before and nobody else had been allocated to share his cell yet.

As he was tying the last knot on his boots, the cell door opened again.

He looked up and saw that instead of the fat prison officer, it was two young, baby-faced inmates who walked in. One white, one black.

As the black youth closed the cell door, the white lad approached Finch, who thought he looked vaguely familiar.

Finch smiled at the white lad and started to say, 'Do I know you—'

His words were cut short when he saw the home-made shiv being held in the lad's right hand.

Before Finch had time to react to the threat, the shiv was plunged deep into his throat. Instinctively, Finch reached up to his badly gashed neck with both hands, trying to stem the blood that was now gushing from his devastated windpipe.

As Finch fell to his knees he tried to speak, but no words formed and he just gurgled out a mouthful of bloody froth.

The man stepped forward again, grabbed a handful of Finch's hair and growled, 'Mr Connor doesn't like grassing bastards.'

As he said the word bastards, the man shoved the shiv deep into Finch's right eye. It was a move intended to kill, not blind, and was quickly followed up by the same movement into his left eye.

The home-made shiv had done its grisly work and Finch fell forward onto the floor. By the time he hit the cell floor, the catastrophic brain injury meant he was already dead.

The black man by the cell door said, 'It's all clear, Jimmy. Let's go.'

Jimmy wiped the handle of the home-made shiv on his prison issue jumper before dropping it on the floor. He took one look down at Dominic Finch who was now bleeding out, spat on his body and growled, 'And such is the end for all grasses.'

EPILOGUE

10am, 26 April 1989
Theydon Bois, Epping Forest, Essex

The old country house was set well back off the road. So far back that only the heaviest trucks using Coppice Row could be heard from the house.

Mason Connor had lived at the Elizabethan manor house for the last six years. It was his place of sanctuary. Somewhere he felt safe enough to relax, surrounded on all four sides by the beauty of Epping Forest.

It was a tranquil location that belied the world of violence, pain, and criminality used to obtain the money needed to purchase it.

Connor's wife, fifteen years his junior, hardly ever left the house. She only ventured out a few times a month, to shop in the West End. She lived a life of luxury, happy to turn a blind eye to her husband's nefarious activities. She was oblivious to the fact that her husband was a vicious gangster engaged in drug dealing, prostitution and violence.

As was his want, Mason Connor was enjoying a full English breakfast on the patio overlooking the luxurious swimming pool at the rear of the house. The manicured gardens beyond the pool stretched for at least another hundred yards before the wild woodland of Epping Forest took over.

He always ate breakfast alone and was never to be disturbed until he'd completed his meal. Only when he started to read the newspaper could his long-suffering housekeeper approach him.

Waiting for her cue, the housekeeper approached as soon as he picked up the newspaper. She started to clear away the empty breakfast crockery and said, 'Would you like some fresh coffee, sir?'

His answer was a terse, 'Yes.'

'I'll bring that right out. Mr Donavon's waiting in the hallway, sir. He's been here since nine thirty. Shall I send him out?'

Connor folded the newspaper and said, 'Tell Finn to wait in the study. I'll take my coffee in there, Rebecca.'

As the housekeeper started to walk away Connor said, 'And bring extra coffee for Finn.'

Finn Donavon was Mason Connor's right-hand man. He dealt with everything Mason Connor needed to distance himself from. He was an Eastender through and through, and rarely ventured out of the city. He'd only made an exception today because he had news he knew his boss would want to hear first-hand.

Mason Connor was acutely aware of police surveillance

tactics and knew there was a remote possibility that any conversation the two of them had outside could be overheard. That was the reason he'd decided to speak with Donavon inside the house.

Connor walked into the study and saw Donavon standing by the fireplace. After an initial greeting, Connor gestured for Donavon to sit in one of the two brown leather Chesterfield chairs.

Both men remained completely silent until Rebecca had brought the fresh coffee into the study.

As soon as the housekeeper had poured the coffees and left, Mason asked, 'So what brings you out here so early?'

Finn took a sip of the piping hot coffee and said, 'I received notification late last night that the problem of Richardson and Finch has been sorted.'

'Have you taken care of the people doing the job?'

'Yes, boss. Their families have been suitably rewarded.'

'That's excellent news. It's always a worry when civilians get involved in our operations. They've got no loyalty. I must say, I was a bit surprised at Dominic grassing like that. Still, lesson learned.'

'What do you want me to give the brief who tipped us off about Richardson wanting to talk to the old bill?'

'What's his usual fee for giving information?'

'A grand.'

Connor was thoughtful for a minute, then said, 'Slip him five grand. He's saved us a mountain of shit with that little golden nugget. What have you arranged for Briar?'

'He was out of reach last night. He's in solitary after slotting a screw. All the information is that he doesn't know anything anyway.'

'Not good enough, Finn. You know I never leave anything

to chance. As soon as he's out of solitary, I want him sorting. Understood?'

'No problem. I'll get that sorted. I'm going to get back to town now, boss. All this fresh air gives me a fucking headache.'

WE HOPE YOU ENJOYED THIS BOOK

If you could spend a moment to write an honest review on Amazon, no matter how short, we would be extremely grateful. They really do help readers discover new authors.

ALSO BY TREVOR NEGUS

EVIL IN MIND

(Book 1 in the DCI Flint series)

DEAD AND GONE

(Book 2 in the DCI Flint series)

A COLD GRAVE

(Book 3 in the DCI Flint series)

TAKEN TO DIE

(Book 4 in the DCI Flint series)

KILL FOR YOU

(Book 5 in the DCI Flint series)

ONE DEADLY LIE

(Book 6 in the DCI Flint series)

A SWEET REVENGE

(Book 7 in the DCI Flint series)

THE DEVIL'S BREATH

(Book 8 in the DCI Flint series)

I AM NUMBER FOUR

(Book 9 in the DCI Flint series)

TIED IN DEATH

(Book 10 in the DCI Flint series)

Printed in Great Britain
by Amazon